INTO THE DARK

Fiona Cummins is an award-winning former *Daily Mirror* showbusiness journalist and a graduate of the Faber Academy Writing a Novel course. She lives in Essex with her family. *Into The Dark* is her fifth novel.

Also by Fiona Cummins

Rattle
The Collector
The Neighbour
When I Was Ten

INTO THE DARK

Fiona Cummins

MACMILLAN

First published 2022 by Macmillan
an imprint of Pan Macmillan
The Smithson, 6 Briset Street, London ECIM 5NR
EU representative: Macmillan Publishers Ireland Ltd, 1st Floor,
The Liffey Trust Centre, 117–126 Sheriff Street Upper,
Dublin 1, DOI YC43
Associated companies throughout the world
www.panmacmillan.com

ISBN 978-1-5290-4016-6

3 5 7 9 8 6 4 2

A CIP catalogue record for this book is available from the British Library.

Typeset in Scala by Palimpsest Book Production Ltd, Falkirk, Stirlingshire
Printed and bound by CPI Group (UK) Ltd, Croydon, CRO 4YY

Visit **www.panmacmillan.com** to read more about all our books
and to buy them. You will also find features, author interviews and
news of any author events, and you can sign up for e-newsletters
so that you're always first to hear about our new releases.

For Steven, Ceinwen and Meredith,
with gratitude and love always

'Women are equal to everything'

                                            – Lady Hale

1

Tuesday morning

The day the Holdens disappeared

The wind sounded like the dead had risen, climbing out of their graves and drumming their bones against the roof.

Julianne Hillier stood on her doorstep and watched the lighthouse beacon dance across the churn of the waves before it swept skywards and was lost to the breaking day.

A curlew dipped its beak at the shoreline, its cry obscured by the push and pull of the tide. A milky sun was burning its way through clouds that raced the advancing light. The beach huts – painted in tasteful hues of Salt Spray and Grey Mist and Hidden Pearl – stood on a spit of sand that over-looked the bay, end-of-season samphire growing from the mudflats.

Even in late autumn, Midtown-on-Sea was the kind of place estate agents called paradise.

Julianne locked the front door behind her and jogged, as she did every Tuesday morning, down Seaview Avenue and left into Marine Parade, where the Holden family lived.

Julianne and Piper Holden had run together every week

since their daughters – now in their fifth year of secondary school – were babies. Their feet had pounded against the pavements of some of Midtown's most exclusive streets, through births and deaths, high days and heartbreaks. These runs had become important to both women, the ritual only interrupted for three reasons: during family holidays; when pneumonia had confined Piper to bed for two weeks; and on the death of Julianne's parents fourteen years ago.

Her mother had been killed by her father's falling chainsaw when he had lost his footing on a ladder while pruning a tree. This shocking accident – and his catastrophic heart attack a few minutes later – triggered a malaise in Julianne that caused her to sit perfectly still for eight days until Piper took control, caring for her children, encouraging her to wash and dress and eat something warm. Julianne owed a great debt to Piper. Their friendship – forged in the fires of early motherhood – was unbreakable after that.

Even the fallen branches and punched-out garden fences, the aftermath of last night's storm, would not stop Julianne today. She'd promised Piper she would call for her, *come what may*, and Julianne did not break her promises.

Despite the enviable location and size of her own home, Julianne often mused that if she could choose any house in this upmarket enclave of beachside properties, it would be Piper's.

The Holden house was an airy art deco wonder, inspired by the prow of an ocean liner. It was double-fronted with two sets of curved bay windows painted white and edged in a glossy black. These windows, lit by the brilliance of vintage chandeliers, bracketed wide stone steps that led up to a front door which opened onto a vast hallway. A spiral staircase twisted upwards to a spacious second floor with six large bedrooms. The two bedrooms at the front of the house – including Piper's opulent master suite – had their own balconies which overlooked the sea. Following the curve of the bay windows and enclosed by safety railings, they were reminiscent of a ship's deck.

When the Holdens had left behind their modest semi-detached in one of Midtown's less salubrious neighbour-hoods and moved here ten years ago, they had filled the garden with palm trees and threaded lights along hidden pathways that wound through the extensive grounds. They'd soon become known for their annual summer party, peopled by well-heeled guests and befitting of a family who glittered with money and success.

A gust of wind whipped Julianne's hair – dark auburn save for the Mallen streak that blazed down from her crown and ran through her left eyebrow – and carried with it a taste of the coast. She upped her pace and less than a minute later found herself outside Seawings.

Piper usually opened the door as soon as Julianne appeared, tossing a cheery goodbye behind her. The children were old enough to walk themselves to school now, the women no longer bound by the strictures of the school run.

Julianne stretched her leg, an old calf injury niggling at her. A woman walked past, her heels clicking against the pavement on her way to the train station. On a strip of grass that ran across the top of the cliff, a grey-haired man in a cap and scarf threw a ball for his spaniel. Adam Moran, a teacher at the children's school. He saw Julianne watching and waved. She waved back.

Gray Holden's Range Rover was parked on the driveway

and the downstairs lights were on. He had an office in town and often drove to work. Seeing his car jolted her, even though he worked from home now and again and its presence was not unexpected. Julianne lingered, uncertain how much longer to wait, but the wind was getting stronger and, after a moment's hesitation, she ran lightly up the steps.

Piper did not answer the first or second ring of the doorbell.

Julianne swivelled on her trainers and scanned the horizon. In the brightening day, the lighthouse beam was no longer visible and the sky was mapped with clouds. The teacher was still throwing the ball for his dog but she saw him glance again in her direction. She wondered whether to wave for a second time but decided it was overkill. He'd acknowledged her already. Once was enough.

With no letter box to lift and shout through – the Holdens had a free-standing mailbox at the edge of their property – Julianne turned back to the door and rapped on the polished wood until her knuckles smarted. But no one – not Piper or Gray or their two children – came to see who it was.

Julianne felt for the mobile tucked in her running belt and called her friend's landline. From inside the house, she heard the phone ringing a dozen times, shrill, sharp. She hung up and the ringing stopped.

Standing on her tiptoes, she peered through the sitting room window but it was empty. *The lights are on but no one's home.* A laugh spilled from her, a high, elastic sound, and then a woman's voice, accented and warm, surprised her, making her jump.

'Ćao, Julianne. Do you need help?'

It was Mila Lovri, Piper's cleaner, her slim body bundled

up in a faux fur jacket, an oversized black patent leather handbag hanging from her arm. Market-chic. Piper called her a 'housekeeper' but Julianne dismissed that as an affectation, although she kept that thought to herself.

'I'm supposed to go running with Piper but no one's answering the door.'

Mila clicked her tongue and rolled her eyes in the manner of an impatient teenager. 'It'll be the radio,' she said confidently. 'Riva likes it loud.'

Julianne was certain that Piper's fifteen-year-old daughter would have her headphones jammed into her ears, streaming music from her phone rather than listening to the radio, but felt churlish to mention it.

The cleaner rummaged in her bag and held up a key, her chipped red nail varnish bright against the dull skies. 'Follow me, *moj prijatelj*. Let's see what's keeping them so busy this morning.'

The house had the feel of the breakfast rush about it. Julianne could smell fresh coffee and burnt toast. An unzipped rucksack was waiting by the front door next to a pair of black school shoes, laces untied. Mila placed her own bag on the hallway floor and hung up her coat. 'Hello,' she called, '*Dòbro jùtro*.' Her Serbian accent, the rising note at the end of her sentence, made her greeting sound like a song. 'It's Mila.'

Julianne followed the cleaner into the kitchen. Mila maintained a steady stream of conversation, interspersed with the occasional phrase Julianne didn't understand, but it died away when she opened the door and saw the empty room. She clicked her tongue again. 'They'll be late for school.'

A china mug rested on the table. Julianne stepped forward and cupped her hand around it. Not warm, exactly, but not cold. 'They must be upstairs,' said Mila, pulling her apron over her head and tying up its strings. She pointed to the ceiling. 'I go up and hurry them along.'

She didn't know how to answer that. During their morning runs, Piper had often complained that Mila embraced her duties a little too enthusiastically at times. 'We pay her to keep the place clean and tidy,' she'd said on one memorable occasion when Mila, concerned that Mr Holden would be late for work, had walked into her employers' bedroom without knocking and caught them *in flagrante.* 'If Gray needs an alarm clock, he's perfectly capable of setting one.'

Julianne wondered if Piper would have been so disapproving if Mila had been less attractive and not quite as young.

She glanced around the kitchen. A half-eaten bowl of cornflakes stood on the table, spoon lolling against the rim, three pearls of spilt milk resting on the wooden grain.

From the radio on the windowsill, the breakfast show chirped its way through an interview with an actor promoting his latest film, an update about traffic on the M25 and the gale-force winds that were pummelling most of the country.

The ceiling light was bright, a talisman against the autumnal murk of morning. A knife, covered in butter and toast crumbs, lay next to an open jar of strawberry jam. A French textbook, a scribbled list of verbs; a script of *The Crucible,* its pages splayed apart.

On the worktop by the bread bin, three mobile phones were charging next to a set of car keys and a wallet. A handbag sat on the chair. By the vegetable rack a second school bag was slumped, books spilling from it, a handwritten history essay on 'The Decline of the British Empire' in a plastic wallet. Wet washing sat in the machine. The detritus of a broken glass filled the dustpan. The clock on the wall read 7.56 a.m.

A snapshot of family life, ordinary and reassuring. Except the Holden family was not there.

'They're not upstairs,' said Mila, slipping back into the kitchen, a frown creasing her usually smooth forehead. 'But Mr Holden's car is still on the driveway. It's most unusual.' Then a smile transformed her face. 'The pool. Of course.' And she was off again, through the back door and down the garden to the pool house.

Piper and the children wouldn't be in the pool. It didn't make sense, not at this time of the morning, but Julianne understood that Mila was grasping at straws, no matter how flimsy.

She sat down at the kitchen table. There was no doubt about it, this behaviour was out of character. Piper was a precise, organized woman who paid her bills on time, cooked meals from scratch, and whose nails and hair were always immaculate. She wouldn't cancel their run without warning. Julianne typed out a message on her mobile. Where are you?

One of the phones on the worktop vibrated with an incoming message.

Julianne stood again, unable to be still. She wandered into the entrance hall and listened to the house she knew almost as well as her own. Apart from the murmur of the radio and the sough of the wind, it was silent.

Several rooms adjoined the cavernous hallway and most

of their doors were closed, apart from what Piper referred to, somewhat grandiloquently, as the drawing room.

Julianne was struck by a stirring of disquietude. This room was only used when the Holdens were entertaining guests, particularly Gray's clients. Piper always kept the door closed. But it was ajar, a glimpse of thick curtains, polished parquet and luxurious sofas covered in striped silk. She loitered, and then, making a decision, closed her fingers around the brass door handle and went in.

Although there were many to choose from, this was Julianne's favourite room in Seawings. A large airy space. Perfectly proportioned. Tastefully decorated. Piper had a weekly delivery of fresh flowers and a large vase of autumn blooms, flashes of burnt orange and fire-engine red, dominated the mantelpiece, their edges beginning to brown and curl.

Behind her, she heard the vague sound of Mila closing the back door and then the younger woman's voice filled the hallway.

'The pool house is locked,' she said, 'but they can't have gone out. They haven't taken their keys or their phones.' She didn't say it but her subtext was clear: *This is strange behaviour. Something is very wrong.*

Julianne sensed movement behind her and Mila appeared in the drawing room. The look of concern on the cleaner's face had been replaced by something darker. In the hollows of her face, fear had made itself at home.

The women stood side by side in the still and greying morning, both lost in thought. As Mila traced a finger across a small table, automatically checking for non-existent dust, her gaze swept the room, settling on the icicle chandelier that had once belonged to a famous London hotel. A strangled sound, a cross between a gasp and a cry of pain, made Julianne jump.

Mila dragged a footstool across the parquet and reached for the crystals, her face crumpled in shock. 'I dusted it last week,' she said. 'But look at it now.' Her hands were trembling and the cut-glass pendants made a tiny clinking sound as they knocked together. '*Look.*'

Fear, a slippery coil of it, tightened in Julianne's stomach. She forced herself to look upwards.

The Holdens had bought the original art deco light fitting from a specialist dealer when the hotel had closed down a couple of years ago. With dozens of antique icicle droplets, it had cost tens of thousands of pounds.

Piper was always complaining that the bottom tier of the chandelier hung too low, especially as she was so tall. But Julianne wasn't thinking about that now.

All she could see was the fine mist of blood that coated the delicate pendalogues.

2

Tuesday morning

The day the Holdens disappeared

The young man slung his rucksack over his shoulder, picked up his holdall with one hand and a small leather-handled wooden chest with the other, and stepped off the train. Even here, inside the station, he caught the taste of brine and stilled, scenting the air like a wolf.

He slid his ticket into the barrier and meandered into the early morning mist, its briskness welcome after the stuffiness of the carriage. It was a while since he'd been this close to the sea – not since the death of his mother Gloria – and already he felt the pull of it.

Not wanting to squander his money on a taxi – he still had a good chunk of the £100,000 reward left but that was not for luxuries – he climbed the steep cliff stairs until his legs began to ache, and followed the rough gravel path that cut above the bay.

The wind pulled at his hair but he barely noticed it. He was intent on the square red-brick building that stood on a distant promontory, edging the salt marshes. He walked on and on, mind empty, relishing the unkind bite of the weather and the way it sharpened his senses.

A froth of gulls – twenty or thirty of them – circled in formation on thermals overhead. Above him, the sky had faded into the nothingness he remembered from the seascape of his childhood. But the house in front of him was nothing like the run-down flat he'd grown up in.

It stood on the cliff's edge, a dwelling with large windows that looked out across the waves. Rising from its castellations was a third storey, encased in tilted glass and a peaked cap of a roof. A radio antenna pointed skywards. The coastguard's lookout, a former wireless station that had intercepted German transmissions in the First World War. Two hundred metres away, the lighthouse rose in proud companionship.

A rusted anchor was propped against the front wall and the key was tucked beneath it, exactly as the landlady had promised. He'd taken the converted tower on a short let, wanting to find his feet in this place before putting down roots. But the taste of salt on his lips and the rough hand of the wind told him he was home.

The kitchen was austere but practical, the sitting room comfortable but cold. He switched on the kettle and carried his bags upstairs. Time for a five-minute shower. He didn't want to be late on his first day.

He pulled the letter from his coat pocket and re-read it for the twentieth time, his eyes alighting on the insignia in the top right-hand corner, confirming his six-month attachment. Three years after entering Essex Police's fast-track programme, eight years after plunging a knife into the hollows of a serial killer's spine, and nine years after watching his father's body disappear beneath the dirty churn of the Thames Estuary, he'd landed on his feet, a coveted position in Midtown-on-Sea's Major Crime Unit.

Detective Constable Saul Anguish.

It had a pleasing ring about it.

3

Tuesday morning

The day the Holdens disappeared

Tea, scalding and sweet, for the shock.

Julianne knew her way around Piper's kitchen better than Mila did. As the cleaner seemed incapable of action, she poured a slug of cooking brandy into a steaming mug, pushed it towards her, turned off the radio and dialled the police.

Mila lapsed into silence, broken by the occasional mutter of words which Julianne didn't understand but suspected were Serbian expletives. When she'd finished on the telephone, she crouched down and clasped the woman's trembling hands in her own.

'The police will find them.'

Mila lifted her tear-streaked face to Julianne, her expression like a stunned animal. 'But what if something has happened?' Her voice shrank. 'Here, in England, they are my family.'

A part of Julianne wanted to shake some sense into the young woman, who was now tearing cellophane from a cigarette packet, despite Piper's strict policy of no smoking in the house. *Of course* something had happened. A family didn't just disappear, mid-breakfast, phones still plugged into chargers, school bag by the front door.

But she forced herself to keep the lid on her own fear, which was threatening to bubble over. Two panicked women would help no one.

A thought struck her and she abruptly left the kitchen, half running down the hallway, through the front door and outside, down the steps, not to Gray's car on the driveway, but around the corner to the property's triple garage.

The doors were open, in preparation for the mobile car valeting service that visited fortnightly, but their other cars – a top-of-the-range Lexus RX, a BMW and a vintage Jaguar – were parked side by side, shiny jewels in the morning grey.

If the Holdens had left by choice, they'd have taken a car, wouldn't they?

Mila was wearing rubber gloves and brandishing disinfectant spray when Julianne walked back into the kitchen. Her defensive half-shrug made her look too young. 'I'm paid to clean.'

Julianne rested a hand on Mila's arm. She was still trembling – shock, Julianne supposed, and she guided the woman back to the table. A wisp of smoke rose from one of Piper's prized olive bowls, a second cigarette already lit and resting next to a small pyramid of ash.

'I don't think cleaning is a good idea. The police might need to take fingerprints or something.'

Mila took another drag on her cigarette, a rubber-gloved

hand rising to her lips. 'But I need money for food. Who is going to pay me?'

'Let's worry about that later, shall we?' said Julianne with the air of one who didn't need to concern herself over such things. After a moment's hesitation, she retrieved a £20 note she kept folded inside her running belt for emergencies. 'Take this. But it's best we don't touch anything for now.'

The women settled into silence again. Neither knew what to say to the other, their shared concern over the Holdens not enough to bridge their differences. Julianne wanted to tell Mila to stop smoking, that Piper would hate it if she knew, but she lacked the appetite for confrontation.

'I wonder how long the police will be?' she said, trying to lighten the awkwardness between them.

'Why? You have somewhere more important to be?' Judging by the edge to her tone, Mila was not afraid to articulate her disapproval.

Her over-confidence irritated Julianne. Piper had complained before that Mila was too sure of herself. Now she could understand why. 'As a matter of fact, I do. I'm supposed to be at a funeral in a couple of hours.'

The cleaner's demeanour visibly altered. 'Oh, *bože*. I am sorry to hear that.' She peeled off her gloves, her bright blue eyes settling on Julianne. 'It was someone you loved?'

Julianne lowered her gaze, not able to find the words to explain.

'I am sorry,' said Mila again, with the stilted formality of one who'd learned almost all her English from black-and-white films of the 1940s. She crossed herself and patted Julianne's hand. Her skin was cool and dry.

As they waited for the police to arrive, each lost to her thoughts, Julianne struggled to ignore the tightening band across her chest, a straitjacket of anxiety. The spray of blood on the chandelier had disturbed her more than she was letting on.

An urge to be sick – to physically expel the sense of foreboding from her body – gripped her until she half rose from the chair, certain she was about to lose control of herself. Several deep breaths later, the sensation had passed, and she watched the hands crawl around the clock, counting the minutes until the authorities knocked on the door.

She didn't tell Mila what Piper Holden had whispered down the telephone last night, that frantic call, mouth close to the receiver, the pull of fear tugging at her words.

'I'm frightened, Julianne. Gray said he's going to kill me.'

4

Thursday afternoon

Five days before the Holdens disappeared

Piper Holden snipped off the thread and admired her handi-
work. Her fingers ached – five hundred sequins was a lot to
sew by hand – but the dress looked stunning. She could
have bought something similar in any one of Midtown's
designer boutiques, but Riva had particular ideas about
colour and cut, and if there was one thing Piper excelled at,
it was making clothes.

She slipped the finished dress carefully onto a padded
hanger, silver sequins flickering in the lamplight like fish
scales. Her daughter – blessed with the fresh complexion
and angular limbs of youth – would cause accidents in that
dress. Men had been looking at her with hunger in their
eyes since she was twelve.

Piper tidied up her box of cotton reels, needles and buttons. Seawings was quiet this afternoon. Riva and her brother
Artie were staying late at school for rehearsals and rugby
practice, and Gray was still at the office, putting the finishing
touches to a deal he was insistent he had to pull off.

She rose from the chaise longue – a French antique shipped in by Gray and upholstered in pale pink silk for her forty-third birthday – and contemplated the decanter of sherry she'd refilled in preparation for the weekend. A mental headshake. *No, too early.* She wasn't an alcoholic, for heaven's sake.

The place was spotless. Mila may be over-familiar at times but she did a wonderful job of keeping their home clean and tidy. So what if she was young and beautiful? So what if she made Piper feel like a spare part? Gray frequently entertained clients at Seawings – keen to show off the abundant fruits of his labour – and with only a few hours' notice, it was important their house always looked its best.

Piper's manicured fingers drifted across the laptop Artie had left on the coffee table. She opened up the slim metallic lid and logged on to one of her favourite sites – a high-end brand famous across the world for its luxury clothing, perfumes and jewellery.

The watch she coveted – black ceramic and steel, and set with fifty-two brilliant-cut diamonds – cost £8,800. Gray had always said she could spend what she liked and although it had taken her years to feel comfortable with his generosity – the lean years of her childhood had instilled in her a sense of frugality – she'd grown used to it. But even she hesitated at this extravagance. Christmas was only a few weeks away. Gray would buy it for her then if she asked.

She gazed at the image and held out her wrist, admiring the elegant nub of bone, imagining the glossy strap encircling it. They were attending a black-tie event at the children's private school in two weeks' time to mark its centenary year, two tickets already bought and paid for. A perfect accessory to the scarlet sheath she was planning to wear. With a decisive nod of her head, she reached for the telephone receiver and punched in a number.

The saleswoman was well spoken and charming. Piper was a returning customer and although the glee in the woman's voice at the prospect of a decent-sized commission was masked, she could not conceal it completely.

'Usual credit card, Mrs Holden?'

'Please.'

A pause for the transaction to go through. Music. Puccini's 'O mio babbino caro'. She examined her nails. One of them had chipped and would need to be redone. She ought to get a hair appointment in the diary too. Her grey roots were pushing through her blonde bob faster than she'd like. The music stopped. A whisper of sharply held breath and then a cooler, more impersonal tone.

'I'm afraid your card has been declined.'

Piper sat upright in the chair, the receiver tucked beneath her chin. A vision of her mother, face blanched a shade paler than the flour coating her hands, popped into her memory. Even twenty-eight years later, she could still see the finely ground dust drifting through the air and settling on the hall carpet as her mother wiped her palms on her apron and took the phone from Piper while the head of the clinic – *Is Mrs Marisa Sharp in? It's urgent* – broke the news that her youngest daughter, Piper's sister Clodagh, had been found dead in her bed. In all the years that followed, Piper had never heard a scream like it, that note of anguish plucked from a shadowy hiding place, distilling the *sensation* of grief into the purest of sounds. The knee-weakening shock of it all.

The saleswoman cleared her throat. Piper remembered herself and gave an embarrassed laugh. 'That must be a mistake.'

A brief silence followed in which Piper sensed her dubiety.

'Please don't worry, Mrs Holden,' said the saleswoman eventually, her words polished with professionalism. Then, still hopeful: 'Do you wish to continue this transaction with another card?'

Piper's cheeks were warm, heart racing. 'Let me get to the bottom of this and then I'll be in touch. I'm so sorry for wasting your time.'

In the study, Piper rifled through the drawer containing bank statements. Gray had wanted to go paperless but she liked the heft of pages in her hand, even if it didn't exactly help the planet.

She ran her finger down last month's transactions on their joint credit card, but there was nothing untoward or unexpected, nothing to suggest they'd tipped over their limit or had got into difficulties. The bill had been paid on time, as it was every month. Apart from their mortgage, Piper had never been in debt. She saw it as a weakness. In her eyes, money was the route to security. And security meant never having to depend on anyone else. Her mother had not taught her much but she had shown her the error in doing that. That last week with Clodagh. Skin and bone. Cold even in the fierceness of high summer, the sips of water, the downy hair on her arms and cheeks. Marisa Sharp begging the bank to extend her overdraft, knowing it wouldn't cover the thousands they'd need to pay for private medical care but focused only on getting her daughter in front of a specialist as soon as possible, worrying about the details later. The empty cupboards. The bedsheets worn thin in places. The too-small shoes and free school meals. Piper had promised herself a life as far away from that as possible. And she had succeeded. With flying colours.

But still she felt the need to be certain – a compulsion to officialize it – so she returned to the sitting room and picked up the telephone again, her hand tightening around the receiver until her knuckles became whitened rocks.

This call is being recorded for training and quality purposes. Why did automated voices sound so bored? She pressed a series of buttons until she was put through to a human instead of a computer.

The man listened to her rushed explanation. *Can't remember my online banking passwords.* (A light laugh.) *My husband deals with all that and he's stuck in an important meeting that can't be interrupted. Could you be a sweetheart and possibly check the most up-to-date transactions for this card and the rest of our joint accounts?* (A well-timed pause.) *I'd be so grateful.*

His fingers made a tapping sound against his keyboard, then silence, the all-consuming kind that comes from being muted. Piper sat very still, waiting. She mentally logged the time: 4.54 p.m. At last, the catch of his breath against the mouth of the receiver, that background chorus of call centre voices.

The Man on the End of the Phone cleared his throat, and when he spoke again, he was hesitant, almost apologetic. 'I'm very sorry, Mrs Holden, but I've checked and rechecked, and I don't think it's a mistake.'

Piper sucked in air. 'What do you mean?'

'There was a period of unusual activity on one of your accounts several months ago – a series of regular large withdrawals – but I can't see anything untoward since then. Until now.'

'And what's happened now?'

'It's clear you have no idea, so I'm sorry to be the one to break it to you, but every one of your accounts has been emptied and closed.'

5

Tuesday morning

The day the Holdens disappeared

Saul followed the cliff path into town. The trees swayed in the wind, last night's storm still making its presence felt. His lungs filled with sea air. For a moment, he was drowning in the past, the coastal brine rinsing the grime of the city from his nostrils and the dark fault-lines from his heart.

The police station was on the main drag into Midtown-on-Sea, sandwiched between a row of exclusive restaurants on one side and a run of expensive boutiques on the other. The pavement was full of women with smart prams and matching nappy bags, striped scarves and thick, stylish coats, reeking of money. A shining bubble of affluence, a world away from the grim reaches of his childhood.

His mother had worn handmade skirts and cheap T-shirts from the market. Gloria: meaning immortal glory. He hoped she'd found it somewhere between the rubbish sacks slumped outside the pub, disguising the shape of her body as the end-of-March snow had fallen, and the treacherous vomit had filled her lungs and choked her.

Her sobriety had been short-lived. Money – Saul's reward money, to be accurate – had meant she'd graduated from separating the alcohol in bottles of mouthwash and hand sanitizer to buying vodka from the off-licence. He'd wanted her to eat nutritious meals, to afford the electricity bill without having to choose between rent or heat, to not barter the secret parts of herself in exchange for dirty notes, touched by lustful fingers. But while she had sometimes attempted to do what he'd asked of her, she'd been unable to resist the siren song of liquid oblivion.

'I don't want it, Saul.' She'd pushed the bank book across the table, the blurred edges of Saturday afternoon darkening her kitchen as rain streamed down the windows and the sea was a coloured-in storm, but he'd paid money into her account every month anyway. Much later, on that vicious April night, while Saul had been on secondment to the traffic division, a fatherly colleague had broken the news of her death to him. The officer had tracked him down to the scene of an RTA where a young driver had wrapped his car round a tree. As sleet was stippling Saul's face, the spring flowers pushing through a bloodied patch of frozen earth, he'd remembered that book. He'd found it a comfort to discover she'd used small amounts of his money here and there while at the same time blaming himself for facilitating her addiction.

Her death – officially recorded as *arterial hypoxemia caused by pulmonary aspiration of vomit* – was the end of everything. She was the only person who knew the truth about his father. He had no brothers or sisters. No relationship with a woman that had lasted more than a few weeks. He didn't know how to let them in and lost interest when they began to ask intimate questions about his past, pushing against a door he didn't want to open. In the end, he would close and lock it, shutting them out without a backward glance. He would not have called it loneliness exactly. But without his mother to anchor him, his place in the world felt insubstantial. As the sole surviving member of his family, he was adrift, alone – and that feeling had carried him along the estuary to Midtown-on-Sea.

Saul was due to report to Detective Inspector Angus O'Neill at 10.30 a.m. sharp. The word *sharp* had been typed in bold in the email and underlined. He tried, without success, not to hate him. He wanted this job more than anything he'd wanted for a long time. Expectations would have to be met, simple as that.

But first, coffee.

The shop was too warm and too busy, the queue snaking almost to the door. He was tempted to leave but he craved the caffeine hit. Saul glanced at the clock on the wall. Twenty minutes to go. Just enough time.

When he was third from the front, the rich smell of coffee beans intensifying with every step, a man with rimless glasses, a forgettable face and carrying a takeaway cardboard cup bumped shoulders with him. The lid was not properly secured and hot liquid spilled over the man's smart jacket.

'For Christ's sake,' he said, glaring at Saul.

The fine hairs at the back of Saul's neck lifted along with his temper. 'You should look where you're going. Could have caused a nasty accident.'

The man took a step towards Saul, staring at him in a way that was designed to intimidate. He was not particularly tall but he carried himself with a hardened ranginess more powerful than height or bulk. But it didn't bother Saul. He squared up to the stranger, shoulders back, palms facing skywards, fingers curving into a 'Come on, then' gesture. The atmosphere bristled with aggression, although not another word had been spoken.

The man held his gaze for a couple of seconds before shaking his head, as if convincing himself not to squander any more of his time on a waste of space like Saul. But Saul recognized that expression, even if the man didn't know it himself: surrender.

The police station was the kind of Tuesday-morning quiet only affluent suburbs at the edge of the Essex coast understood. Saul waited for the desk sergeant to sign him in.

'What kind of a name is Anguish?' the officer asked with a smirk. 'Oh, wait. You're the kid who nailed that psycho.'

Saul refused to bite. He leaned forward and made a show of reading the sergeant's name badge. 'Everhard.' He raised an eyebrow. The sergeant coloured and shut up.

For all his determination to become a detective, Saul was not comfortable in police stations. He'd had more experience than most.

At the age of eleven, he was caught stealing a can of Shandy Bass, and the corner shop owner had dragged him all the way to Elm Road by his ear. The officer manning the desk had threatened arrest to 'teach him a lesson' and given him a stern talking to, but there had been no formal punishment. The council mowers had been trimming the cliff gardens that afternoon and a drunk had vomited in the stairwell. Even now, the smell of freshly cut grass and the scent of pine disinfectant and parmesan could throw him back to that memory.

When he was fifteen, he'd accompanied his mother to file a missing person's report following the disappearance of his father, even though they'd both known he was lost to the dark embrace of the estuary.

The last statement he'd given – eight years ago now, when he was sixteen – had forensically detailed his courage in plunging a knife into a serial killer's back and saving the lives of two young children. Not the whole story, though. He would hold that secret to himself until he was cold in the ground.

As far as the police, the newspapers, the wider community were concerned, Saul Anguish was a hero. Some days, he even believed it himself.

The desk sergeant was talking to someone. Detective Inspector Angus O'Neill. Saul heard his name mentioned and smoothed down his trousers. No jeans, his line manager had said. He turned, a quarter-smile of greeting lighting his face.

The man from the coffee shop stared back.

6

The day the Holdens disappeared

'I'm sorry,' said Julianne, glancing at the clock. 'I can't stay any longer. I need to go home.'

The young cleaner looked aghast. '*Jebiga*. You can't leave me on my own. There's' – she gave a weak shudder – 'blood.'

Julianne crouched and retied the lace of her left trainer. 'The police will be here soon. I'll be back as soon as I can, I promise.'

Before Mila had a chance to protest further, Julianne had shut the door behind her and was running down the wide steps of Seawings and back to her own house, feet slamming against the pavement, sloughing off Mila's bleak proclamations like dead skin.

She breathed in the sea air, shivered in the wind. A headache throbbed between her eyes. *Where are they? What if Piper or the children are hurt? What's happened to Gray?* Her stomach twisted at the unanswered questions.

It was one thing for an adult to vanish – people walked away from their lives all the time – but for a wealthy family

28

to disappear, leaving their cars and phones and wallets behind them? That hinted at something much darker. As for the blood, she couldn't bear to think of what it might mean.

Her own house was silent when she let herself in.

'It's only me.' Julianne waited a beat for an answer that didn't come. 'You won't believe what's happened.' The words tumbled from her, impossible to contain. 'The Holdens – all four of them – are missing.'

Her voice echoed around the walls. The children would be at school, but she'd thought Quiller might pop home to check how things were after last night's phone call. His appointment would be over by now and he knew she might need support.

But there was no answering hello, no request for coffee or a shoulder massage, or that familiar creak as he rose from the chair in his light-filled office overlooking the bay to hug her too tightly, fingers pinching her skin.

She had stayed at Seawings longer than she'd planned to and now she would have to hurry. She stripped off her running clothes and stepped into the rainforest shower Quiller had spent hours choosing online. Interior design interested her too, but she was realistic enough to know that her husband always had the last word. Even if she didn't like it, he would overrule her because, as he often reminded her, he was the one who earned all the money. On the rare occasion she brought home a scented candle or pretty cushion that had caught her eye, he would demand receipts and click his tongue at the *exorbitant* price. Even the food shopping was an ordeal of its own. If she hadn't filled her trolley with three-for-two offers and kept within a strictly allocated budget, there would be a post-mortem. On one occasion, he'd stopped her from going out with her friends, confiscating the credit card he permitted her to use on trips to the supermarket. 'If you can't budget properly, Julianne, I'm afraid you can't afford to have a meal out.'

But this didn't stop *him* from spending money. They had plenty of it, after all. And he would gift her nice things – clothes and jewellery, mostly – and pay for haircuts and beauty treatments to maintain appearances. It was just that he liked to be the one in charge of their bank accounts and decide how it was spent.

Julianne dried herself off and dressed with care. A tailored suit – classic, not showy. Black sheer tights. A platinum watch and a silver locket at her throat. Heeled boots, but not too high. A soft grey leather clutch bag.

She called a taxi – she would need a glass of wine at the wake and anyway, what choice did she have? – and while she waited for it to arrive, she cast an appraising eye over her reflection.

Her hair was in a sleek bun at the nape of her neck, accentuating the flash of her Mallen streak. A suggestion of eyeshadow, a light sweep of blusher and lipstick, nothing gaudy or bold. She drew the tip of her manicured forefinger beneath her eye to remove a smudge of mascara and checked her teeth. Julianne stared at the mirror and an attractive woman, expensive and groomed, stared back.

A text informed her that her taxi was waiting outside. She would pay with the cash she'd taken out of Quiller's wallet last night. With a last check of her bag – comb, tissues, keys – she was gone.

* * *

The church and cemetery were stitched into the cliffs, over-looking the bay. Quiller said it was ironic the dead occupied Midtown's most sought-after location when they were not able to appreciate its multi-million-pound view. But Quiller was an estate agent. That was the way his mind worked: it was all about the money. As someone whose parents were buried here, Julianne disapproved of his ethos. The curve of the sandy beach and wide mouth of the sea, the wind's kick and the fluctuations of light, were a balm to those tethered to this graveyard by the death of their loved ones. Mourners, whether coping with the open sore of fresh grief or the scars of older losses, deserved to find comfort in the majesty of the seascape.

St Mary's Church was the sort of place one might find on a film set. It was a white clapboard building – an odd choice, given the relentless buffeting of the elements – with a grey spire and a cemetery enclosed by a white picket fence. It was surrounded by long grasses which bowed when the wind raced through them. The air often tasted of salt. Sea-birds wheeled across a sky which changed its clothes by the hour. A place of peace in a world that had all but forgotten how to respect death.

Seventy or so people were clustered on the porch at the front of the church, the queue inching its way inside. They had the look of blackbirds about them, hushed and flutter-ing in their funereal clothes.

As Julianne walked along the path towards the building, the cortège pulled up by the gate and she quickened her pace until she became part of the crowd, turning in silence to watch the family arrive.

A woman wearing pearl earrings and a navy raincoat leaned into Julianne. 'Awful, isn't it?' She squeezed her arm.

'How did you know her? Are you one of the mothers from school?'

'No.' Julianne offered a faint smile. 'We were friends a long time ago.' She was prevented from answering more fully by an usher, who held out an Order of Service and directed her to a pew.

The church was cold and perfumed with flowers. The vicar cleared his throat and asked the congregation to rise.

Music. The slow procession of a father and his two young sons walking behind a coffin with polished handles and bedecked with lilies. Julianne traced the smiling face of a woman, freckles sprinkled across her nose and sun-bleached hair. *In Loving Memory of Anoushka Thornton, 14 July 1979– 27 October 2021.* From somewhere in front of her, Julianne caught the sound of muffled sobbing. She reached into her bag for a tissue and dabbed at her eyes.

After the service, a flautist played the coffin to the grave-side. Mourners clustered around the freshly turned earth, no longer fluttering blackbirds but ants in a colony, pur-poseful, each with their role to perform. Julianne stood near the back, the wind snatching strands of hair from her bun. Anoushka's husband, known to his friends as Thorne, bent and whispered something to the coffin as it was lowered into the ground. Her sons – Seb and Thomas – tossed handwritten letters and a sprig of lily of the valley after their mother.

After her stellar fifteen-year career at Barclays, Anoushka was ready for a different type of challenge. She moved back to Midtown, where she'd attended Southcliffe High School for Girls as a teenager, and devoted her life to her family.

Julianne had paid careful attention to the eulogy. The

words played on a loop in her memory. *Southcliffe. Barclays. Devoted to family.*

As the vicar committed Anoushka Thornton's body to the dirt, her younger son let out a thin wail. His father put an arm around him. The boy's cry reminded Julianne of a sandpiper chick, calling for its mother, and it made her think of Riva and Artie Holden, missing from their home for several hours now. For the first time since arriving at the church, emotion swelled her throat.

The pub was thick with laughter and whisky fumes by the time Julianne arrived, even though it was not yet lunchtime.

Men in dark suits stood unmoving as rocks while their wives eddied around them, checking on the Thornton boys and removing cling-film from plates of sandwiches. The conversation was louder now, broken by the occasional huff of laughter, an inevitable lightening of the funeral tension that Julianne had witnessed before. One or two of those men in dark suits followed Julianne with their eyes as she made her way to the bar. Julianne ignored them. She was used to it.

'Can I get you a drink?' He was tall – six foot two, at least – with tired eyes and a salt-and-pepper quiff, and he was leaning against the wooden counter, sipping a pint of Guinness.

'Your speech was beautiful,' she said.

He smiled at her but there was no joy in it. 'My *sister* was beautiful. We're going to miss her horribly.' He put down his glass and gestured to the bartender. 'My friend here would like a . . . ?' He turned to her with a question mark in his eyes.

Julianne ordered a vodka and soda with fresh lime. She

waited for the man – his name was Ben – to fill the silence and he obliged. He studied her face, an expression of interest on his own.

'How did you know Anoushka?'

She swallowed a large mouthful of her drink, bubbles tickling her nose. She had expected this question but it didn't stop her from stumbling over the answer.

'From school. A long time ago. I saw the Death Notice in the newspaper and I wanted to come and pay my respects.'

'That's lovely. So you were at Southcliffe too?'

Julianne nodded and his face brightened, a glimpse of sun in the rain. He laid his hand on her arm. 'There's a whole gang of her old school friends here. Would you like me to take you over to them?'

'Thank you, but I doubt they'd remember me. I was only there for a year but Anoushka was very kind to me.'

His eyes filled. 'She always was.' He released a shaky breath. 'Why don't you come and say hello to Thorne instead? I know he'd love to meet you.'

Five minutes later, Julianne was being introduced to Anoushka's husband. He was inspecting a card attached to one of the floral displays the funeral directors had brought with them from the church. Thorne's eyes were red-rimmed and bloodshot but he cut a striking figure in his immaculate white shirt and black silk tie.

'I'm sorry for your loss,' said Julianne, extending her hand to shake his. He ignored it. Too late, she smelled the wall of alcohol on his breath and realized he was several miles down the road to drunkenness. To cover her embarrassment, she cast around for a distraction. Behind him, amongst the photographs that charted Anoushka's life, she noticed a bouquet of ivory roses and vivid lilacs in the shape of a teardrop. 'What stunning flowers.'

Thorne swayed, draining his goblet of red wine. His fist was curled around its stem and Julianne wondered whether the fury of his grief might break it. He waved the card at her, his words rough and slurred, but she couldn't make out what he was saying.

'Let's get you some coffee,' said Ben, trying to ease the empty glass from his grip. 'And what about a sandwich? When did you last eat something?'

Thorne shook off his brother-in-law. 'Not hungry.' He turned the card over and over in his hand.

The wine had loosened his boundaries, liquefied them. He waved the card again, his unfocused gaze roaming around the room, his words tinged with suspicion. 'Who sent these?'

Julianne glanced at Ben, who looked as uncomfortable as she felt. A stab of compassion for Thorne surprised her. The widower was unsteady on his feet, lurching to his left. She wanted to slip away but she was trapped, a deer frozen in front of an incoming car. He repeated the question, and his voice, rising, inflected with confusion and an undercurrent of anger, turned heads in their direction. One of his sons – the older boy – put down his cake, a wariness in his eyes.

'Listen to this,' said Thorne, holding the card in the air with an exaggerated flourish. Julianne could see 'Masterson's', the name of the local florist's, printed on the back. *'Darling Anoushka, my heart will never stop looking for you, with all my love.* Unsigned. Three kisses.' He spat out the last two words, as if they tasted of something spoiled and rancid.

'Come on, buddy,' said Ben, more firmly this time.

But Thorne wrenched his arm free, turning the force of his ire on his brother-in-law. 'What do you know about it? Who was she fucking behind my back?'

'Hey,' said Ben, cold and sharp as a surgeon's scalpel. 'That's my sister you're talking about.'

Julianne felt the air thicken between the men, a bolus of anxiety forming in her stomach. Thorne was still swaying, Ben observing him with a hardness in his expression. Thorne took a step towards his wife's brother and Julianne noticed Ben's fists were clenched. She glanced around, seeking help, but most had returned to their conversations and the function room was filling with the smell of hot food, and no one was looking in their direction except Thorne's eldest son.

In desperation, she scanned the mourners for his mother or sister, an aunt or a cousin. Any female relative would be better placed than she was to cool the tension with a compress of empathy and understanding, but the women were gathered together in tight knots, tending to children released from the formality of church or passing around plates of honey-glazed cocktail sausages and slabs of sponge cake.

Julianne hadn't met either of the men until ten minutes ago but now she found herself stepping between these strangers, calming the heat of their anger with her body and her voice.

'Come on,' she said, a softness to her. 'You're both on the same side.' She was standing face to face with Thorne, so close she could feel his hectic breath against her skin. Ben was somewhere behind her, but she focused her attention on the widower, waiting for him to gather himself. 'What about that coffee?' she said. He dipped his head a quarter of an inch and followed her to the rows of ugly cups squatting in their saucers, and a stainless steel urn.

She lingered nearby as he sipped his hot drink – but not too close. That was not her place. Friends and family whirled up and away again in a never-ending parade of platitudes. She drank her vodka – the ice had melted and watered it down – and watched him from her chair. As the coffee worked its way through his system, Thorne began to sober up. He was polite but his smile didn't reach his eyes. Not for the first time, Julianne understood a funeral was the darker sister to a wedding. The same guests, the same sense of ritual and formality, except only one half of the couple was in attendance, clothed in black, not ivory or white, looking to the past, not the future.

An hour passed. Then another forty minutes. The crowd began to thin. Those who had come for the free drinks and buffet – acquaintances and distant colleagues, not those entwined with the family through the deep roots of loyalty that come from years of friendship – slipped away.

Julianne's gaze flicked to the clock on the wall. Time to leave. She had drunk too much and chatted to a few guests, but now she needed to return to Seawings, to see if there was any news on Piper and her family. She glanced around, wanting to say goodbye to Thorne. If she didn't act now, there might not be another chance.

He was standing by the flowers again, shoulders slumped like a collapsed puppet. A woman touched him on the shoulder and then disappeared to the bar. Julianne seized her moment. On his cheek, a shaving cut had scabbed over but she could see its bloody crust.

'It was good to meet you. I just wish it wasn't under such dreadful circumstances.'

'Sorry about earlier.' His apology was gruff, a hint of embarrassment. 'I don't know what came over me.'

'Don't apologize,' said Julianne. 'It's completely understandable.'

'I'm not being an idiot, am I?' His eyes, red-streaked with grief and seeking reassurance, found hers. As a neutral party, she supposed she was easier to talk to than his family. 'I just want to know who sent them.'

'Most of us would feel the same way. It's a very human response.'

The woman at the bar mimed drinking from a glass. 'That's my cousin. She's getting me a drink.' The ghost of a smile. 'A *soft* one. I think she's asking if you'd like one.'

'Thank you, but I'd better not. I've got to head off now.' The colour of the day had changed and she could tell by the grey light filtering through the windows that the temperature had dropped. She buttoned up her coat and felt in her pocket for her gloves.

'I don't think I'm ever going to find out.' His eyes filled again.

Julianne wasn't sure whether she ought to get involved. David Thornton was in a great deal of distress, that much was clear. She wondered what Piper would do in her position. To speak up now felt too forward, over-familiar even. But she had no idea if they would meet again, and from what she'd witnessed so far, he was a widower stumbling through a maze of grief. The public-spirited response would be to offer to help in any way she could.

'Listen, I'm not sure whether I should suggest this or

not, but a close friend of mine works at the florist that sent the arrangement. If you let me have the card, I could try and find out for you.'

'Really?' His voice lifted in grateful surprise.

She shrugged, an *it's nothing* gesture. 'It's no trouble. I'm not sure if I'll get anywhere, but it's the least I can do.'

From inside his suit jacket, Thorne withdrew the rectangular card bordered with printed flowers. He photographed it, and then scrawled his email address on the back and thanked her.

'So, you'll be in touch if you manage to find something out?'

For the first time that day, she smiled. 'I promise you'll be the first to know.'

As Julianne waited for her taxi to arrive, it was a relief to feel the chill afternoon air against her skin. She hadn't known what to expect – wasn't sure if she'd be welcomed – but Anoushka Thornton's funeral had gone more smoothly than she'd dared to hope.

Julianne's manicured nails clicked against the screen as she checked her messages for the twentieth time. Quiller had sent a terse missive mid-morning asking why this month's heating bill was so high and could she please wear an extra cardigan at home, but there was still no word from Piper. Not that she'd expected to hear anything. As soon as she'd realized her friend's phone had been abandoned at Seawings, she knew she was in trouble.

In the distance, a taxi barrelled up the hill towards the pub. The last few hours had been a distraction, but the events of early this morning – and late last night – came crashing down, suffocating her. She stiffened, the lapels of her black suit lifting in the wind. *Open. Close. Open. Close.* Her fingers worked her leather phone case, an obsessive action, the truth twisting her insides.

Now the funeral was over, she couldn't delay any longer. As she'd known from the moment she'd stepped into the odd stillness of Seawings that morning, she would have to tell the police everything: that chilling call from Piper at 2.31 a.m. and the voicemail she'd left over an hour later, when the rest of Midtown was sleeping, the violent sound of movement and her best friend's final gut-wrenching words: *God help us all.*

7

Friday evening

Four days before the Holdens disappeared

The audience was on its feet. Piper and Artie rose with them. Her son clapped so hard the palms of his hands stung. The theatre swelled with the sound of rapturous applause.

In the seat behind her, Miranda Colman – Scarlett's mother – leaned over and poked her in the shoulder. Piper half turned to see who was bothering her. Miranda beamed at her and mouthed, 'She's a star, darling. You must be so proud.' Piper gave her a polite nod and turned her attention back to the stage.

The cast had gathered for the curtain call and Riva was standing amongst them, her silver sequins catching the lights, her cheeks flushed from pleasure or exertion, Piper couldn't tell.

One by one, the principals waited for their moment in the sun. When it was Riva's turn, she jogged to the front of the stage and gave an extravagant bow, flinging her arms out to her sides. Piper applauded wildly, torn between those familiar feelings of pride and envy. Someone nearby whistled through their fingers and the auditorium was filled with cheering, a roar of appreciation that made the skin on the back of Piper's neck tingle.

The clapping seemed to last forever. With her long hair and lengthening limbs, Riva, on the cusp of womanhood, was transformed by the acclaim. She was more than her looks, more than the part she had just played. She was changed, made dazzling by that indefinable quality, charisma.

Piper watched her daughter soak up the glory and bit her lip.

She had wanted to be an actor. When she was a child, a talent scout had invited her to audition for a television series after watching a showcase at the Royal Albert Hall by her Saturday theatre school, the only extra-curricular club her mother could afford because she qualified for a council grant.

'She's good,' he'd said to her parents afterwards. 'Better than good. And she's exactly what they're looking for.' Piper had begged her parents to let her try out. The scout, so convinced of her star quality, had even persuaded the producer to call them and work his magic. He'd cajoled, charmed and pleaded with them for half an hour to allow their daughter her big break, but her father had refused, insisting it was too precarious, too risky. They'd struggled for money all their lives – despite his wife's extraordinarily wealthy mother – and he ordered Piper to focus on her studies and get a proper job in the real world, not 'bloody fantasy land'. As she'd sat, white-lipped, on the bus home, her father had polished his glasses. 'If you're that good, there'll be other opportunities.'

The television show became a global success, launching

the Hollywood careers of several of its child stars. The *other opportunities* failed to materialize. A part of Piper resented her father's lack of ambition because she knew, if given half a chance, she would have excelled, that scrappy little girl with sharp elbows from the Chilvers estate. And she *had* survived, hadn't she? More than survived. *Succeeded.* She was wealthier than she could have dreamed of. She lived in a glorious home and enjoyed all the luxuries that money could buy. But she had dreamed of acting. For that reason alone, and although she would never admit it, Riva's triumph clogged her throat like dust.

Miranda Colman's index finger was poking her shoulder again. Piper tried to ignore her but, as chair of the Parents' Association, Miranda was one of those overbearing women with a skin so thick she did not feel the poison darts fired in her direction by the other mothers.

Piper had no desire to run the gauntlet of this woman's insistent questioning but she took a deep breath and forced herself to paste on a smile. 'What's up, Miranda?'

'Where's Gray?' she said, her voice strident enough to be heard over the applause, and then, with customary bluntness, 'He ought to be here with you and Artie, supporting Riva.'

Yes, he bloody well should. In the same way he *should* have returned the dozens of frantic phone calls she'd made since yesterday afternoon and he *should* have answered her panicked questions about the missing money, and he *should* have been brave enough to face her last night instead of hiding at the office as he usually did when things became difficult or messy or complicated.

But he hadn't done any of those things.

As for Miranda, she and Gray might be old friends but Piper bristled at her proprietorial tone. As if she needed reminding her husband hadn't bothered to show up for the most important night of his daughter's life. And that wasn't the worst of it. Even though their empty bank accounts had dominated her thoughts for the last twenty-four hours, she'd managed to push those worries to one side while she'd watched Riva's show, and she resented Miranda for bringing it up. She was too shrewd to chastise the other woman though, and made herself look away from the empty seat next to her, pasting on a rueful smile.

'Gray's away on business. He was hoping to get here in time, but unfortunately he's been held up.'

In truth, she had no idea where Gray was at this particular moment, but she wasn't about to tell Miranda Colman that.

'Business more important than his daughter, is it?' said Miranda, arching a perfectly shaped eyebrow. 'On a Friday night? I shall have to have words with that husband of yours.'

Piper bit her tongue to stop herself from retaliating and turned her attention back to the stage. Riva had stepped back-wards and a young man was grinning at her. He grabbed her daughter's hand and Riva laughed, and there they were, young and beautiful, dancing and singing with the last beats of music, the grand finale, and something inside Piper bent at the sight of them.

'Is it true Riva has an agent?' Miranda's breath was hot in her ear, wine-flavoured, hungry for information. 'I mean, I can see why after that performance, but I was surprised when Scarlett told me. I thought you'd want to concentrate on her education. That's what we're paying for, after all.' A silky laugh to soften the jab of her sabre.

Whatever Piper told Miranda, it would spread around the school community within a matter of hours. She and Julianne had often thought about challenging Queen Mimi of Midtown, their secret nickname, but agreed it would be a fruitless exercise. Miranda knew *everyone*. She would blacklist them. Not overtly, but in that insidious way that seems ridiculous until all the lunch and coffee invitations dry up and no one returns your call. And while Piper wouldn't consider herself one of *those* mothers, it had been a surprise to discover that Bay College, an academically selective independent secondary school, boasted a thriving PA and, even while she scoffed at it privately, she recognized the importance of not alienating its committee. With that in mind, she chose her next words with precision.

'It's about options,' she said, watching the students leave the stage, energy fizzing from them in that way unique to the young. 'Riva has exams coming up and we wouldn't want to jeopardize those, of course, but this is an opportunity that might not come again.'

Miranda clicked her tongue, her disapproval apparent. 'Scarlett won't be getting an agent until after her exams.' Artie rolled his eyes at his mother. It would have been uncharitable for Piper to suggest that judging by Scarlett's performance she wouldn't be getting one at all, so she said nothing, letting her voice lose itself in the stamping feet and cheers of the audience.

As soon as the curtain came down, Artie slid away to meet friends and Piper rose from her own seat, waving goodbye to Miranda without waiting to see if she waved back.

She ignored the crowds making their way towards the

front of Bay College's purpose-built theatre – officially opened by Dame Maggie Smith five years earlier – and headed for the back staircase which led to the bowels of the building.

It was quiet here, and smelled of paint and new books. Piper hurried along the corridor and down three flights of stairs before she came to the double doors that led backstage and to the dressing rooms.

She knew where she was going because she'd sneaked down here during the afternoon dress-run to make sure the flowers had arrived. A card and bouquet of white roses for the leading lady. *Break a leg, darling. Love Mum, Dad and Artie x x x*

A tall girl in a jumper and jeans hurried past, still wearing her stage make-up, bag slung over her shoulder. She blinked when she saw Piper. 'Riva's just coming, she's, um . . .' The girl tailed off.

Piper felt certain the girl was embarrassed for them both. *Look at Riva Holden's mother loitering in the corridor as if she's five instead of fifteen.* Gripped by a compulsion to confide the truth of why she was there – to explain to Riva her father hadn't made it before the likes of Miranda Colman did – she resisted the impulse for her daughter's sake. 'Thanks,' she said instead. 'Great show.'

More students spilled from backstage in twos and threes. Piper recognized some girls from Riva's year group – a half-hearted wave from Julianne's daughter Emelie – and a handful of older boys. After a while, their chatter faded and Piper checked her watch. Its hands were frozen at seven o'clock. For some reason, the stopped watch reminded her of the pity in the voice of the saleswoman yesterday – and the flat surprise of the customer service advisor when he'd informed her their accounts were empty.

If Gray didn't come home this evening, she would flay him alive. For a long time, she had loved him. More than she'd loved any man. Which wasn't saying much, if she was being honest in that brutal manner she sometimes had. She'd always struggled with the kind of romantic love her friends had talked about. While they had swooned over Valentine roses and diamond earrings, she was drawn to practicality. What he could do for her and what she could do for him. Almost transactional. Shared life goals and ambitions with an agreed endgame in sight. In Gray, she recognized a man with the same glint in his eye as she had. And she did love him in her way. Enough to share almost all of the secret parts of herself. But there was at least one secret she had never told him: the significant sum of cash she had, until recently, kept hidden in the zip pocket of a Louis Vuitton suitcase in her dressing room at home.

A glimpse of Clodagh's face in the last weeks of her life – the planes of her cheekbones, the sunken pools of her eyes where the flesh around the orbital cavities had shrunk away to nothing except a translucent covering of skin – filled her vision. Too late for the expensive private specialist treatment that might have saved her from the muscle wastage that triggered a sudden and cataclysmic failure of her heart. The money promised to her mother to pay for it had never materialized. Even now, the fury of that injustice burned inside her. She blinked, remembering the vicious jut of shoulder blades beneath a cotton T-shirt, and her sister was gone again.

The loss of Clodagh had taught her a painful but important lesson: the value of always having her own money. But she'd never discussed her Fuck You fund with anyone, except Julianne. That was her private safety net and hers alone.

Still, she did admit to experiencing a particular kind of thrill from watching the vast sums generated by Gray's business accrue in their bank accounts. She was grateful for it. But even as someone who believed in the sanctity of rational explanation and cool-headed discussion, the missing money – hundreds of thousands of pounds of it – had now become a matter of extreme urgency. Every time she allowed herself to think about it, cortisol thrummed through her, a spike of anxiety. She messaged Gray for the umpteenth time. Where the hell are you? You missed Riva's opening night. What have you done with our money?

The corridors were quiet. Had she somehow missed her daughter? She would check the dressing rooms and if Riva was not there, she would head upstairs and wait for her in the lobby.

At Piper's inner city comprehensive school, offensive graffiti had decorated the toilet doors and its prison-grey walls, and a threadbare patch of grass was their only sports field. But at Bay College, money talked – and loudly. Expensive prints of students' artwork lined the corridors. The walls were clean and painted in soothing tones of pale blue. The music rooms were like professional studios, kitted out with recording equipment and sound desks and so many instruments. Impressive sporting facilities greeted visitors as they drove up the tree-lined drive; sprawling fields of perfectly mown grass, a running track, and football and rugby pitches. A gym. Swimming pool. Tennis courts. All against the glorious backdrop of the sea.

The girls' dressing room was deserted. Piper caught the thick smell of stage make-up. A faint mist of body spray lingered about the place. Costumes hung in neat rows ready for the next night's performance. Everything was tidy apart from a rose gold holdall she recognized as Riva's on the floor.

The room was squared by make-up benches and mirrors crowned with individual lightbulbs. She poked her head around the corner and saw her daughter sitting on a stool, bent over one of the benches, head resting on her crossed arms.

'Hello, love,' she said, her soft tone disguising the sharp needles of concern that pricked at her. 'You were outstanding tonight.'

Riva lifted her tear-stained face towards her mother, pale rivers tracking down her face, mascara bruises beneath her eyes. A heady aroma – part sweet, but mostly spoiling mulch – filled the air.

Piper went to her, folded the sobbing teenage girl into her arms. 'What on earth has happened?' But she didn't need an answer. The cause of Riva's distress was apparent for everyone to see. And that, suspected Piper, was a large part of the problem. All of Riva's classmates would have witnessed her humiliation.

Throughout her life, Piper had often encountered the uglier side of human nature, and she accepted it as a necessary – an inevitable – evil. She had developed an impenetrable shell, learned how to harden herself to the emotion of a situation, gauging only the practicalities, divorcing herself from the repercussions of other people's actions and her own. But seeing her daughter so upset pierced her with an unexpected arrow of guilt.

She glanced over Riva's head, heart pounding, a dozen feet marching through her chest.

Lying on the make-up bench like a frothy pile of feathers was the bouquet Piper had chosen for her daughter's opening night. But it was no longer the image of floral perfection collected from Masterson's a few hours earlier.

Feeling her daughter's eyes upon her, Piper covered her mouth with her hand, exhaling a murmur of shock at the savagery that lay before them.

Each of the flower heads had been hacked to pieces, visible slashes in the translucent petals weeping like blood from a wound, browning their edges and corrupting them. Scattered amongst these ruined calyxes was a harvest of rose thorns, dozens and dozens of them, curated into a spiteful rebuke.

8

Two months before the Holdens disappeared

The coffee shop was full of Bay College students. Emelie scanned the tables, looking for Riva, but her friend hadn't arrived yet.

She ordered them both a chocolate milkshake and a bottle of water. She was never sure if Riva was on a health kick or in need of a blow-out, so she got one of each to cover the possibilities.

The girls had been best friends forever, since pre-school where they'd played dressing up, through all those happy years at primary school and now at secondary school, where the waters were shark-infested. But they'd always had each other.

'God, Mrs Sampson wanted to talk about doing French at A-Level and I couldn't get away fast enough,' said Riva, dumping her school bag on the table and uncapping the water without saying thank you. 'She says I have natural talent.'

Health kick.

None of the teachers ever pressed Emelie into taking their subjects because of her *natural talent*. She was proud of her friend but sometimes it was a little exhausting to bear witness to Riva's continued brilliance. When the auditions for the school play had been announced, Emelie had felt that familiar pang of – what? It wasn't jealousy so much as envy. Covetousness. She didn't want to deprive Riva of her triumphs but she wanted to savour the taste of her own.

She was as good at acting as Riva. Maybe even better. Mr Moran had asked her if she was planning to try out for the main part and she was going to. She might be too self-conscious to raise her hand in class but the stage was different: she dreamed of the applause.

'You wanted to have a chat?' She flashed her friend a mischievous grin. 'Which boy is it about now?'

But Riva didn't answer with a smile. She looked sombre. Emelie's stomach folded over. Riva could occasionally lack consistency. Yes, she was Emelie's best friend, but every now and then she could be offhand and dismissive, and Emelie would have no idea what she had done. But she wasn't perfect either. Sometimes she wondered what would happen if she stopped being friends with Riva and told her what she really thought. That she was spoilt and petty. That she trampled over the feelings of others in favour of her own. That Emelie had fantasized about taking her down a peg or two. That sometimes she didn't like her at all.

Riva fixed Emelie with a look and a flower of anxiety unfurled itself inside her stomach.

'Nothing like that.' Riva waved a hand. 'I was wondering if you were planning to audition for the role of Sally Bowles, that's all.'

Emelie almost laughed in relief. 'I am, actually. Thought I'd finally pluck up the courage and have a go. Do you want to work on our audition pieces together?'

Riva was silent. A drop of milkshake had slid down the side of her glass and she wiped it away with a fingertip which she popped into her mouth. Then she took another swig of water.

'Do you think that part is right for you?' She waved to a schoolmate, not meeting Emelie's eye. 'You're such a great actor but there's a *lot* of singing and dancing.'

Emelie bit her lip. 'I think it'll be fine.' An embarrassed smile. 'I've been having singing lessons.'

'You didn't tell me.'

Emelie wanted to say that she didn't have to tell her everything. That she was allowed to keep some parts of herself secret from her friend. But Riva liked to know everything. Sometimes she used that knowledge against her.

'Don't you think your skills would be better suited backstage? You're so good at art – you'd be such an asset to the set design team.'

Emelie swallowed, mouth dry. Palms sweating. Even when they were small, Riva had always bullied her a little. She didn't know why, it was just the way it was. Easy to manipulate, although that made her sound more malleable than she was. She could be tough if she needed to be. But most of the time she couldn't be bothered.

But she wanted this. More than her friend did. She steeled herself against Riva's entreaties.

'All the same, I think I'll give it a try.'

Riva didn't respond but a couple of minutes later when some of the boys from their science class walked into the cafe, she joined them without a word to her friend. When Emelie shouldered her bag, ready to leave, she lingered, waiting to see if she wanted to walk home with her, but Riva didn't glance in her direction again.

9

Tuesday morning

The day the Holdens disappeared

The room was filled with voices and the ringing of telephones, buzzing, swelling with noise. Saul smoothed his
damp palms against his trousers and absorbed it all.

The far wall was plastered with images of a man who had
been suffocated and drowned on his way home from the
pub. On a separate wall, a woman was smiling, waving a
kayak paddle in her right hand. The next photograph showed
a blood-stained kitchen floor. She'd died there, by the still-
warm oven door, after her husband had stoved in her head
with a propane cylinder during a family barbecue.

Saul waited for Detective Inspector Angus O'Neill to
decide what to do with him. The day had got off to a terrible
start – and showed no signs of improving. O'Neill hadn't
thawed. In fact, his demeanour had grown colder as the
morning had progressed. He'd hardly said a word to his new
recruit, except to check he'd brought his personal protective
equipment – handcuffs, baton, spray and body armour. Saul
had wanted to drag his personal radio from his rucksack too,

shove it in his face – he wasn't an idiot, he'd carried his equipment since it was issued during his first placement at the Essex Training Centre – but he didn't think that would improve the poor impression he'd already made.

He loitered by a long table with a telephone and an empty chair. O'Neill was talking to two male officers and they glanced in his direction. He bit down on his instinct to stare back, challenging them, and forced his gaze away.

A young woman he hadn't noticed before was leaning against the wall, not far from him. He wasn't a sleaze, not like some of the dirty old fuckers he'd met during his training, who'd take a statement from a woman in distress, all compassionate concern, and jerk off over her ten minutes later while describing her 'tits' to his colleagues. But she was something else.

She was much smaller than he was, shoulder-height, possibly even smaller than that, and there was a restless energy to her he found appealing. She was jiggling her left leg, but paused the movement every now and then before restarting it. Her white cotton shirt was oversized and she wore a loose houndstooth jacket over it and a tight black skirt which stopped halfway down her thighs, thick black tights and leather biker boots. Her hair was pastel blue, the precise shade of a dextroamphetamine pill.

When she felt him staring at her, she turned to face him and his breath caught in his throat. Her eyes were grey, but as far from dull as possible: the colour of the sea on an overcast day or the flat silver of a newly minted sky.

She acknowledged him with a roll of those spellbinding eyes, as if to say she was bored of waiting for the goons to get it together. A snort of amusement spilled from him before he could hold it in. He liked her just from looking at her.

O'Neill called to him, the sharpness of his tone cutting Saul back down to size. He eye-rolled in return at the young woman before sauntering over to the detective inspector with just enough pace to avoid appearing insubordinate.

'We'll be pairing you up with DC Eliot Williams,' said O'Neill, the longest sentence he'd spoken to Saul in the last hour. 'He's an experienced officer with a history of mentoring new recruits. I'm sure you'll get on famously.'

DC Williams grinned at Saul and stuck out his hand. 'Welcome to the Murder Club, son.' Saul did not enjoy that kind of faux bonhomie from strangers. He resisted the urge to say the last man to call him son had ended up dying with a knife between his shoulder blades.

Out of the corner of his eye, he was aware the other male detective had approached the young woman and was introducing himself. The man was laughing over-loudly at something and Blue – he was too far away to catch her name – smiled politely. For an instant, she lifted her gaze to Saul and he read a trifecta of emotions – discomfort, amusement, solidarity – and then she looked away again.

Williams was droning on about house-to-house enquiries and Saul forced himself to tune in. After all his training, the assessments and exams, the two weeks he'd spent with the community policing unit, a month with Safeguarding and the depressing litany of sexual assaults and hate crime, and double that with the Domestic Abuse team, investigating the shit that some people had to endure on a daily basis, and the months and months he'd spent in a series of shit-hole Essex towns, he couldn't afford to blow this opportunity now.

He asked sensible questions and jotted down notes and gave the appearance of being an interested and diligent young police officer.

When he looked for Blue again, she was gone.

10

Tuesday afternoon

The day the Holdens disappeared

A flock of dark-bellied brent geese was resting on the salt marshes when Julianne arrived home. Although she was desperate to change out of her funeral clothes and return to Seawings, she stopped for long enough to watch the birds, specks of dirt against the sludgy landscape, and feel the freshening wind on her face. The sky was a blank page until the birds took flight, filling the whiteness with inky scrawls. She envied them their freedom.

The house was exactly as she'd left it and it rang with the silence of daytime routine. A whirring dishwasher was the only sign Quiller had nipped home for lunch, and it was too early for the children to be back from school. The heating had switched itself off – Quiller's economy drive again – and she shivered, the airy rooms making it seem colder inside than out. A bit like their marriage.

Over the years, their relationship had settled into something she tolerated. She might have loved him in the beginning. She couldn't remember now. It was like a memory viewed through frosted glass. She could still recall the first time he'd challenged her over money though. In vivid, painful flashes.

A toaster. Something so silly and mundane. It had been in the window of a hardware store and the colour matched the kitchen in their old house. Expensive, yes. But perfect. She'd been looking for one like it for a long time.

It was snowing. That detail was important. She had put the plastic bag on the table and called out to him, excited, rubbing her swollen stomach. Eight months and twelve days. The baby would come early although she hadn't known that then.

'What's this?' His lip had curled in a way she had only noticed once or twice before. She'd seen it a thousand times since, but back then, this expression was still new and incomprehensible.

'A toaster. Look at the colour. Isn't it lovely?' Mint and cream. Shiny. Designer.

'We don't need a new toaster.' His voice was flat and lacked emotion, and he had a pen mark on his cheek. His hair was pushed upwards as if he'd been tugging at it. Tired and stressed from running his fledgling estate agency.

'Yes, but—'

'It's too expensive. Take it back to the shop.'

She had laughed, thinking he was joking, putting on an act for some bizarre reason she hadn't been able to fathom. 'No. I like it.'

Quiller's eyes had narrowed. 'You like it, do you? Let's see how much you fucking like this.' He pulled the toaster from the bag, plugged it into the wall and grabbed his pregnant wife by the wrist, jamming her hand into the slot for bread, pressing down on the lever mechanism and forcing her to stay there until the filaments burned her skin.

She cried out in pain, an animalistic yelp of distress, and then he'd been overcome with contrition, rushing her outside to press her wounded hand into the snow, skirt hem wet against her frozen thighs, belly heavy and cold as she kneeled on the ground.

The toaster went back to the shop, Henry was born the next day, and Julianne learned not to challenge her husband again.

Upstairs, she stripped off her black suit and pulled on her jeans and a cashmere jumper, thick socks and a lightweight cotton wrap.

At her dressing table, she sat on the stool and wiped away the mascara that had collected in the corners of her eyes and removed the hair grips from her bun. In the unforgiving natural light of her bedroom, she looked tired, dried up. Worry could do that to you.

Piper. Riva. Artie. She repeated their names again and again, as if that mantra would protect them all. Her feelings about Gray were more ambiguous. In spite of his public devotion to Piper, she didn't trust him.

The clutch bag she'd taken to the funeral was lying in the middle of her bed where she'd tossed it before getting changed. She sat on the edge of the duvet and opened its magnetic catch.

Inside was her purse, a lipstick, some tissues and the florist's card that David Thornton had given her.

She withdrew it and laid it on the bed. It was a tasteful, classic design and she knew the florist was expensive because Piper used her regularly. When she'd carefully copied his email address into her mobile phone, she rummaged in the drawers for a pair of nail scissors and lifted the card aloft, cutting it into a dozen tiny pieces.

Two squad cars were parked outside Piper's house when Julianne arrived there in the dying light of the afternoon. Even though she'd expected some kind of police presence, the sight of them jolted her into a new understanding. This was happening. It was real.

She hesitated on the doorstep, breathing in the smoked air of autumn, knowing that what she was about to share with the police would electrify their investigation. She'd wanted to call Mila during the wake, to ask what was happening at Seawings, but realized she'd left in such a hurry, she didn't have her number.

No word yet from Quiller, not even a text or WhatsApp message to see how she was feeling. She'd left him a voicemail, explaining the Holdens were missing, but it was clear he hadn't listened to it. For all his self-absorption, even Quiller wouldn't ignore news of this magnitude. Not for the first time, Julianne acknowledged she was the last item on his to-do list, coming in well below: 1) his job, 2) his passion for cycling, 3) his children. As each day passed, their marriage was emptying of all that was nourishing, like the skin of an apple that had wrinkled and loosened. It was still there, it *existed*, but it had been sucked dry of everything that made it palatable.

A couple of officers in uniform were talking into their phones when the third, a woman with several moles and a gap between her teeth, opened the front door to Seawings, a question in her face.

'I'm Julianne Hillier,' she said. The female officer stared

blankly at her. Struck by a need to explain herself, she pressed on. 'Piper Holden's best friend.'

'Have you given a statement yet?' The police officer was not looking at Julianne, but over her right shoulder, distracted by the officers behind her. She sounded bored, more interested in eavesdropping on their conversations than this stranger on the doorstep.

'No, I had to go to a funeral this morning. I left before the police got here.'

The woman's head snapped back. 'You were here this morning?'

Something in her expression made Julianne feel defensive. 'Yes, we'd planned to go for a run. I spend a lot of my time here.'

'Sarge,' said the female officer, waving a hand at one of her colleagues. And when he didn't reply, she called him again with sharper emphasis. '*Sarge.*'

The detective sergeant, who was putting his phone into his pocket, walked over, his face unreadable.

The woman explained who Julianne was. Although an experienced officer, he was not able to contain the briefest flicker of pity that crossed his face before he tucked his feelings away.

'Mrs . . . ?'

'Hillier.'

'Mrs Hillier, I'm afraid things are moving rapidly at the moment. When we arrived here this morning, this was a Missing Persons investigation, but that has changed in the last couple of hours.'

Julianne stilled, unconsciously holding her breath. 'Have you found them?'

The detective shook his head and his tone, when he spoke, was gentle. 'I'm afraid not. In fact, I'm sorry to have to tell you this, but we've discovered traces of blood in a bedroom and bathroom upstairs, and other disturbing evidence I'm not currently at liberty to share.' He fixed his brown eyes on hers, unreadable. 'This has just been upgraded to a murder investigation.'

Saul was sitting at a desk in the Major Crime Unit's incident room on the instructions of DC Williams. So far, his first day had been spent conducting interviews with the father and mother of Austin Kellaway, the man whose picture he'd noticed on the wall earlier, and the bar staff on duty on the night of his murder. Nothing worth getting worked up about there. Daft kids with not much between their ears and a landlord who was more concerned about losing his licence than paying attention to his clientele.

At one point, he'd been dispatched to the canteen for six Styrofoam cups of tea. He'd glimpsed a flash of blue in the distance and his heart had leapt. Her smile had cut across the wall of noise until she was all he could see. But then she'd slipped away, kingfisher-quick, to whatever corner of the station she was working in before he'd had a chance to talk to her.

When he returned, one of the team wandered over and passed him a scrap of paper with a message written on it. *Call Mr C. Lyons urgently.* Followed by a landline telephone number. The name wasn't familiar but as he didn't have anything else to do, Saul punched in the digits and listened to it ring out.

'Welcome to Colchester Zoo,' said an automated voice.

'If you know the extension you require, please press it now. Or dial zero for other options.'

Saul followed the instructions until he got through to a pleasantly spoken man in his fifties. 'How can I help you today?'

'This is DC Saul Anguish from Essex Police. Can I speak to Mr C. Lyons please?' As soon as the words were out of his mouth, he realized what he'd said and was halfway to an apology when the man said in a terse voice, 'Very funny,' and hung up.

Out of the corner of his eye, he saw the officer who'd handed him the note, a couple of the squad he didn't recognize and DC Williams, all pissing themselves. He kicked himself for being so gullible. Having a respectable job for all these months had blunted his instincts. The mention of a zoo should have been an immediate giveaway. *Sea lions, for fuck's sake.*

He forced himself to grin and shrug it off, even though the Other Thoughts, those tendrils of darkness, itchy and twisting, whispered to him about humiliation and reprisal, about driving his fingers into the soft space behind DC Williams's eyes. He wouldn't be laughing then.

But instead he clapped Williams on the back. 'Good one,' he said, shaking his head in mock disbelief at his own naiveté, trying to be one of the lads. Chuckled again. 'Good one.'

The officers were still high on their prank when DI O'Neill strode into the incident room and beckoned to Williams, his face serious.

Williams started towards him, turned and looked for Saul, still lingering by his desk. 'What are you waiting for?' he said. 'Let's see what the old bastard wants.'

The old bastard, it turned out, had an address he needed them to visit, and a troubling mystery to untangle.

'A family of four, missing from their home. No apparent signs of a struggle,' said O'Neill. 'Apart from some blood residue on one of the lights.'

DC Williams rubbed the heel of his palm against his nose. It made an unfortunate squeaking sound. 'But that's not enough for the MCU, is it?' He nudged Saul in a *listen-up, son* fashion, digging an elbow into the new recruit's ribs. 'So what are you not telling us, boss?'

O'Neill grimaced and opened up his phone, showing the detective constable a photograph he'd been sent a few minutes earlier.

DC Williams's face turned the colour of soured milk. His eyes were too wide, as if a caricaturist's pen had slipped and she was trying to over-correct her mistake. Saul leaned in, instincts sharpening, greedy for a closer look.

A girl's bedroom, a teenager, most likely. Posters on the wall. A dressing table festooned with scarves and hair ties and cosmetics spilling from designer-branded make-up bags.

In the oval of the glass mirror, beyond the reflection of her unmade bed, was something that made his heart flutter against his chest, a delicious quickstep of adrenalin, and beneath that an undercurrent of something thicker, a swell of anticipation, of dark longing.

Written on the glass, in the unmistakeable viscosity of blood, were three words.

Make Them Stop.

11

Saturday afternoon

Three days before the Holdens disappeared

Gray Holden pressed send on the email he'd spent almost an hour composing and leaned back in his office chair, fingers laced behind his head.

The afternoon sun was filtering through a large window which offered a glimpse of the sea. A boat bobbed on waves of liquid silver. For a while, he sat and watched the lone craft, wondering about the skipper and his crew, and how freeing it must feel to spend a working life pressed up to the elements, not worrying about financial deals and markets and awkward clients, but the rise of the tides and the changing direction of the wind.

He hadn't confided in Piper – he didn't want to worry her yet – but everything hinged on the next couple of days. If – no, he couldn't allow himself to think that – *when* he pulled it off, they would be wealthier than they could imagine. But he hadn't heard from the old man in a while. Which alarmed him, because he'd been expecting another hefty bank transfer. Or a call, at the very least. But so far, there had been nothing – and that made him nervous. He wasn't deliberately ignoring his wife's messages. But there were certain obstacles that needed surmounting first. Nice and easy does it.

Gray enjoyed his work. He'd often considered a base in London – he travelled there for meetings several times a week – but his office by the sea was too appealing to give up.

Holden Investments was run from a narrow townhouse tucked down one of Midtown's smartest commercial streets, a two-mile run or drive from Seawings, and befitting of a bespoke agency such as his, offering a wide range of financial services and open six days a week.

The team was small – just him, one other financial consultant who ran the insurance side of the business and worked from home in Edinburgh, and Charlotte, their PA-cum-receptionist.

And it was Charlotte's well-modulated voice he could hear now, except it was much louder than her usual polite tone.

'I'm afraid you need an appointment. Mr Holden is busy at the moment.'

The telephone on his desk began to buzz. Stopped. Buzzed again, aggressively insistent. Before Gray had the chance to answer it or to push back his chair and go and see if Charlotte needed help, his office door opened.

The man was short and muscular, the kind of physique honed by hours in the gym using weights. His suit was tailored, immaculately cut, but his shaved head and the twist of his mouth gave him a feral look, savage and unrestrained.

Gray had never seen him before.

The man planted his palms on the edge of Gray's desk

and leaned over until his face was centimetres away. Gray could smell his aftershave, citrussy and fresh, and beneath that the foul rush of his breath, his teeth covered in a sticky biofilm of plaque. A discordant cocktail of scents.

Gray, who was much taller, rose from his chair, his fingers splayed on the desk in symmetry. 'You can't just burst in here—'

In one fluid sweep of motion, the man picked up Gray's fountain pen and drove it into the thin webbing of skin between his index and middle fingers. A white hole of pain opened up inside Gray.

The man smiled. 'Mr Moore's changed his mind. He'd like his money back.'

Gray tried to reply but was so shocked by the pen sticking out of his hand, the violent, unprovoked assault of it, that he could not speak. Even as a schoolboy, he'd never been in a fight. Before he'd set up his own financial consultancy, his particular brand of scrapping had been with rivals on the trading floor, not strangers at the taxi rank on a Saturday night.

Distracted by the fire burning in his hand, he forced himself to formulate a response, trying to buy himself some time and prevent this lunatic from inflicting more damage.

'I'm not authorized to speak about my clients for reasons of confidentiality,' he said, knowing the man would not be fobbed off with such a weak explanation, but with fear and disbelief clouding his mind, it was the best he could come up with.

The stranger smiled again but it didn't soften the stones of his eyes. 'I don't need you to talk about your client. I know who he is. Passing on a message, that's all.'

Gray stared at the man, dredging his memory for his

brief interactions with Patton Moore. An elderly widower with a large country estate about thirty miles from Midtown, Mr Moore was considering transferring Power of Attorney to his son, but had wanted to make some prudent investments first while he was still *compos mentis*.

A couple of months ago, Gray had driven out to Bradbury Manor and talked to Mr Moore about ways he might invest his substantial fortune. He'd found him charming company, a gentleman of the old-school variety, his manners almost courtly, but with an occasional barbed edge to his personality. They'd shared tea and cake, served by one of Mr Moore's housekeeping staff, and wandered the gardens together. The old man was vague about his fortune, not entirely sure how much he was worth, which was less of a surprise to Gray than some might think. His clients were a mixed bunch and fell into two camps: the financially savvy who were aware of every last penny and those who were so rich they could not keep track of their wealth.

The elderly man had leaned on his stick as they had surveyed the blousy end-of-season roses, their scent rising powerfully in the autumn sun.

'I've had a good life,' he said. 'But I want to make sure my investments continue to provide my children and grandchildren with a generous income when I'm gone.'

Gray had smiled at him. 'Well, I hope they realize how lucky they are.'

Mr Moore bent over to smell a yellow tea rose at its peak moment of glory. Tomorrow the petals would fall, but for now, it was as close to perfection as it would get. 'Do our children ever truly appreciate what they have?' His chuckle, although warm, contained a wry note.

'But they visit you regularly? Make sure that you're OK?' Although it felt intrusive, Gray pressed on with his question because the answer was important.

The pensioner shrugged. 'When they can. They all have busy lives.' He touched the tip of his finger to the petal. 'This variety is called Golden Celebration. My wife bought it for me on our fiftieth wedding anniversary.'

Gray touched his arm. 'It must be hard for you. I can tell how much you miss her.'

Mr Moore's expression clouded. 'Gone, just like that.' He clicked his fingers at the same time he said 'that'. 'Pulmonary embolism. Two years ago now.' He frowned. 'Or is it three? That's the funny thing about time, I can't always remember. Sometimes, it's as clear as the horizon on a sunny day, but then the weeks seem to roll into one and it's winter instead of spring.' He pushed his glasses back up the bridge of his nose, confusion corrugating his forehead. Wincing, he shifted his weight onto his other leg, knuckles gripping his stick.

Gray clapped him on the shoulder and together they walked back to the manor house.

A week later, Mr Moore had transferred an extremely large sum of money to Gray's company so he could make a start on building his portfolio, with the promise of much more to come. He hadn't heard from the old man since.

The stranger in Gray's office leaned forward and picked up a framed photograph of the Holden family. Piper, Riva and Artie, sun-kissed and laughing on a beach in Florida Keys.

'What an attractive family you have, Mr Holden.'

He didn't say anything else but the threat was implicit.

'Look—' said Gray, but the man interrupted him.

'Just make sure Mr Moore gets his money. I don't want to have to come back.' The stranger returned the photograph to Gray's desk and sauntered towards the door. With one hand on the handle, he turned back towards Gray, his tone light and conversational. 'Nice place you have, by the way. Great views. Seawings, isn't it?' And with that, he was gone.

Fear – a thick, dark entity – closed up Gray's throat, suffocating him, and all he could do in that moment was to concentrate on the in-out of his breath and the blur of pain in his hand.

He was still standing motionless when the door to his office was flung open and Charlotte let out a scream. 'Oh God, your hand.' And then, 'I'll call the police.'

'No.' Gray's refusal was a whip-crack across the room.

His personal assistant looked horrified. 'Of course we have to call them. That *animal*' – she spat out the word – 'attacked you.'

'I said no.'

Although Charlotte was a woman who could hold her own with anyone – she'd kept the wolf from the door more times than Gray could remember – she was smart enough to acknowledge he paid her salary, and that was enough to pause her in her tracks, despite her better judgement. A range of emotions played across her face, her hand hovering over the telephone on his desk before she let it fall to her side.

'Pass the brandy.' Pain made him economical with words.

Charlotte handed him the bottle he kept in the cabinet for clients. He unscrewed the cap and drank straight from the bottle.

'Pull it out,' he said.

His secretary paled. Blood was staining the edges of the wound, the creeping spread of bruising already discolouring his skin. 'I can't,' she said, shaking her head, and with a rush of memory, Gray recalled the time she'd had to go home after fainting in the phlebotomy department of Midtown Hospital during a pregnancy check-up.

He took another swig, the alcohol burning a hole in the centre of his chest. 'For Christ's sake.' A mutter, too low for Charlotte to hear and feel guilty about, but enough for him to vent his fear, to steel himself against the pain.

Breathing in, filling his lungs with as much air as possible, Gray gripped the pen and eased its bloodied tip out of his hand.

The pain was a flower, opening up inside him, spreading its roots through his wrist and up his forearm. Blood spilled through his fingers. Charlotte rushed forward with a neat rectangle of white towelling she'd retrieved from the client restrooms, the type stacked high in upmarket hotels and used for drying wealthy hands. Charlotte upended the bottle, soaked the cloth with brandy and pressed it against his wound.

His body bucked, the heat of alcohol inflaming the rawness, but he did not cry out. Instead he shook his head, trying to communicate that disinfecting an open wound with alcohol was an old wives' tale, more likely to traumatize the skin than heal it. But he could not shape the words, could do little more than exhale sharply, and the scent of grapes and winter wheat rose together in a potent mix.

An hour later, when the wound had stopped bleeding and Charlotte was on her way home through the violet twilight, her silence greased with an extra week's holiday and a generous bonus, Gray sat alone in the still of his office.

A heavy-duty dose of codeine had temporarily reduced the fire to dulled-down embers, but his mind was alive, sharpened and hyper-alert. The stranger would make good on his promise to return if Gray Holden didn't repay Mr Moore's money. He was as certain of that as the setting of the sun.

But Gray was sure of something else too: Mr Moore was never getting his money back.

12

Tuesday afternoon

The day the Holdens disappeared

The debris from last night's storm had left a tidemark of scum and seaweed on Midtown beach. Saul Anguish had a thing about beaches, ever since he'd hefted his father's body down to the water's edge and watched the sea swallow him. As they passed along the coast road, he gave himself over to the rush of waves lapping the curve of the bay, seduced by their promise of secrecy and the memory of salt drying on his sun-warmed skin all those years ago.

He was in the passenger seat while DC Williams was driving and whistling through his teeth. Saul wondered if anyone had been convicted of murder – or the lesser charge of manslaughter – for silencing a man who whistled through his teeth. Taking a hammer to his mouth would be satisfying but messy. Removing them one by one with a pair of pliers would be his preferred method, twisting each by its root as he went.

DC Williams turned his head towards him, grinning, his mouth full and gleaming. 'It's the big one, kiddo. Excited?'

The younger detective couldn't help thinking Williams would not be smiling if he knew what was going on in Saul's head. Instead he pushed his hands beneath his thighs and offered a non-committal murmur in reply.

Seawings was the biggest house Saul had ever seen, quadruple the size of the coastguard's lookout. DC Williams whistled again, but this time in admiration. 'Christ alive, how the other half live.'

Saul, who'd spent much of his life with nothing, had never been ashamed by his lack of material possessions, but even he was surprised into quiet as they pulled up outside the house.

Two police cars with their Battenberg markings were already parked in the sweeping driveway and across the street, a small knot of neighbours had gathered, anxious for news. 'Has there been a robbery?' said an older woman with a string of saltwater pearls at her throat and a plum inside it. She shook her head, irritated. 'I *told* everyone we needed to hire private security but they didn't want to hear it. This will be the tip of the iceberg, mark my words.'

'I'm afraid we can't comment at the moment,' said DC Williams with a practised smile, 'but we'll let you know as soon as things change.'

The two men walked up the path, unwittingly following the same route Julianne Hillier had taken a few hours earlier. The front lawn was littered with leaves and branches, the aftermath of the storm. Above their heads, the sky was heavy with the promise of rain. Saul knew from his training that both last night's wind and the imminent wet weather were bad news for a murder investigation, obscuring forensic evidence or destroying it. If the Holden family *had* been killed, the police were already many hours behind, and at a serious disadvantage.

DC Williams was striding ahead, exuding officiousness. Saul had come across men like him before and, while his instincts told him he was not a threat exactly, he recognized a slyness in his fellow officer, a warning that he was not a team player but intent on furthering his own career, whatever the cost to others. Saul let him go. He was not one for politics, and Williams was not the type to hang around waiting for those who were slowing him down. That suited Saul. Something in the grass had caught his eye and he didn't want the other detective to see it.

Saul crouched against the damp earth, the smell of it rising and catching at the back of his throat. A frisson – rarer these days but still as powerful – rushed through him. With infinite tenderness, he flattened his palm above the ground and, with his other hand, he lifted up the gleaming black exoskeleton of a devil's coach horse. The now-dead beetle – once a fearsome hunter in the dark – was about the most perfectly preserved specimen he had ever seen. And a first for his collection.

Saul, who had scavenged the remains of dead insects since he was a boy, slipped it into the matchbox he always carried with him and followed DC Williams into the house.

His first impression was that it was full of expensive things. Paintings, silk curtains and antique furnishings, an impressive collection of clocks, a grand piano and, although he was no expert, a vast ebony cabinet inlaid with what looked like precious stones. The house smelled of money, or how he had always imagined wealth might smell: of polished parquet and expensive paint and the sweetly cloying scent of fresh flowers.

Three police officers – with DC Williams at the centre – were clustered by the foot of the staircase that dominated the hallway. A woman with a sweep of white running down the front of her hair was being shown out.

Williams raised his eyebrows at him, a question in his face. Saul read the rebuke and mouthed his apology, and the older man let it slide, intent on the handover from the senior officer at his side.

'It's a mystery,' said a detective sergeant Saul had not met before. 'They disappeared in the clothes they were wearing – and with nothing else. No phones, wallets, coats or bags. The cars – as far as we can ascertain – are still here. Passports in the drawer. Breakfast on the table, half eaten. It's as if they've been wiped off the face of the earth.'

'Apart from the blood,' said DC Williams.

'Which is a puzzle in itself. There's some indication a clumsy attempt at a clean-up has been made, but we'll know more later, once forensics have done their bit.'

'What about the writing?' said Williams.

The detective sergeant grimaced. 'I think you need to see it for yourselves.'

A young woman's voice was drifting along the landing as DC Williams and Saul climbed the vast staircase towards Riva Holden's bedroom. In the family's deserted house, it was an eerie sound, as if some imprint of the missing girl remained, even if she did not.

Upstairs, the smell of money was stronger. It was in the thick pile of luxury carpet and the stiff silk of the drapes that swathed the ceiling-height windows spaced along the corridor. These days, Saul didn't bother to shut his curtains. He liked to let the light in – he'd spent too long in the dark.

Riva's bedroom was busier than the rest of the vast house. Four officers – all men – were standing in a circle but none of them were talking. Instead, a woman's voice – confident and impressive – rang out.

'Trust me. I know I'm right.'

'That might be so,' said one of the older men, his voice laced with amusement. 'But do we?'

Her reply cut through their laughter. 'I can wait for you to catch up, if you like. But I was under the impression this was an urgent inquiry.'

Three of the men laughed again. 'Ouch,' said one of them, nudging the target of her scorn, who scowled. Saul didn't let himself react, not outwardly at least, but inside he was laughing too. He wanted to buy her a beer for puncturing the officer's self-righteous condescension, whoever she was.

Detective Constable Williams cleared his throat. By the third hour in his company, Saul had deduced this was his way of attracting the attention of those he considered subordinate, in standing, if not official rank. It indicated his time was important and he did not wish to be kept waiting for longer than was necessary. The three officers moved apart to make way for Williams, but Saul, who was squeezed in behind him, couldn't see much except a glimpse of colour.

Blue.

She gazed around the men who encircled her, her winter-sky eyes daring them to argue. Saul inched forward for a better look.

'What have we missed?' said DC Williams. 'Fill us in.' It sounded like an order instead of a polite request.

'I'm sure you *meant* to say please,' said Blue, so sweetly that Saul's teeth ached in sympathy. Williams's eyes narrowed but she didn't give him a chance to speak again. 'For those of you who don't know me, I'm Dr Clover March, and my job as a forensic linguist means I use the written word to help solve any crimes that may have been committed. DI O'Neill asked me to take a look at this.'

The officer closest to Saul – he didn't know his name – muttered something under his breath. Saul didn't catch it, but he could tell it was derogatory by his tone. Blue – she might be a doctor called Clover March but in his head she was colour – did not let it slide. A cold fire burned in her eyes. 'I'll be happy to answer any questions you have, DC Niranajan.' A perfectly timed pause. 'Or is the science beyond you?'

Brushing off her jibe, Niranajan laughed too loudly, but when Blue looked away, his lips thinned into disdain. Saul admired Blue's confidence – some might argue it bordered on arrogance – but he felt certain of one thing: her attitude would make her enemies, particularly amongst the older members of the team, who would not enjoy being intellectually and verbally bested by a woman – and a young one, at that.

Blue, who looked barely older than the teenager whose bedroom they were standing in, stepped aside to let DC Williams and Saul – newcomers to the scene – examine the evidence.

The pale walls of Riva Holden's bedroom – the posters and photographs pinned to a corkboard and a printed-out school timetable – were in sobering contrast to the mirror on her dressing table.

Saul had seen this image once before on O'Neill's phone but, like many things viewed through a screen, it was no match for real life in all its technicolour glory.

Here, in a place where the scent of Riva's perfume still lingered, the truth of it loomed over everything, a dark and malignant heart.

Up close, the blood had darkened into rusty smears. Saul bent towards the glass and noticed how it was thicker in places, viscous pockets that had coagulated and hardened. He knew about blood. So much had been spilled at his hands. But where he might have expected muscular clots, he noticed only paper-thin scabs of blood. Something inside him clanged but he didn't know why.

He caught a glimpse of himself in the mirror, a sweep of white-blond hair and the pencil line of his jaw. Adulthood had turned him from a surly, troubled boy into a young man who'd turned down the advances of many women and some men, drawn by the intoxicating cocktail of his striking looks and the air of invulnerability he'd learned to project to deflect the interest of school teachers and social services.

The letters were written in a style bordering on cursive. *Make Them Stop.* Beneath the floral notes of Riva's scent, Saul smelled not the metallic tang of dirty pennies, but something sweeter. He pictured Riva tracing the tip of a bloodied finger across the face of the mirror. Was this show-manship, a statement or a last act of desperation?

'So,' said Williams, 'initial thoughts?'

Saul considered the question. As his mentor, Williams would provide detailed feedback on Saul's performance to

O'Neill. Although the older officers had yet to earn his respect, Saul recognized the need to play this particular chess match with appropriate consideration for the rules. At this stage of the game, impressing Williams and O'Neill was the shrewdest move he could make.

'Why is it written in blood?' he said. 'Why didn't she leave a note? And if this was a violent abduction, how did she have time to write a message at all?'

Williams was nodding, jotting notes in his pad. 'Keep going, lad.'

Saul frowned, trying to organize the questions that jumped around in his head. 'There's blood on the glass and some in the bathroom, but none on the carpet or the walls. Why is that? And perhaps the most important question of all, whose blood is it?'

'Not bad,' said DC Williams with a hint of grudging admiration. 'Better than I expected.'

Blue, who had been listening to their exchange, gave Saul a level look. 'All valid questions, but you're wrong, I'm afraid.'

Saul met her gaze, not offended by her combativeness like the others, but intrigued. 'Go on, then. What have I missed?'

'The most pressing question is not the origin of the blood used in that message' – she smiled at him and he was lost – 'but finding the person who wrote it.'

13

Two days before the Holdens disappeared

When Riva Holden was twelve, life changed. She'd always been tall but when she started to fill out, the trouble began: catcalls from construction workers; cars crawling along the kerb, offering her a lift as she walked to school in her plaid skirt and ponytail; the young guy at the auction house Kenilworths pressing a scrap of paper into her hand when she went to a sale with her father, his telephone number an eager scrawl; and the endless unsolicited approaches over social media from men old enough to know better.

Piper Holden minded very much, although not for the reasons she ought to. Naturally, she voiced outrage at the inappropriate attention her pre-teen garnered, wrote furious letters to site managers, reported fragments of half-remembered number plates to school and the police, and tore up the hopeful scraps of paper. *You are not here for the pleasure of men* was a frequent mantra. *You are entitled to walk the streets without harassment.* And only when she was sure her daughter understood the importance of valuing herself without validation from the opposite sex did she allow herself space to examine her own feelings.

She recognized it was a negative trait to feel envy towards her own daughter and yet she could not stop herself. As her once-upon-a-time child, all grass-stained knees and bedtime stories, abandoned her toys and grew into her beauty, her own feelings had distorted into something ugly. Riva shone with the impossible luminosity of youth. Her skin was fresh, unmarked. No teenage acne for Riva. Her legs had length-ened until she was taller and slimmer than Piper, and, sweet Jesus, her hair. So thick and plentiful, not thinning in places like her middle-aged mother's, which fell in flat hanks around her shoulders.

Piper did not think that Riva had the slightest awareness of her inner conflict. She fought hard to disguise it, lavish-ing too much praise on her daughter, who accepted it in good grace, but with a sense of youthful superiority that compliments were nothing more than she was due. In spite of this, a distance had crept between them. Perhaps it was a subconscious instinct for her mother's envy or perhaps it was because they were so alike, but Riva's closest bond was now with her father.

As a child, she had told her mother everything. Now she kept secrets from her, folded away in the distant reaches of herself, thrilling in the knowledge that her mother had no access to.

Because of this, Piper knew nothing of Riva's trip to Gray Holden's office the previous afternoon, in the hours after his hand was impaled with a pen by a stranger. Riva had arrived after his secretary Charlotte had been sent home, and so she'd waltzed in without announcement, laden down with shopping bags, as he was binding his wound with a fresh bandage.

'What are you doing here?' He was startled to see her, but there was weariness instead of sharpness in his tone. He rose from his chair and crossed the room, locking the office door to prevent any other unexpected visitors. He'd had more than enough for one day.

Her eyes settled on his hand and she swerved his question with one of her own. 'Oh God, Dad, what did you do?'

His explanation – that he'd cut his hand on a broken tumbler – was a lie, but in that self-absorbed way of teenagers, Riva accepted it without argument or challenge.

His face, pale and drawn, she blamed on loss of blood, and it didn't occur to her to look for the glass shards or to notice the bloodied nib of the pen on his desk. She had other concerns on her mind.

'Daddy?' She spoke in a voice her mother would never allow.

'Hmmmm.' He was adjusting the tightness of the bandage, his mind full of the stranger and Mr Moore's money and the threat to his family, too distracted to answer more fully.

'Why didn't you come home last night?'

He stilled but didn't look up, his fingers fiddling with the safety pin. 'I did – but it was late. You were asleep.'

She rested her hands on her narrow hips and pouted. 'I'm not stupid. I heard Mum on the phone to Julianne this morning.' She looked around the office for signs of occupation and noticed a blanket folded in the corner. Her voice kinked in disbelief. 'Did you sleep *here*?'

'Does your mother know where you are?'

'I won't tell her, if that's what you're worried about.' A flash of chiding humour. 'Chill, Dad.'

Gray leaned back in his chair. The pain in his hand was hampering his ability to think clearly and while he wanted his daughter to leave, he couldn't tell her that because he was besotted with her in the way some fathers are.

He loved his son, their mutual appreciation of cricket and films by the Farrelly brothers, that natural sense of brotherliness that was developing between them as Artie grew older and they became more like equals.

But his relationship with Riva was different. It was a base thing. Not in any kind of sexual way, although he recognized his daughter was beautiful, but an instinct – an imperative – to protect her above all else, even his marriage. His love for her was without strictures or conditions, it simply was. Although he loved his wife, their relationship had dulled into a comfortable familiarity. If he was forced to choose between Piper and Riva, his daughter would always come first.

'I'm "chill",' he said, forcing out a laugh. 'Now what can I do for you? Haven't you got homework or rehearsals, or something?'

Her face darkened. 'The play's finishing tonight, remember? Oh, that's right. You didn't come.'

'I'm sorry, honey. You know I would have made it if I could.' He shrugged, helpless. 'It's work.'

'You're always working.' She was not accusatory or antagonistic but stating a truth that knifed him in the heart. 'Anyway,' she said, a shadow passing across her face, fingers pulling the ends of her hair, 'that's not why I'm here.'

'Ah, I see.' He rolled his eyes, his mouth flattening, as if he already knew what she was going to say.

'I don't want money,' she said quickly. He raised his eyebrows, surprised, and crossed his arms. She took a deep breath. 'I want to talk to you about Piper.'

He couldn't help but laugh. 'Why are you calling your mother that?'

Riva flicked her hair over her shoulders. 'It's her name, isn't it?' She watched her father carefully.

'You're a funny thing,' he said, affection softening his words. 'Come on then. Spit it out. What's on your mind?'

Riva widened her eyes and pushed out her lower lip. It was a look she used on the boys at school to get them to pay attention.

'I think something's the matter. She's being' – she fished around for the word – 'weird.'

Gray's face was a motion picture of laughter lines. 'No change there then.'

'I'm being serious, Dad. She's' – a hesitation – '*different.*'

'Different how?' Gray's hand was alive with pain, and his patience was thinning and stretching. He loved his daughter and always had time for her, but all he wanted was to down half a bottle of brandy and a double dose of painkillers, and to be alone. 'Look, it's getting dark. Shouldn't you be getting home, love?'

Riva continued as if she hadn't heard him, the words tumbling out in a rush. 'She's distracted and she was on the phone to Julianne the other day, and she stopped talking when I came in, so I listened at the door this morning and she's up to something, Dad, but I don't know what. She told Julianne that she was—' The silence said more than her words.

'She was what?'

Riva had flicked an anxious glance at her father, sitting in the gathering dusk of his office. Her voice dropped and he had to lean forward to hear what she was saying, the shadows casting a darkness across his face.

'That she was leaving.'

Twenty-four hours later, standing in the middle of the supermarket aisle, that conversation played in Gray's brain on a continual loop. He'd managed to avoid Piper at bedtime, but only because he'd slept in one of their spare rooms and was gone by the time she got up. He knew the children would notice he was not there but they would have to live with that. He was avoiding their mother for a reason. He knew it, and she knew it too.

Piper had sent him seventeen texts and left five voicemails over the last two days. He had listened to a couple of the messages and scanned all of the texts, just in case, but had answered only one.

I have nothing to say to you.

Seven words. Eight syllables. A lifetime together. They'd been married for sixteen years. Christ, where had that time gone? Best friends. Lovers. Partners in crime.

A hungry darkness pressed against the glass windows of the supermarket and he caught sight of his reflection, a washed-out smudgy outline. Overhead, a fluorescent light flickered and jumped, a loose connection somewhere, and the deserted aisles made him think this was how it would feel to be trapped in an apocalypse.

He walked up and down with purpose, past the expensive cheese and olives, the bottles of wine and spirits, the packets of biscuits and confectionery. He caught sight of a bag of chocolate limes and it threw him back down the years, the sticky wrapper, the acid-sweetness dissolving on his tongue.

The first time he'd glimpsed Piper, she'd been sitting in the same Elements of Drama lecture, a couple of seats along from him. He'd risked several glances, admiring the faded Nirvana T-shirt, the Doc Marten boots, the badges pinned to her Army & Navy satchel. She'd caught him watching and gifted him a smile. When she glanced up again, and he was still looking, she dipped her hand into her satchel and slid a chocolate lime along the bench to him. In return, he'd handed her a flyer to a Magic Society social that night. When she'd walked into the dingy pub, cool and confident, a different T-shirt this time – the Ramones – his stomach had lurched with excitement and lust. Three pints of snakebite later, they'd shared their first kiss.

Two students from impoverished backgrounds. Both determined to climb out of the poverty trap they'd been born into. They'd drifted away from each other after university but had stayed in touch and found their way back to each other a few years later. Seawings was a bricks-and-mortar reminder of how far they'd come.

In the cleaning aisle, he grabbed three bottles of bleach and several packets of blue-and-white absorbent cloths. Supplies for the office. A middle-aged man was unloading packets of toilet rolls onto the shelves. Gray envied him the mindlessness of a task that would be forgotten as soon as his shift was over. His own head was full of tangled strings.

He knew Piper was furious with him for obfuscating about the money, but it was too late now. He'd already closed their accounts and withdrawn all their savings. Multiple withdrawals of £10,000 or less over a handful of days from different branches.

A few of the tellers had asked him where the money was going – money-laundering regulations, he knew the drill – but a couple recognized him, used to the large sums he deposited, and barely raised an eyebrow.

A young man – new to the job – quizzed him relentlessly about what he was spending the money on. A car, he explained. A top-of-the-range Mercedes. He was paying for some of it in cash. An excellent diversionary tactic he'd used before on naive twenty-somethings. The young man lapped up the details; the colour, the model, the top speed.

Some of the money he'd transferred to other accounts at different banks. Overseas. Sleight of hand. The art of misdirection.

The supermarket was almost empty. Every now and then, he came across someone else but they were intent on their own shopping. He lifted his eyes upwards, seeking out the position of the security cameras. When he reached the homewares aisle, he ducked his head. Baking trays, saucepans, glasses, crockery, tea towels. He scanned the shelves until he found what he was looking for.

He picked it up. Stainless steel, cool and heavy. He held the weight of it in his hand for a few seconds, his fingers tightening around the handle. The cameras were behind him, to the left. He angled his body away from them and placed the meat hammer back on the shelf.

14

Tuesday evening

The day the Holdens disappeared

The branches of the oak tree in Julianne's front garden were moving so wildly she feared they might break apart in the wind.

As she watched them submit to the weather from an upstairs window, rain spitting against the glass, Quiller's car pulled into the driveway. Instead of waving to her husband, Julianne ducked beneath the sill, crawled across the carpet and bolted down the stairs. By the time she heard his key in the lock, the radio was playing and she was chopping spring onions for their stir fry.

It was a while before he came to find her. He hung up his coat, placed his keys in the drawer and dumped his bag in the study. She heard him climb the stairs and the creak of the floorboards told her he'd gone into their bedroom to get changed. Back down the stairs and into the study. He put on a record, turning up the volume, and the sound drowned out the news programme she was listening to. By the time he appeared in the kitchen, she'd chopped all the vegetables and was cubing chicken breasts.

'Where's your car?'

No *hello* or *how was your day?* No kiss or embrace. Julianne turned to face him, pasting on a smile. Her husband hated moodiness. And dull-wittedness. But this time, he didn't wait for her answer, instead rolling on to his next question.

'Where are the children?'

'Music practice and Debating Society.'

Quiller grunted and poured himself a glass of orange juice without offering her one.

'You're home early. Good day?' She wanted to ask if he'd sold any houses but feared a thirty-minute monologue on indecisive vendors. He grunted again and opened his mouth to say something more, but the doorbell rang and he went to answer it.

When he returned, he was flanked by two men. Julianne recognized them as the police officers from Piper's house. They'd turned up as she was being sent home because Seawings was now a crime scene. Those two words had made her shudder.

'We've come to take your statement,' said the older one. The younger officer stared at her with serious eyes.

'What's this about?' said Quiller, looking from the police officers to Julianne and back again.

'The Holdens,' she said quickly. 'I told you, remember?'

Quiller settled himself in a chair at the kitchen table and cupped his chin in his palm, as if preparing to watch an interesting film. 'Bloody hell, I didn't realize it was *this* serious.' And then, as an afterthought, he flapped his other hand at the detectives. 'Sit down, sit down.'

Julianne willed him to leave the room. She couldn't

speak as frankly as she might with Quiller listening in but she knew it would irk him to the point of sulkiness if she asked him to go away.

'Would you prefer to make a statement on your own?' said the white-blond detective, his eyes trapping and holding hers, a pin in a butterfly's thorax. When he'd introduced himself as Detective Constable Anguish, she'd thought how well his name suited the sorrowful tilt of his mouth. But his eyes held a darker knowledge. He was clever, she realized. Watchful. She would have to be careful.

'Julianne won't mind.' Quiller was dismissive. 'We don't have secrets in this house.'

'Righto,' said the older officer, DC Williams. 'Let's get cracking, shall we?' He pulled out a chair and settled himself at the kitchen table. 'Any chance of a brew?' he said to Quiller with a pointed glance.

'Julianne makes the best tea in this house,' said Quiller with a laugh. 'Don't you?'

It was a standing joke between them. Quiller was hopeless at making tea. And coffee. He was also hopeless at cooking and loading the dishwasher and putting the laundry away. Now she came to think about it, there was nothing funny in that at all.

But it was easier for her to fill the kettle and warm the pot and lay out biscuits, so she did.

When she was finished, she sat opposite the detectives and sipped the hot liquid. She pressed her middle finger against the bridge of her nose and rubbed it in a circular motion. The vodka she'd drunk earlier was giving her a headache.

'Let's start at the beginning,' said DC Williams, dipping

a biscuit into his tea. 'You raised the alarm when you realized the Holdens were missing, is that right?'

DC Anguish's pen was poised over his notepad. His
junior status meant he'd drawn the short straw.

'Yes,' said Julianne. 'I usually meet Piper for a run on
Tuesdays but she wasn't answering the door, which was very
unusual. Their cleaner arrived and she had a key, so we let
ourselves in, and when it was clear something untoward had
happened, we called you.'

DC Williams fired off many questions. What was Piper's
usual routine? What about the rest of the family? How long
had they lived here? Did they have other properties else-
where? What about extended family? Had Piper – or any of
the Holdens – mentioned the possibility of leaving town?
What kind of work did they do? Had they ever disappeared
before? To the best of her knowledge, did the family have
any enemies? What about the state of Piper and Gray Hold-
en's marriage? The children?

While he waited for Julianne to answer his last question,
the older detective helped himself to another biscuit, slop-
ping it into his almost-empty mug and then into his
colleague's full one.

DC Anguish had not touched his tea. He was watching
her. Despite her efforts to maintain a neutral expression, she
couldn't hide the indecision that flickered across her face.
She knew he'd noticed it when he said, 'Is there something
you'd like to tell us?'

Quiller, who until now had stayed mostly silent, looked
up from his own tea with interest.

Julianne closed her eyes. Bit the inside of her cheek.
Drew in a breath until it filled her lungs and calmed her.

'Actually, that's why I came back to Seawings this afternoon. I wanted to speak to you.'

'After the funeral?' DC Anguish's voice was encouraging but he was looking at her intently.

'Whose funeral?' said Quiller.

'I told you,' said Julianne, irritation edging her tone. 'Anoushka Thornton's.'

'Never heard of her.'

'We were at school together.'

'Not another bloody school friend. They're dropping like flies.' He sounded outraged, as if dying prematurely was somehow the fault of the women themselves. He flicked his gaze to the detectives, seeking validation. DC Williams smirked, then remembered himself. Quiller slurped his tea. 'Is that where your car is then? Still at the pub or something?'

Julianne stilled. Williams and Quiller watched her. A silence settled over the room.

DC Anguish did not look at any of them but made a note in his pad and urged Julianne to continue, unable to disguise his frustration at the interruption. 'Let's not worry about that now. Please go on.'

'Piper was frightened.' Her eyes were fixed on her lap. 'Gray had moved some large sums of money out of their accounts. She called me late last night to say she was scared he was going to hurt her.'

DC Williams looked up sharply. 'Has he been violent before?'

Julianne gave a helpless shrug. 'Not that she's mentioned to me, but that doesn't mean it hasn't happened. It's not the sort of thing she'd necessarily want to talk about, even to her best friend. From the outside her life is pretty enviable, I think she'd be embarrassed.'

'Gray wouldn't hurt Piper,' said Quiller. 'That's not his style. He can be a sanctimonious bastard at times, but I don't think he'd hit her.'

A rush of anger, fierce and sudden and hot as a burn, spread through her. *Shut up.* She wanted to shake it into him. *Shut up. Shut up.* But she didn't. Instead she quietly disagreed.

'He's got a temper,' she said. 'I wouldn't want to cross him.'

DC Williams was interested by this revelation, she could tell. More than interested. Excited. Buzzing with an energy that had been absent when he'd arrived. DC Anguish was different. He was sizing her up, weighing her truths. His scrutiny made her feel exposed.

'Can you think of anywhere the Holdens might have gone? Do they have a holiday home, for example?'

Julianne frowned, concentrating hard. 'They've got an apartment in New York, but their passports are still at Sea-wings. There's family in Northumberland, but Mila rang them this morning and they haven't seen them. Her mother lived a couple of hours from here but the farm was sold when she died.' In truth, she had no idea where her friend might be.

'Did Piper Holden ever have any unexplained bruises or injuries?' DC Williams was alert now, poised, his whole demeanour changed.

Julianne was at a crossroads. But which path to take? A memory of a video of Piper at university – reading aloud from a script, stunning her tutor into a rare silence and mesmerizing her classmates – popped into her head. Gray had played it to her one drunken night a few years ago, all of them laughing at the dated camcorder footage and Piper's crimped hair. A second recollection hit her sideways. Last week, when she'd bumped into her friend on the high street, Piper was wearing a silk scarf around her neck. 'Very Audrey Hepburn,' she'd said, reaching up to touch her fingers to the fabric, and Piper had smiled and then winced. But she never usually wore scarves, silk or otherwise.

Julianne reached a decision and dropped her words like a series of tiny bombs.

'I'm afraid so. She always brushed it off as being clumsy but she seemed to have a lot of accidents. When we were late home from a shopping trip a few months ago – horrendous traffic – Gray was furious because he was hosting a client that night, and he practically dragged her from the car. When I saw her for a run the next morning, he'd left bruises on her forearm in the shape of finger marks.'

'Really?' said Quiller, surprised. 'I would never have expected that of Gray.' He looked at his wife. 'You didn't mention it.'

'None of us knows what goes on behind closed doors, Mr Hillier,' said DC Williams.

The three men sat around the kitchen table, watching her. Julianne was used to male attention – craved it, even – but she was uncomfortable with their scrutiny and got up abruptly from the table.

'There's something else you should probably hear,' she said. She grabbed her mobile from the worktop and scrolled through it, searching for the voicemail that had come in from Piper's home telephone number at 3.37 a.m., a few

short hours ago. She hadn't told the officers about it yet –
she hadn't told anyone, even though she should have done
so by now – but from the moment they'd stepped through
her front door, the interview had been building towards this
and she was relieved to share the burden of it at last.

She placed the handset on the table, unexploded ord-
nance resting amongst the floral plates and biscuit crumbs,
put it on speakerphone and pressed play.

The kitchen was silent apart from the angry song of the
wind, drumming against the windows and walls.

Julianne had listened to the message several times now
but, watching the expression on the faces of the men opposite her, it felt like she was hearing it for the first time.

For the first couple of seconds, the recording was quiet,
like the calm before the storm. And then the storm made
landfall.

A sound – not a scream, more guttural than that, but not
a shout either – made them all jump and was over so quickly
it was impossible to tell if it came from a man or a woman.
A muffled voice – rising in volume but not clarity – was
followed by a crash, like the sound of furniture being turned
over. Quiller opened his mouth to speak but DC Williams
held his hand up to silence him. The noises grew louder, as
if this microcosm of violence – the eye of the storm – was
moving closer to the telephone. Julianne imagined the
receiver lying on its side, on a table in the sitting room or
the nightstand by Piper's bed, listening and recording the
secrets of Seawings.

Then, even though she knew it was coming, a wet sound
that made the blood run hard and fast through her veins.
The thud of something heavy hitting something tender and

vulnerable, and a woman's scream, as cold as the stars that squatted in the clouded darkness above the Holden house.

And Piper's cracked voice pressed up to the mouthpiece, 'God help us all,' before the call cut out and the sound of dead air filled the room.

15

Two months before the Holdens disappeared

When their English class had finished, Riva lingered by her seat until the room emptied. She wanted to catch Mr Moran before the after-school auditions began but she didn't want her classmates to know.

He was sitting at his desk behind a pile of exercise books, head bent, intent on marking, and didn't look up until she cleared her throat. Students moved through the corridors, their footsteps a percussion of dozens of individual drum beats. He peered at her over his glasses.

'What can I do for you? Do you need a copy of the homework sheet?'

'No, thanks, sir. I've got one.'

'Spit it out then. What's on your mind?'

She adopted her most anxious expression, eyes wide, a sincere yet tremulous grin. 'It's a bit of an awkward one and I don't want it to go any further, if that's OK.'

'Go on.' He put down his pen.

'It's about Emelie Hillier.'

Mr Moran gathered the exercise books into a pile and shoved them into his work satchel. 'Your friend?'

Riva nodded. 'She said you'd encouraged her to try out for the show.'

'That's right.' Mr Moran checked his watch and smiled at her. 'And thank you for reminding me. The auditions start in ten minutes.'

'The thing is, she feels a bit pressured into it. She doesn't want to let you down but she doesn't want to audition. She'd prefer to work on the set design. But she doesn't want a big drama about it. She's too embarrassed to talk to you, so I said I'd do it for her.'

Mr Moran got up from his desk and slung his bag over his shoulder. 'I'm sorry to hear that. As it happens, I think she's got a lot of talent but we haven't had a chance to see it yet.'

Riva swallowed down the bitter rise of jealousy. 'I agree. I tried to persuade her to have a rethink but she's made up her mind. She feels bad for not telling you herself but you know what she's like.'

'It's a shame she didn't feel able to approach me herself though. I'm not *that* terrifying.'

'Not at all, sir. But she's always avoided confrontation, ever since we were little. You won't tell her about this, will you?'

'Thank you for telling me. I don't want to push her into anything she doesn't want to do. But I hope you're not planning to bail on me too, Riva.'

She gave him one of her most dazzling smiles in return. 'Of course not. You can count on me, sir.'

16

The day the Holdens disappeared

'But there were no signs of a struggle,' said Saul to DC Williams as they walked back to Seawings through Midtown-on-Sea's early evening streets. 'Apart from the blood on the chandelier.'

'And the mirror. Don't forget that.'

'Even so.'

'Gray Holden tidied up before he left,' said Williams. 'Kicked the shit out of her, cleaned up his mess, did a runner – the oldest trick in the book.'

'But what about the children?' said Saul. 'Are you suggesting he killed them too?'

'It's been known.'

'But they're not little, are they? They're teenagers. Big enough to put up some kind of fight.'

'Not if he killed them while they were sleeping in their beds.'

'So why leave the message on Riva Holden's mirror? What's the point of that?'

DC Williams didn't seem bothered by it. 'She might have been messing about. You know what teenagers are like. We don't how long it's been there until forensics tell us.' He glanced sideways at Saul. 'Was it my imagination or was it hot in there? Julianne Hillier is—' He blew out a breath and fanned himself, seemingly oblivious to Saul's distaste at his misjudged attempt at sexualized banter.

'Don't be grim,' said Saul, risking his mentor's ire but unable to let it pass without comment. He swerved the conversation back to the investigation. 'You think Piper Holden's dead, don't you?'

'We'll find out soon enough,' said Williams, taking a flat metallic water bottle from inside his pocket and drinking deeply, 'but if I was a betting man, I'd say yes.'

A police cordon had been put in place at Seawings by the time the two men arrived back at the house and DI Angus O'Neill was standing on the entrance steps, staring up at a wall-mounted camera above the front door.

Saul ducked under the blue-and-white tape that had been pulled so taut it snapped in the wind. 'Put on some fucking shoe covers,' said the detective inspector, pointing to a plastic box inside the cordon that Saul hadn't noticed. He blushed. Rookie mistake.

'They've got closed circuit television cameras trained on the front and back,' said O'Neill in lieu of a greeting. He turned, grinned unexpectedly at them. 'This is going to change everything.'

His boss crackled with energy and purpose in the same way Williams had when Julianne Hillier had hinted at Gray Holden's predilection for violence an hour or so earlier. But as far as Saul was concerned, nothing much had changed. The Holdens were still missing.

Williams and O'Neill were deep in conversation, exchanging intelligence gathered so far. 'I'm just going inside,' said Saul. 'There's something I'd like to check in Riva Holden's room.'

His two superiors barely acknowledged him. They wandered off together, heads bowed, towards the end of the front garden, leaving Saul standing by himself. As an afterthought, Williams called out to him, not bothering to glance back at his young colleague. 'Don't take too long, Anguish. We've got a lot of work to do.'

A Forensic Investigation van was pulling up outside Seawings as Saul climbed the entrance steps and disappeared into the house. A few officers milled around but they didn't pay any attention to him. He jogged lightly up the stairs and made his way along the corridor that led to the bedrooms. Such a beautiful house. The child in him felt a thin prick of envy. Imagine growing up in a place like this. And then he remembered why he was here and it chastened him. As he retraced his steps to Riva's bedroom, the sounds of activity from downstairs dulled into silence and he pushed the door open.

Her bedroom was vast, like something from an interior design magazine, the walls decorated with hand-painted paper that would probably cost Saul a month's salary. A king-sized bed dominated the space, which was larger than the flat he'd shared with his mother. In one corner was the door to a walk-in wardrobe, and on the opposite side, an en-suite bathroom.

The dressing table with its bloody message had already

been dusted for prints and scavenged for samples of DNA, but he slipped on the pair of latex gloves he was carrying in his pocket and pressed one hand against the solid oak, working quickly.

The brush was clogged with strands of thick hair and he dragged them free from the bristles until he was sure he had enough. Forensics had left plenty behind but he took only as much as he dared, making sure its absence wouldn't be noticed. He was stuffing Riva Holden's hair into a plastic evidence bag when someone cleared their throat.

He jumped and spun around, half expecting to see one of the detectives standing in the doorway, finger pointing and asking difficult questions, but there was no one there.

His eyes strayed around Riva's bedroom, seeking the source of the noise. Thirty seconds later, he found it. Lying on the carpet, in the gap between the bed and the bathroom that had been hidden from view when he'd stepped through the door, was Blue.

She was pulling herself into a sitting position, rubbing her eyes, as if she'd been asleep. When she caught him staring at her, she froze. Her gaze travelled down to his gloved hands and he realized he was still holding Riva's hair and the plastic bag.

'What are you doing? Forensics have already taken Riva's samples.'

'What are *you* doing? Heavy night?' He smiled to show she had nothing to fear from him. Grassing to DI O'Neill was not his style.

A frown creased her forehead. She stood up, hair falling around her face, and lost her balance, tipping heavily to her right. Saul stepped forward to steady her. Their hands touched by accident and electricity ran through him, like the grind of sparks against railway tracks.

'No, it was not,' she said softly, and he glimpsed something fleeting in her expression. Defiance, perhaps. And shame.

'Are you sure you're OK?' Although he hardly knew her, Saul was compelled by a need he didn't fully understand to confirm the status of her well-being.

Blue flashed a sardonic grin. 'Peachy keen.' Then she lifted one hand in farewell and walked out of the room.

Night was bruising the sky when Saul took the path back to the coastguard's lookout. In the hook of the bay, distant lights stopped the darkness from swallowing him whole. The day had been long, full of new people and experiences, and he needed time to hold still and catch his breath.

Using his police torch, he picked his way along the muddy track. His hair was wet by the time he arrived at the cottage, the rising wind seasoned with salt and rain.

He'd forgotten to leave on the lights and the brick edifice was a smudge against the brushed darkness. He fumbled with his key twice before managing to fit it in the lock and open the door. An unfamiliar smell greeted him, not yet of home: musty dampness with an undercurrent of bleach and brine.

His stomach rumbled, reminding him it was many hours since he'd eaten. He'd thought about asking Blue to show him somewhere decent for dinner, perhaps even asking her to join him, but she'd left Seawings by the time he'd gone downstairs and he didn't want to ask DC Williams about her. He'd look her up on the internet later. Most people left a trace these days.

The landlord had left a basket of essentials for him on the kitchen table – crusty bread, cereal, cheese, fruit, a bottle of wine – and for that, Saul was grateful. He'd had no time to shop and no energy to cook. He retrieved milk from the fridge and poured out a bowl of expensive granola he'd never buy for himself. When he'd finished that, he cut a wedge of cheese and tore some bread from the loaf, and ate it standing by the window, listening to the crash of the waves.

His rucksack and holdall were upstairs on the bedroom floor where he'd left them when he'd arrived that morning. The room was a third of the size of Riva Holden's but the heating had come on automatically and it was warm enough to keep the night at bay.

Saul unpacked his meagre collection of clothes and placed his book and laptop on the bedside table. When all that was done, he carried the hand-carved wooden chest with careful hands to the box room at the back of the cottage.

He'd always owned a receptacle of some kind, even as a boy. His first had been a jewellery box. But as the years had rolled on, it was no longer big enough to hold his collection. When he was seventeen and the reward money had come through, he'd commissioned a joiner friend of his mother's to make a portable apothecary chest in miniature with bespoke drawers and hidden compartments.

He withdrew the matchbox from his pocket and pulled out the third drawer from the top. His eyes travelled over the *Coleoptera* specimens lying against the wood and velvet flocking. With careful fingers, he searched for the smaller members of the *Staphylinidae* family and placed the devil's coach horse amongst them. *Ocypus olens.* He whispered the name to himself. The finest specimen in the order of beetles.

His collection housed many insects. A queen bee and her foot soldiers. The exoskeletons of several crickets. A locust. The dusty husk of a *Catocala fraxini* with its smoky-blue underwing, the rarest of moths.

When he'd placed the beetle in its final resting place, he closed the drawer and fished for the tiny key he wore on a chain around his neck.

At the bottom of the chest, inlaid into the wood and disguised by an ornate carved panel that slid across its length, was a deep, wide drawer with a lock mechanism. The throaty click it made when he opened it reminded him of a gun being cocked.

The drawer had been partitioned into compartments and each of these had been divided into four squares, a quartet of tiny rooms.

Saul withdrew the evidence bag from his pocket and chose an empty one. He touched Riva Holden's hair with a reverence reserved for the dead.

When he was a boy, he'd made a pipe-cleaner worry doll to share his secrets and fears. He'd carried it around for years, a place to hide himself. That dolly, with her wool strands for hair and scrap-of-felt face, had been his talisman until, in a fit of pique, he'd cut off its head. The frayed remnants of its body now occupied one of the quarters, tucked under a poplin blanket like the one he used to fold over his mother.

In the square next to it lay another pipe-cleaner doll, crowned with hair as blond as Saul's own, rubied spotting on the platinum shafts of keratin, an antique doll-sized knife buried in its chest. A bible in miniature sat next to it, opened at the Song of Solomon. Solomon Anguish. Long gone now, his body lost to the sea. But the strands of hair were real. Saul remembered the feel of his father flinching beneath his curled fist as he pulled them out, his look of pain and surprise as his life leaked onto the linoleum floor.

Third quarter, third pipe-cleaner creation, its black strands of hair streaked with silver. A ghost from the past. A killer who'd deserved to be killed. A bone fragment – the stapes of a rabbit, the ear bone, the smallest in its body – was tucked into its pipe-cleaner fist. Face down, another tiny knife sticking out of its back. Saul's little joke.

As the years had passed, he'd refined his collection and it had grown beyond his family and the men he'd killed from a sense of morality. Murder, some might call it. But he preferred to think of it as his duty. He did not regret his actions. As far as he was concerned, he'd had no other choice. He'd been too young, not a boy, but not yet the man he'd become. Even now, he'd do it again.

He could not explain the compulsion that drove him to keep these trophies, only that it calmed him. Reminded him of how far he'd come. And what he'd left behind.

The first time he'd stolen hair from a crime scene as a police officer was eight months ago, a year after starting his training. It had belonged to a woman, beaten and strangled, turned inside out by the brutal violence of her boyfriend. Saul had been attached to the Domestic Violence unit and they'd warned him of the darkness at the heart of the home. They didn't need to tell him. He knew all about it. But the sight of the woman – nineteen, a mother herself when she'd barely stopped being a child – slumped at the foot of her daughter's cot in an act of protective sacrifice had stopped him in his tracks.

The female police officer – his mentor on this secondment – had ordered him to take care of the crying baby while she radioed through for an ambulance.

He'd gathered up the child, curls sticking damply to her forehead, cheeks wet with tears. She was no older than eight or nine months, and as he held her close, waiting for her shuddering breaths to subside, a fury burned inside him.

Saul was supposed to take the child downstairs, away from her unconscious mother, a bloodied doll with the strings cut. And he'd intended to.

But his gaze had settled on a pair of nail scissors sitting on the chest of drawers, next to nappy cream and a teething ring, and Saul had picked them up, weighed them in his palm. He shifted the child to his left hip and leaned over to clip a lock of the woman's hair: a token, a marker of her suffering.

The baby watched, eyes wide. On impulse, he cut some strands from the back of her head too.

Months later, when the investigation into her assault had concluded and the man who'd beaten her halfway to death had expressed his carefully calculated remorse, and the judge, weighing all the evidence, had taken the exceptional step of granting a conditional discharge, Saul unearthed the address he'd copied from the man's police files, biding his time.

Over the last few months, Saul had visited many crime scenes, scavenging bits of hair, acting outside the law when keeping inside it was an affront to the victims.

But the jury was still out in the case of the Holden family.

Saul removed Riva's hair from the evidence bag and placed it in the box for safekeeping. Strange to think it had been part of her once. He stared into the blackness outside his window. Was she dead? Was the family dead? He would not make her pipe-cleaner doll until he was certain of her fate.

Unlike Detective Constable Williams, Saul had learned not to make assumptions. The good guys were not always good. He was living proof of that.

Saul leaned back in his chair, the old floorboards of the lookout creaking. He considered the way Julianne Hillier's eyes had slid away from his, and her unusual stillness when recounting Piper's disappearance, as if trying too hard, and the way she sometimes covered her mouth with her hand.

He had no idea what had happened to the Holdens. But he was sure of one truth: Julianne Hillier was lying.

17

Wednesday morning

The day after the Holdens disappeared

The morning after the Holdens disappeared, Julianne waited for Quiller and the children to leave before she got out of bed, citing a terrible headache.

Quiller, smelling of aftershave and self-importance, set a glass of lukewarm water and a couple of painkillers on her bedside table. 'I'll call you later. I've got an appointment at nine.'

She murmured something in return, making her voice inaudible. The bedroom had that stuffy, filtered dimness that comes from morning light pressing against closed curtains. Julianne could smell her own body, the unwashed scent of it. She'd hardly slept, replaying the events of the last thirty-six hours over and over again until every sinew in her was strained with tension and she lay rigid against the sheets, listening to Quiller breathe. She envied his untroubled sleep.

When she was sure the house was empty, Julianne showered and dressed. She couldn't stomach breakfast but made coffee, black and burning, and scanned online sites for stories about their missing friends, but the news hadn't broken yet.

At half past nine, she picked up her keys and purse, put on her coat and hat, and closed the door behind her.

The short but picturesque route along the cliffs into the bustling high street was one of the many reasons Julianne had fallen in love with their house.

As owner of an estate agency, Quiller had first look at properties coming onto the market and when he'd called her sixteen years ago, excited in a way he never seemed to manage these days, she'd shared his enthusiasm.

After the first night in their new home, they'd strolled along the cliff path into town for lunch. She remembered every step: the open sky, the dramatic fall away of the rocks and the sight of the sailing boats, a row of folded handkerchiefs floating on the water, breath catching in her throat.

Even now, when it was as familiar as her own face, the view across the bay awed her. As she walked into town, the tall, expensive houses with their manicured front lawns turned into artisan bakeries, designer boutiques and tasteful homeware stores selling soft blankets and decorative anchors. An old-fashioned ice-cream parlour and countless coffee shops. Two butcher's shops, a greengrocer's, a specialist wine shop and a confectionery shop with rows of jars filled with a rainbow of sweets and sherbet.

The florist's was situated on the corner with a glimpse of the sea between its own brick building and the hair salon next door.

The bell jangled as Julianne pushed her way in. Corinne

Masterson had inherited the shop from her mother and run it for twenty years. The interior was cool – it helped to keep the flowers fresh – and it smelled earthy and damp and sweet all at once.

Corinne's smile was broad. She snipped a length of ribbon. 'I didn't expect to see you again this week.'

Julianne bent over a long stem of pale lilac stocks. 'These are beautiful.'

'Did Piper like her flowers?'

Piper had ordered flowers from Masterson's every week for years. Sometimes, when they were going for coffee, Julianne went with her to choose them or settle the bill, and sometimes she collected them for her friend, as she'd done twice already in the last few days.

Every now and then, if it was close to her lunch break, Corinne would join them. As the only florist in the town, she knew everyone and everything. Celebrations and sorrows, loves won and lost – and all the secrets in between.

But then Julianne remembered why she'd come. She took a deep breath and steeled herself. 'I've got some bad news, I'm afraid. You might need to sit down.' Exhale. 'Piper's missing. The whole family's gone.'

Corinne's jaw slackened in shock. She dropped her scissors on the counter. 'Missing? What do you mean?'

Of unknown whereabouts. What else could it mean? Julianne bit back the retort that rose inside her. Alienating Corinne wouldn't help.

She explained the events of the previous day, the abandoned breakfast, the blood on the chandelier. Corinne drank down every detail with the thirst of a gossip and actually licked her lips when Julianne had finished.

'But she seemed OK last week. Perhaps they've gone on holiday.' Corinne answered her own question. 'No, you said the cars and passports were still at the house.' She leaned forward, eyes gleaming. 'You don't think Gray's involved somehow?'

Julianne raised her eyebrows, weighing her words. 'Stranger things have happened. The police are considering all possibilities.'

Corinne's top was clinging to her stomach and she plucked at the fabric, drawing it away from the soft rolls of flesh. 'I've never liked that man.'

'Between you and me,' said Julianne, moving closer, confiding, 'neither have I.'

The women chatted for a few more minutes. Corinne told Julianne about the wedding bouquets she was designing. 'The bride wants twelve yellow roses. I've told her even numbers of flowers at weddings – especially yellow – are considered bad luck, but she won't listen. It's odd for weddings, even for funerals. Everyone knows that.'

In turn, Julianne told Corinne how beautiful her floral arrangements had looked at Anoushka Thornton's funeral, how everyone had commented on the thoughtful details of the wreaths and family flowers. Corinne beamed, flattered. 'Oh, wait,' she said. 'I've got this for you.' And she opened the till and handed her friend a receipt.

'That reminds me,' said Julianne. 'Do you keep a list of all the flowers you send and the names and addresses of the people who order them?'

The florist looked puzzled. 'Not as a matter of course.' She indicated the hard-backed notebook, open on the counter. 'I do have some paperwork, often just a name and phone number, and the type of arrangement they've asked for, but it depends on whether they've come into the shop or if the flowers have been ordered online. Why do you ask?'

At that moment, the telephone rang. Corinne disappeared into the back to answer it. As soon as she'd gone, Julianne reached for the book, scanning it for personal information on the sender of the teardrop bouquet. By the time Corinne returned, she'd found what she was looking for, heart jumping in her chest.

'Listen, I know it's a bit cheeky but do you have a home address for David Thornton? I need to drop something off to him, but I'm not sure where he lives.'

Corinne's expression clouded. 'I'm not supposed to give out delivery addresses. Client confidentiality, I'm afraid.'

'Of course,' said Julianne. 'I'll email him and ask instead. I was trying to save him from having to deal with unnecessary correspondence, that's all. Especially with those poor boys.'

Corinne bit her lip.

'I'm sorry,' said Julianne, resting her hand on Corinne's. 'I shouldn't have asked, I'd hate you to think I was taking advantage of our friendship. It's just there's so much on my mind with Piper gone.' She lowered her voice. 'I keep thinking of how frightened she sounded in her last message.'

If Corinne had been an animal, her ears would have pricked up. 'Why, what did she say?'

Julianne met her gaze. 'I probably shouldn't talk about it. The police are investigating, as a matter of priority.'

The women stared at each other, an unspoken understanding flowing between them like an electrical current.

Five minutes later, Julianne left Masterson's with David

Thornton's address written on a piece of paper and Corinne knew exactly what Piper had whispered down the telephone to Julianne.

By the end of the day, half of Midtown would know that Piper and her children were missing and Gray Holden, husband and father, was the police's chief suspect.

A closed sign hung on the door at Holden Investments and it gave Julianne an odd jolt as she walked past. She couldn't see inside. It was one of those places that looked like a private members' club. Sleek black front door with a brass handle at its centre, clean brickwork and large windows covered by blinds. She hurried by, unsettled by the sight of it. She'd half expected to see Gray's assistant at work, manning the telephones, but then she remembered Piper telling her how – as a point of principle – Gray insisted on opening up every day. And calls could easily be diverted to his PA's mobile phone.

David Thornton lived a few streets away from Gray's office in what Quiller would describe as the cultural quarter. With a more bohemian feel to it, the coffee shops and boutiques of Midtown's main drag were replaced by artist studios and writing spaces, galleries and community arts hubs.

The houses here were not as grand as Julianne's or Piper's, but they were most typically described as Arts and Crafts, made from natural wood and stone with airy, light-filled rooms and intricate stained-glass designs.

Number fifty-seven was larger than average, and Julianne noted a new Mercedes parked in the driveway and an expensive security system. Before she rang the bell, she smoothed down her dress and ran the tip of her finger around her mouth to make sure her lipstick hadn't smudged.

David Thornton was wearing a blue checked shirt and jeans. Barefoot. His hair was wet and it was clear he'd just got out of the shower. Lack of sleep had hollowed out his eyes.

'I'm so sorry,' said Julianne, 'I should have called first.'

Thorne smiled at her. 'I'm glad of the company, to be honest. The children have gone back to school today and my mother-in-law is threatening to come over.'

Julianne grinned back. 'I promise I won't take up too much of your time. But I wanted to let you know as soon as I could that I've been to see my florist friend today.'

He didn't ask her how she'd found out his home address but she was quietly satisfied her instincts on that front had proved sound. His grief was too big for him to care about unimportant details.

'Already?' He smiled again. 'That's kind of you.' A gust of wind made a grab at her hat. Thorne shivered in the open door. 'Do you want to come in for a minute?'

His house surprised her. For all its stylish exterior, the inside was a hotch-potch of discarded shoes and coats, untidy stacks of mail and unironed washing. But it was warm and homely, lived in.

'Sorry about the mess,' said Thorne, pushing a pile of Lego bricks on the sofa to one side. 'Things have been—' All of a sudden he looked stricken, the words petering into silence.

'Of course they have,' said Julianne. His wife stared down at them from the mantelpiece and she turned away from the photograph. She touched his hand, offering up a chaste physical comfort, but he jerked away and she cursed herself, sensing she'd been intrusive and over-familiar. They hardly knew each other, after all.

Thorne didn't offer her tea or coffee, but she wouldn't have accepted, even if he had. This visit was about something else entirely.

'Did you . . . ?' He hesitated, not quite sure how to go on. His eyes dropped to his lap where he spun his wedding ring in an endless circle. Her own hands were trembling and she sat on them.

'I've made some enquiries for you. Those flowers *were* sent by a man.'

Thorne didn't swear or cry or do any of those things she might have expected him to. Instead his expression sagged, hope escaping from him like air from a pricked balloon. When he spoke, his voice was controlled but quiet. 'Did you happen to get his name?'

Despite the rawness of her own distress, Julianne composed her face into an expression of tenderness. She glanced at her lap, and then back up at Thorne, meeting his eyes with her own, radiating sincerity.

'Actually, I did. It's Gray Holden. Does that ring a bell?' The words sounded wrong to her, freighted with intensity. She couldn't believe she was saying his name.

He frowned, trawling the corridor of his memory. 'Never heard of him.'

Julianne didn't reply. As far as she was concerned, Thorne wasn't emotionally ready to know the truth about her relationship with the Holden family yet. In time, but not now. He frowned. 'I've been thinking about this a lot. I'm almost certain Anoushka wasn't having an affair. It goes against everything she stood for.' She could tell how much he wanted to believe that.

'If you'd like' – *careful now, Julianne, don't blow it* – 'I could do a bit of digging for you. Find out what I can about him.' She smiled. 'I'll be very discreet.'

He flashed a grateful smile in return.

As Thorne was processing the enormity of her revelation, Julianne reached for the widower's hand again and gently squeezed his fingers. This time, he squeezed them back.

18

Wednesday morning

The day after the Holdens disappeared

Dr Clover March tipped the tiny blue pill that matched the colour of her hair into her palm and observed it.

Although she'd gone to bed early the night before – or early for her, at least – she'd slept poorly. Now her eyelids were closing with a heavy familiarity and she rubbed at them before taking a single step backwards and folding herself into her desk chair.

Her flat was silent apart from the drone of traffic from the street below and the shallow push of her breath. Fifteen minutes later, her pupils began to move beneath her eyelids, rapid flicks from side to side. A string of saliva escaped from the corner of her slightly open mouth.

During yet another argument about her lack of focus, her ex-boyfriend James had described these episodes as a light going out, but she preferred her mother's take on it: a dimming of energy, like a bulb on the wane.

When she woke up, the shadows in the room had

lengthened and her palm had uncurled, the tiny blue pill rolled under her chair.

Fully alert – it didn't take long, three or four seconds – she ran through her regular checks. Was she hurt? Exactly *where* was she? Was she in any kind of compromising or dangerous position? And lastly, what time was it?

'Crap.'

Clover grabbed at the paperwork strewn across her desk, stuffing it into her satchel. She closed the files she'd been reading and threw them into her bag. Purse. Water bottle. Medication.

She groped on the floor for the fallen pill – she didn't want Miss Meow swallowing it; another vet's bill would topple her precarious finances and she still had to buy a new toaster after the cat had pissed in it – and dropped it in the bin. With a lurch of trepidation, she braced herself and glanced at her phone. Two missed calls. Not bad, considering. Her all-time record was fifteen.

Hopping about on her left foot, she pulled on one leather boot, then swapped over, repeating the motion. Her keys – a symbol of her doctor-mandated freedom – were on the hall table where she'd discarded them earlier. She was allowed to drive because she'd convinced her neurologist her symptoms were well controlled. But that was when she was taking her tablets. Now she was sick of them. And their side effects. She considered the tiny pill in the bin, a flash of colour amongst the rubbish. Although the keys felt light in her hand, the decision weighed on her. A throw of the dice. She'd be all right, she decided. The drugs stayed in her system for thirty hours. It had only been a couple of days. And it was a short journey.

Her Honda Shadow motorbike was parked outside her flat, which was ten minutes' drive from Midtown police station. Her street was on the outskirts of the affluent seaside town, the ragged hem of it. Kebab shops and launderettes and display windows with metal shutters instead of artisan bakeries and the candy-striped awning of the ice-cream parlour. She revved the engine and next door's curtain twitched into life. She raised a hand to Mrs Nolan and, through grimy glass, the pensioner waved back. With a final rev of her bike, Clover was gone.

The briefing was already underway when she slipped in behind a constable carrying a stack of pages still warm from the photocopier. Unfortunately for Clover, DI Angus O'Neill's observational skills were as sharp as his tongue. 'Thanks for joining us, Dr March. Punctual as ever.'

'I got caught on a call.' The lie came to her with practised ease. 'I thought it was better to hear what they had to say in case it was pertinent to the investigation – but if punctuality's more important to you, I'll cut it short next time.' She smiled, a counterweight to her impudence.

O'Neill narrowed his eyes, picking his way through the pleasant valley of her tone for the slight he was certain she'd dealt him. She braced herself for the comeback, limbering up for a verbal confrontation. A small part of her – scratch that, a *large* part of her – knew it was foolish to goad him, especially given her circumstances, but she couldn't abide his officiousness or that of the other detectives, drawing authority from their maleness like blood from a vein. It was such a cliché. Except the blond boy. He was smiling in that vague way of his, but his eyes, when they met hers, were amused and watchful.

O'Neill clapped his hands to disrupt the buzz of conversation and the room snapped into a silence so absolute it was like a wire had been cut. Clover hadn't worked with this detective inspector before but it was clear to her that even if he'd earned the respect of his colleagues, their fear of him was greater.

She'd been in the briefing room for less than two minutes when she realized O'Neill was in a foul mood. He stank of it. The senior officer stood in front of the gathered team with his arms folded, the air stretched and uncomfortable.

He waved a piece of paper at the room. 'Do you know what this is?'

One or two of the officers shifted in their seats. Another cleared his throat. Clover watched a female constable lower her eyes to her lap and guessed, correctly as it turned out, that she knew exactly what it was.

'It's a log sent to us by UK Power Networks,' said DI O'Neill. 'As I'm sure most of you know, they supply electricity to this part of the country.'

Nobody spoke. A gust of rain-filled wind threw itself again the window. It made the same sound as the confetti of uncooked rice that had hit the dusty pavement at Clover's brother's wedding.

'At 3.49 a.m. on the night the Holden family disappeared there was a power outage affecting the south-eastern edge of Midtown.' O'Neill didn't need to look at his notes, the timings burned into his memory. 'It was a busy night. As some of you may remember, there were strong winds affecting power lines all over the bay. Power was restored at 4.43 a.m.'

The briefing room was still.

O'Neill's voice was cool and measured. 'Anita, would you care to elaborate to everyone exactly why this is such a fucking disaster?'

DC Anita Laghari, the officer Clover had noticed earlier, unfolded herself from her chair. Shoulders down, she faced the room. 'We were confident the CCTV cameras at the front and back of Seawings would offer us a clearer picture of what happened to the Holdens. But the power cut means we have no footage of their disappearance. We have a recording of Gray Holden arriving home after midnight but it cuts out, as the boss explained.'

'That's right,' said O'Neill, 'and the wind and rain means we'll have to work much harder to find any forensic traces.' His grimace spoke more eloquently than he did.

The detective she'd met in Riva Holden's bedroom – DC Williams – leaned back and steepled his fingers. 'What about the problems in the Holden marriage? Shouldn't we be focusing on those?'

O'Neill gestured to the blond boy who'd found her asleep behind Riva's bed. 'Saul, care to fill in the rest of the team?'

He blushed, roses at his cheeks. Clover willed him to get himself together, a pang of solidarity surprising her. She recognized the awkward tilt of his head, the discomfort of being new and the focus of scrutiny.

DC Anguish clasped his hands. He didn't look at the officers in front of him but at a spot in the corner of the far wall. 'We interviewed Julianne Hillier – Piper Holden's best friend – last night. She indicated Gray Holden was violent towards his wife on more than one occasion.' He glanced at DC Williams, who nodded. 'Piper called her in the early hours of Tuesday morning. She later left this message on Julianne's voicemail using the landline at Seawings at' – he checked his notes – '3.37 a.m.'

He withdrew his police-issue mobile. The briefing room slumped into a silence thickened by expectation. As he played the recording he'd made the evening before, in the Hilliers' kitchen, one of the female officers exhaled a surprised pocket of air. The sound seemed to speak for them all.

'So this has just become our most pressing line of inquiry,' said O'Neill. 'Find out everything you can about Gray Holden. Turn him inside out. His workplace, his friends, his movements. Was he involved with another woman? What's the state of his finances? Any enemies? I want to know what he had for breakfast, lunch and dinner, and when he last took a shit.'

Clover was not a prude but she winced at his coarseness. O'Neill stopped his monologue for long enough to take a breath and she raised a hand. The blond boy raised his too. The detective inspector ignored them both and resumed talking.

'Find out what you can about Piper Holden. Talk to her friends and family. Let's see what else we can tease from Julianne Hillier. But tread lightly. I don't want her spooked. And I want to know what the children's friends and teachers have to say. Did Riva or Artie mention difficulties in their parents' marriage?'

He threw a look at the young recruit, the jerk of his head betraying his impatience. 'What is it, Saul?' His tone was short, as if he didn't have time for pointless interruptions.

Saul's gaze flicked to DC Williams, who was staring at

him with a fixed expression. Clover tried to interpret what it meant – there was something written in his face – but she couldn't decipher the undercurrent between them.

'Julianne Hillier's husband says Gray Holden isn't the type of man to hurt his wife.'

'Wake the fuck up, kiddo.' Williams couldn't contain himself. 'Of course he's going to say that. He's a mate. He probably doesn't have a bloody clue. Women talk to each other, don't they? Most men can't be arsed.'

Clover wanted to say he was wrong about that – that some men talked to their friends more candidly than their wives – but that didn't fall 'under her remit', according to O'Neill, who'd reminded her more than once that she was only here in her capacity as the most gifted forensic linguist the Chief Constable had seen in several years. She waited for O'Neill to acknowledge that all statements from potential witnesses should be treated with caution – that these statements, however well meaning, were coloured by a million tiny prejudices – but he said nothing except a brusque, 'This is the best lead we have so don't waste it.' He clapped his hands. 'Let's get to work, people.'

All around her officers were standing up and talking in low voices, waiting for more specific orders. Clover cleared her throat.

'Is there something I can help you with, Dr March?'

She couldn't decide if O'Neill's hostility was because she was young and outspoken or because her blue hair did not conform to his traditional view of how a woman should look. Both, probably.

She smiled, arms folded across her chest. From the corner of her eye, she could see the blond boy watching her.

She took a deep breath and stuck out her chin. 'You invited me to this briefing but you haven't asked for my update yet.'

O'Neill had the audacity to look at his watch. 'How important is it? We need to get back to work.'

Although it would have given her considerable pleasure to tell him exactly where to stick his investigation, she resisted the temptation. Even she was aware of the need to maintain a professional relationship, however reluctant she might be. She bit down her natural urge for sarcasm.

'I think it's pretty important, actually.'

An expression rolled across O'Neill's face, the kind that suggested he didn't approve of the new brand of investigator the young woman standing in front of him represented. He was a believer in the old ways, the more traditional methods, but he was ruthless enough to listen. Just in case.

'So, we've been examining the handwriting on the mirror,' said Clover.

O'Neill looked up sharply. 'In Riva's bedroom?'

A brisk nod of assent instead of vocalizing her first reaction, *Where the hell else?* 'That's right.' She paused to see if he had anything to add, but he was watching her, just like the blond boy. A desire for him to think well of her surprised her and sharpened her delivery. 'The sample of text on the mirror is quite small. Three words. But enough to tell us something.'

O'Neill watched her carefully while she spoke. 'This is more graphology than linguistics, but we'll get to that later,' she said. She showed him a photograph of the bloodied writing. 'See the bar across the letter T – the way there's a tiny flick on the left, where it ends. Hardly noticeable, really.' O'Neill was blank-faced but she pressed on. 'This indicates it was written by someone whose instinctive hand is their left.'

DI O'Neill shrugged. 'O-kay, and that means exactly what?'

She chose her next words with precision, weighing them out and offering them up like plump fruits. 'That it was almost certainly written by someone who's left-handed.'

She waited for him to catch up but the silence became awkward, loaded with her expert knowledge and his lack of understanding.

'We've managed to examine samples of each member of the Holden family's handwriting since their disappearance,' said Clover. 'A shopping list, a couple of birthday cards, school books, that sort of thing.' O'Neill was nodding impatiently now and she sensed he didn't share her enthusiasm for detail, that she was losing his attention. She cursed her self-indulgence and finally said what she ought to have done at the beginning.

'Piper, Gray, Riva and Artie – they're all right-handed. Which means whoever wrote that message on the mirror, it definitely *wasn't* one of the Holdens.'

19

Two months before the Holdens disappeared

Emelie sat in one of the seats in the school's purpose-built theatre, the churn of nerves in her stomach. Several girls had auditioned for the part of Sally Bowles but no one stood out. A crowd of students had gathered to watch the try-outs but Emelie's singing teacher had taught her to drown out the noise and focus on the performance. Mr Moran had a list of auditionees in front of him and when she saw him glance at it, her stomach flipped over.

'Riva Holden. Please take your place on the stage.'

Not her turn yet. But she would be next. As far as she could tell, everyone else had been given their chance.

Riva stood in the centre of the stage. Mr Moran had arranged for a spotlight for each of them and it highlighted her cheekbones, those sharp edges that could cut like her tongue. A few whispered conversations between friends continued but when she started to sing, the auditorium fell silent. Riva leaked charisma from every pore. She was mesmerizing. Even Emelie couldn't deny it. But she could do better. She knew it even if no one else did.

When Riva had finished her audition, the students clapped wildly and, with a grin, she performed a mock bow.

Emelie's palms were sticky and she wiped them on her thighs. She would have to hit it out of the park to follow that but she'd been practising for weeks, and she was confident she could impress.

She was half out of her seat when Mr Moran put down his list and stood up, a broad smile on his face.

'Wow, what a way to finish. Thank you to everyone for attending this afternoon. The list of names will go up tomorrow. Remember, it doesn't matter if you don't get one of the main parts – it's a team effort. And the stage crew is just as important as the principals.' He glanced at Emelie when he said that.

Emelie felt like she'd been struck across the face. She wanted to shout at Mr Moran – to remind him that he'd forgotten about her – but the theatre was filled with chatter, the lights had come up and she couldn't find it within herself to challenge him. Her mouth dried and she wanted to cry.

She looked for Riva – her loud, confident friend who would think nothing of speaking up – but she was surrounded by a knot of students, congratulating her. She caught snatches of their conversation. *Mad not to cast you. In the bag. Brilliant.* And something inside her died.

She waited for everyone to leave. Even Riva didn't hang around, swept away by other friends on the tidal wave of her success.

There was an air of wistfulness about a deserted theatre. The abandoned stage and empty seats. It was the kind of place that needed to be filled. She sat in the front row for a while, wondering why she was always overlooked.

'Still here, Emelie?'

It was Mr Moran, making sure all the students had left the building. She rose quickly, wiping the tears that had spilled out, and hurried up the centre aisle. 'Just leaving.'

He held the door open for her, chatty now his working day was almost finished. 'It's a shame you didn't want to audition today. But I understand. Perhaps you'll be ready next time we put on a production. I'm thinking of *Fame: The Musical*.'

She stilled, doubting whether she'd heard him correctly. He carried on, oblivious to her turmoil. 'I'll make you head of the set design team, OK? But next time come and talk to me yourself. Don't send Riva.' He smiled at her. 'Have a good evening. We've got a lot of hard work ahead.'

She watched him walk down the corridor, his shoes squeaking against the polished floor. Everything fell into place. She had always suspected Riva capable of treachery but this was the first occasion she'd been on the receiving end of it. And this time, Emelie Hillier wasn't going to roll over like a good girl.

20

Wednesday lunchtime

The day after the Holdens disappeared

Blue was in a side room, making some notes, when she heard the door close. She looked up, surprised, not expecting to see anybody because she'd deliberately sought out a quiet place to collect her thoughts. She preferred to work alone, so that if she fell asleep, as she often did, it would be on her terms.

It was an officer she didn't know but recognized from yesterday. He was attached to a neighbouring force – Kent Police, she recalled – and had been drafted in to help with an ongoing murder investigation that neither Blue nor the blond boy had been allocated.

He grinned at her. 'How are you getting on?'

She took a sip from her Styrofoam cup. The tea was hot and tasted faintly of chemicals. She eyed him warily, wondering what he wanted. 'Not too bad.'

'I saw you staring at me in the canteen.'

The implication was so wide of the mark that she was shocked into silence. But that meant he must have followed her. No, of course he hadn't. She berated herself for being too sensitive. She'd only been here a few times before. Not new like the blondie. But *newish*. Still finding her feet. He was being polite, that was all. Making conversation.

She put down the file she was preparing. 'How can I help you?'

He raised his eyebrows. Flicked a glance to the closed door and back again, and then straight at her in a way that made her feel uncomfortable. 'I don't know.' He was flirty. 'What did you have in mind?'

He bristled with an arrogance she found repellent.

She frowned, confusion laced with sarcasm. 'Um – nothing.' Her cheeks grew hot. She didn't want to be here with this stranger whose behaviour was beginning to disturb her. But why should she have to move? She was here first.

He took a step towards her. She tried to remember his name, reached into the recesses of her memory, but it eluded her. Her body's stress response kicked in. Heart rate elevated. Dry mouth. Hormones flooding her system. She tried to avoid situations such as these because there was an inevitability to her response that was beyond her control. She hadn't checked the floor for obstacles yet and she wasn't convinced she was in a safe place and— Her head lolled forward.

When she woke up, she was lying on the floor, a pain in her hip. She assessed her surroundings. The room was empty. She could tell by the way the air was still. But her stomach felt cold and she wasn't sure why. Blue glanced down at herself.

Her shirt was untucked and its buttons had been undone, revealing her bra. One of her breasts was partially out of its cup, the nipple exposed. There was a tenderness to it, like the budding of a new bruise. She closed her eyes. Breathed. Processed the feelings that were swarming around her brain like angry bees.

Humiliation. Embarrassment. Shame.

And most potent of all, fury.

Blue adjusted her bra and did up her shirt. Three of the buttons were missing. She found one of them on the floor but no sign of the others. It was clear it had been ripped open in a hurry. Her stomach and the band of her bra were visible through a gape in the fabric. She would have to go home and change.

A tear welled in the corner of her right eye. She swiped at it, annoyed with herself, and it was gone. She would not buckle under the weight of what had just happened. She refused to give him that satisfaction. Her body was her own. He had no right to touch it without her permission. But he hadn't *claimed* it. She wouldn't allow that, whatever he'd done. It was hers. *It was still hers.*

Caressing her in intimate places while she was vulnerable and asleep, lost in a narcoleptic episode, was the lowest of the low. It breached every faith she had in humankind. But if she reported him, she would have to tell them about her condition and she had no intention of doing that. Still, there were other ways of making someone pay.

She stumbled into the corridor, holding her shirt together with one hand, a fire raging inside her. Every instinct in her burned to march into the Major Crime Unit and confront the officer in question. But she fought against it. The idea of such a performative action in front of her male colleagues, leaving some – not all, but some of them – to sneer and laugh at her expense, left her cold. No, she would have to be clever about it. Find out who he was and plan her revenge.

Her head was bent, lost in thought, and so she almost bumped into the blond boy – his name was Saul, she remembered – who was walking along the corridor in the opposite direction. He put out his hands to stop her – the lightest of touches – and she flinched, then relaxed when she saw who it was. 'Are you OK? You're as white as a sheet.'

She almost broke at the kindness in his voice. 'I'm fine.'

He took in the way she was holding her shirt, the guarded expression on her face. Her hands were trembling and she tried to steady them, but couldn't manage it. She watched him do the calculation but he didn't press her. 'Do you want to get some fresh air?'

She did. That's exactly what she wanted. She was usually so independent but she let him lead her out of the building and onto the street. There was a small park close to the station that overlooked the bay and they sat side by side on a bench. The grey water calmed her.

Saul had stopped to buy two cans of Coke. Her hands were still shaking and so he opened the tab before passing one to her. When she had taken a drink and the colour had returned her to face, he said, 'If you want to tell me what happened, I want to listen.'

In the past, she had struggled to share the hurts of her life with others, afraid of ridicule or gossip, determined to cope on her own, but there was something about him that compelled her to trust him, and so, with faltering words, she explained the events of the last half-hour, telling him she had been asleep but without mentioning her condition.

His face hardened but he did not speak. At least not for a bit. And when he had checked for a second time how she was feeling, he said, 'So you don't know who he is?'

'Only what he looks like.'

He gazed at her, an unreadable expression on his face. But she saw something in him she recognized in herself. A desire for vengeance. To balance the scales. 'We better do something about that then.'

Without needing to say anything further, they both knew exactly what that meant.

21

Monday afternoon

The day before the Holdens disappeared

Gray's hand was hurting but he ignored it in the same way he ignored many important things in his life. Piper had rung him at lunchtime and he'd ignored her too, leaving his phone in the office, preferring to eat his sandwich on a bench in the park and mull over the columns of figures in the ledger he carried about him at all times.

No evidence on the computer. That was their agreement, although he knew it was impossible to erase a paper trail altogether. But he'd done his best. He couldn't have done any more. And despite everything, the shit was already beginning to hit the fan.

Gray checked the time. If Mr Moore was on to him, there wasn't much of it left. He'd been so careful. At least, he thought he had. But the events of Saturday – and the pain in his hand – were evidence he hadn't been careful enough. When the man came back – and Gray knew he would – he wouldn't be so generous.

The afternoon sun was flooding the office, touching the

photograph of his family on the desk. Piper was still a beautiful woman, even after all these years together. He remembered the smile on his face when he'd come back after lunch to find her twirling in his chair. She dazzled him. But in the dark hours of the night – those moments of clarity when everything was pin-sharp and the taste of the future flooded his mouth – there was so much about his wife he didn't understand.

And she drove him fucking nuts, always asking him about the business, wanting to know the ins and outs of the way it worked. 'I make the money, sweetheart,' he wanted to say, 'and you spend it.' But Piper wanted to know about his clients and his deals. She was sharper than he was, often spotting a way to exploit a client or the careful wording of a legal contract that he hadn't considered. But the business was *his*. He didn't know how to explain that he wanted her sticky fingers out. Sometimes, he forced them out and she didn't like that one bit.

He withdrew his notebook and laid it on the desk in front of him. Underneath *Mr Moore* was a list of figures. Gray tapped them with the lid end of his pen. He did a quick mental calculation. Six million, give or take. It was a decent enough amount but he'd hoped for more. Still, there wasn't time to worry about that now. The money had been moved to a safe place. As long as Mr Moore's men didn't kill him for it first.

That grim thought forced a bark of laughter from him. Gray had always known his method of conducting business was a risk, but it had been a calculated one. His model was predicated on the idea of not getting caught. This was much closer to home than he would have preferred.

Gray could pinpoint the exact moment he realized that

stealing money from a wealthy clientele was much easier than working hard for a living. When he was the Chief Financial Officer – full of corporate group-think and over-blown bullshit – of a juggernaut of a company specializing in Investor Relations, he'd toed the line for a good many years. But an unexpected opportunity had come his way and Gray had seized it with both hands. Systematically, he'd stolen hundreds of thousands of pounds of company wages, diverting – and re-diverting – them into several different bank accounts, painstakingly creaming off amounts here and there. The blame – because Gray had left a breadcrumb trail of clues leading in that direction – had fallen squarely on the shoulders of his number two, Alan Myles. As far as Gray was aware, Myles, who had served three years in prison for fraud and lost his house under the Proceeds of Crime Act – and then his wife – had been released a few years ago.

A handful of old work contacts kept him informed, although they had no idea that was the reason Gray carefully bought them a beer and dinner every financial quarter.

A few months later, Gray had left the company and set up his own business. He'd cherry-picked stupidly wealthy clients – or their friends and families – from the address book of contacts he'd helped himself to, scoping them out for potential opportunities, biding his time.

The first one had been easy. Too easy, almost. Dorothy Randall. In her eighties. Widowed. Malleable. Filthy stinking rich.

She'd liked him. He'd sensed that almost as soon as he'd met her. He took her to lunch at Truly Scrumptious. She appreciated his almost courtly behaviour, the politely extended elbow, his tailored suit and the endless supply of tea and cream cakes. By the end of their afternoon together, he'd convinced her to let him invest several hundred thousand pounds of her considerable fortune with a promise of more to come. She was too trusting to query the disappearing money, her 'under-performing' investment portfolio, and he was just the right side of charming to avoid suspicion.

He'd repeated this trick several times – and with such significant success it had surprised him. His fortune grew and his business assumed a veneer of respectability that almost persuaded him he was above both law and retribution. Until Mr Moore and his muscular emissary.

Gray cast a critical eye around his office. He'd spent a fortune doing it up: expensive furnishings, top-of-the-range speakers and a cherrywood desk that cost more than his PA's car. He would do everything within his power to cling to all that he'd worked for, even if it meant skewing his moral compass still further.

Gray rose from his chair, a twinge of pain in his injured hand. The late afternoon shadows were licking the walls with their dark tongues and the street outside was quiet.

He would have to go home and face Piper. Not that he felt much like doing that. She would want to talk about the attack and Mr Moore's visitor, and ask endless questions about the six million pounds. All he wanted was a short glass and a long drink to help him punch his way through the pain of the night and straight on until morning.

A sigh, as leaden as the skies, slid from him. Charlotte had gone to the doctor's – Piper said she'd got some 'women's problems' and needed the afternoon off – and it was his turn to lock up. He picked up his ledger and slipped it into his jacket. Pocketed his keys. Turned to switch off the lights.

A noise – intrusive in the quiet of the closing minutes of the day – stilled him. His palm rested on the handle of the door. Fear closed its fingers around his throat.

He looked around for a weapon – anything – to defend himself and crossed the office to pick up the millefiori paperweight Piper had bought him to celebrate winning his first client. The glass was cool and satisfyingly heavy in his hand. Raising it above his head, Gray turned in the direction of the hallway, straining for the sound of movement, waiting for Mr Moore's messenger.

His left palm had just made contact with the door handle again when he felt it shift beneath him, dragging his hand down with it. He jerked away, as if the metal was live, electrified. His mouth dried and he tasted dust and fear. The band of muscles that ran between his shoulders tensed as he prepared himself to fight off a brutal beating, wondering if, when the moment came, he would have what it took to drive the paperweight into the flesh of a stranger's face in order to save his own life.

Time slowed to the beats of his heart and the thunder of blood in his ears. He heard the thrum of rush-hour traffic and the clunk of the central heating turning itself off. The hitch of his own breathing.

Gray Holden tightened his fingers around the orb of glass in his hand.

The door opened and two things happened: the first, a woman who was standing in the shadowed light of the late afternoon, a hand tucked behind her back, called out to him, her voice melodic and familiar.

He blanched, convinced he was seeing things. That the woman standing in front of him was the product of his tired but overactive imagination, or that he had somehow dozed off at his desk without realizing it and was trapped in a nightmare he'd left in his past. She walked towards him, a smile playing about her lips, the buttons on her shirt undone, a glimpse of skin visible beneath her coat.

'I came,' she said. 'I always promised I would. Remember, Gray?'

The second, over before she'd even finished speaking aloud that last blunt *ay*, stunned him. With a fury that possessed every blood vessel, every thump and beat of his heart, he imagined himself bringing the paperweight down, transforming her mouth, her tongue, into a running red river, fragments of teeth scattered like shingle.

In the beginning, she would fight back, nails clawing at his face, an elegant hand clutching the cuff of his suit jacket, the front of his shirt, the expensive silk tie. But it would be a fruitless exercise, her efforts no match for the compulsion that drove him to repeat that single violent movement again and again.

Gray wouldn't stop until the woman had collapsed beneath him, her legs splayed across the floor, a glimpse of bone visible beneath her ruined face and the matted strands of hair that stuck to her temple. Only when her body was as still as death would he lift the paperweight, stippled with blood, to stare at it in a kind of dazed shock, as if he couldn't quite believe what he'd done.

Instead he said, 'What are you doing here?'

She reached for him, her slim fingers trailing down his

arm, an amused light in her eyes. 'Don't be silly. You know exactly why I'm here.'

One hand tightened around the paperweight. With the other, he shoved her away. 'Get off.'

He was rougher than he'd intended and she stumbled backwards, knocked off balance. Under different circumstances she would have righted herself, but he'd left a pile of files on the floor and she tripped over them, falling backwards, arms flailing, mouth open in an expression of surprise.

Even then, it might have been all right. But she caught her shoulder on the corner of the filing cabinet and a plant pot, made of stone and too close to the edge, toppled and fell off, striking the side of her head with blunt force.

She crumpled to the floor without making a sound, eyes closed, a trickle of blood streaking her hair, dark and sticky.

Gray recoiled, horrified at the sight of the woman lying unconscious in his office. He willed her to open those eyes, to move, to talk – *shout* – at him. But she did not.

He crouched down, not quite able to bring himself to touch her. A pulse fluttered in her throat. He watched its erratic rise and fall. Should he call for an ambulance? That would be disastrous, the questions from paramedics – and then police – destabilizing everything he'd worked for. But he was compelled to do something.

'Ice.' He said the word out loud. Wasn't that the treatment for a head injury?

In the deepening shadows of the afternoon, she moaned, making him jump. Gray made a split-second decision.

He would run to the convenience store down the street

for a bag of ice, and if she was still in such a bad way when he returned, he would call an ambulance and deal with the consequences.

The queue was longer than he'd expected, and on the way back he bumped into a client who wanted to chat. By the time Gray returned to his office, almost half an hour had elapsed.

Afternoon had tipped into evening and the air had bite. He let himself in, almost expecting her to have upped and gone. But she was lying in the same position he'd left her, a halo of blood around her head.

He dropped the carrier bag and kneeled by her side, steeling himself to touch. Her amber eyes looked into his and her skin was warm. But he knew, even before he pressed his fingers into the pulse point of her neck, that she was dead.

22

Wednesday afternoon

The day after the Holdens disappeared

The day had left a sour aftertaste. Julianne contemplated pouring herself a gin, to coat her tongue in a fresh kind of bitterness, but she resisted, knowing her children would be home from their clubs before long. Reeking of alcohol was never a good look and, besides, it had a habit of loosening her lips, which would be a Very Bad Thing under the current circumstances.

To distract herself, she ran upstairs, intending to change out of the clingy dress she'd worn to David Thornton's house. Seated at her dressing table, she stared at herself in the oval mirror, scrubbing the red lipstick from her mouth until every trace was gone from the pale shadow of her mouth. The stained tissue made her think of the blood on the chandelier and the echoing rooms of the Holden house. Worry, a thin, crawling thing that began in her stomach, inched its way through the rest of her body. They'd been gone for almost two days now. *Ring me, Piper.*

She wondered how her children were coping with the

news about Artie and Riva. The families had been friends for years, sharing holidays and New Year's Eves, but the four teenagers had become more distant lately, their paths forking in opposite directions. The boys had always rubbed along well, despite being very different creatures. Henry, a couple of years older, was a quiet, studious boy who preferred his own company and despised team sports while Artie, taller and broader than most of his classmates, was the star of both the rugby field and many fevered conversations in the girls' changing room.

Emelie and Riva had been close since they were little – a passionate, loyal friendship – but something had changed in the last couple of months and the girls were now vicious rivals, a fact Julianne had discovered by accident when she'd suggested Riva stay the night at the Hilliers'. Her daughter had rolled her eyes, drawing her top lip into a Pink Candy-painted pout. 'I don't want that infection in my bedroom.'

Julianne, shocked by this brutal dismissal of a childhood friend, had remonstrated with Emelie. 'That's an awful thing to say. Don't speak about her like that.' But her sharpness failed to penetrate the hide of her daughter's self-righteous anger.

'She deserves it, Mum.'

When Julianne had attempted to probe the reasons for their falling-out, Emelie had clammed up and refused to say anything else. She'd considered asking Piper but the women had always vowed to remain friends in spite of their children, not because of them. And so she had left it alone, a decision she now regretted.

The front doorbell rang. It would be Emelie. She was

first home on Wednesdays and almost always forgot her key, a continuing source of irritation for her mother. Julianne ran back down the stairs she'd climbed a few seconds ago.

'Jeez, Mother, what are you wearing?' Emelie dumped her bag in the hallway. *As charming as ever.* Julianne squashed down that uncharitable thought and bit back her instinct to reply with the same question. Her daughter was dressed in her PE kit but had customized it by tying her T-shirt into a knot at her midriff and rolling over the waistband of her already too-short skirt. Julianne smoothed her hands over the fabric of her dress, the swell of her hips.

'I had a coffee with a friend. I was just getting changed, actually, before I was so rudely interrupted.' Her tone was even but pointed.

Emelie raised her eyebrows. 'Bit full-on *sexy times* for coffee.'

Julianne reddened. 'That's enough, Em. It's perfectly acceptable.'

'Uh-uh. Of course it is. Better not let Dad see you in that. He'll think you're having an affair or something.' Emelie laughed, as if that was a ridiculous notion. 'I'm starving. Can I make a sandwich?' She didn't bother to wait for her mother's reply.

Julianne trailed her daughter to the kitchen and winced as she carved rough slices from the loaf. 'Riva wasn't at school again today, was she?'

Emelie's hand stilled on the knife but the hesitation was short-lived. 'I didn't see her, no. But she's not in many of my classes so it's hardly a surprise.' She heaped pickle onto a slice of cheese, pressed down on the top layer of bread with the heel of her hand.

Julianne saw no point in beating about the bush. 'She's still missing, sweetheart. All of the Holdens are. The police have launched a murder investigation.'

The girl swung around to face her mother, her mouth widening into an oval of shock. 'Seriously? That is so messed up.'

She threw out questions, not quite able to disguise the undercurrent of excitement and relish that ran through her. Julianne answered them as best she could. 'The police will want to speak to you, I expect,' she said when Emelie had run out of steam.

The change in her daughter was instantaneous. She turned away from her mother, her long hair hiding her face. 'But I don't know anything.' She lifted her sandwich and took a half-hearted bite, but Julianne could see she'd lost her appetite.

She laid a hand across the girl's wrist. Beneath warm skin, she could feel the frantic pulse of Emelie's radial artery. 'If there's anything you think I should know, now's the time to tell me.'

For a moment, the space between them thickened with possibility, that knowing charge between mother and daughter. Julianne braced herself for a revelation and counselled herself to remain calm, whatever Emelie told her, but when the girl spoke it was not what she'd expected at all. Her daughter's eyes, blue and steady, caught her mother's and pinned her in place. A smile, thin and sly, carved her face into something ugly.

'Why don't you tell me, Mum? I mean, aren't you the one with all the secrets?'

* * *

Three miles away from the scene unfolding in the Hillier household, Saul Anguish found himself an unlikely ally to Blue.

O'Neill was still chewing over the forensic linguist's latest revelation. 'Why didn't you tell us at the start of the briefing this morning? This is significant information. It would have been useful to discuss it with the rest of the team.'

Blue rolled her eyes at Saul, but he shook his head, trying to warn her off. She ignored him. 'Well, I tried to, but—'

O'Neill raised his hand to silence her. He might as well have put a gag across her mouth. She started to say something else and then bit her lip. Saul was discomforted by their exchange, particularly as O'Neill was much older than Blue, and seemed well practised in using his seniority to bully younger colleagues into submission. But then Blue laughed – a low, bright sound that punctured the detective's pomposity – and Saul realized, not for the first time, that this woman could look after herself, especially after the traumatic events of that lunchtime. He stared at the faces of his fellow officers milling around, wondering which of them had been responsible.

Blue's low-key amusement flustered O'Neill. He removed his glasses and polished them in slow circles. An awkward quiet descended while they waited for him to clean each lens before folding the cloth into a square and putting it away, patting his pocket twice.

Saul risked another look at Blue. She tapped her forefinger lightly against the watch on her wrist, a comical expression on her face, the message unmistakeable. *Hurry up, DI O'Neill. Don't keep us waiting.* He stifled his own laugh.

'Right,' said O'Neill, sliding his glasses back on and regaining his composure. 'Here's what I want you to do now. Anguish, go back to the scene. See who turns up at Sea-wings. Chat to neighbours, friends or any Tom, Dick or Harriet who shows their face, you know the drill.'

'What about Williams?' Saul liked the idea of striking out on his own but thought he'd better feign at least some interest in his mentor.

'Williams is staying here, for the time being. I need him to follow something up.'

'I'll give you a lift if you like,' said Blue unexpectedly. 'I want to head back there myself and take some more photographs before I finish my report.'

O'Neill didn't bother with niceties like goodbyes and was already striding across the briefing room with Williams, their heads bent together, by the time Saul had accepted Blue's offer. Not for the first time, Saul was on his own.

When they stepped outside, the sea had salted the air. Above the bay, the clouds were streaked with golden threads of late afternoon sunlight. Saul could taste the incoming tide in the creeping dusk and he drew in several lungfuls, enjoying the respite from the stale atmosphere of the police headquarters.

Blue was already walking down the street at pace and he lengthened his stride to catch her up. He followed her until she stopped by a motorbike. When she unhooked a helmet from the sissy bar and handed it to him, his stomach lurched, an uncomfortable memory rearing its head. 'I thought we were going by car.'

She unzipped her rucksack and pulled out her own

helmet. 'Bike,' she said. 'But feel free to walk if that doesn't suit you.'

Saul couldn't bring himself to tell her the last time he'd ridden a bike was as an underage boy with a death wish, but she must have sensed his unease. 'Look, riding pillion is easy. Put your hands around my waist and follow the movement of the bike.'

It was a while since Saul had touched a woman in this oddly intimate way. A one-night stand here and there, yes, but mostly he'd forced himself to avoid the opposite sex. He didn't want the complication of falling in love.

His hands spanned her narrow waist. He was tentative at first, holding her gingerly, as if she might break. Her voice echoed through the Bluetooth speaker. 'You need to hold on a bit tighter than that, otherwise we'll both come off.' He closed his eyes, feeling the heat of her, aware of the curve of her hips and the proximity of her body. She revved the engine and then the world began to spin past.

The sensation of speed and movement floored him. Blue was a careful driver, he could tell from the way she handled the bike, but the absence of solid ground beneath his feet was disconcerting. It was years since he'd ridden but, as Blue negotiated the clogged streets of rush-hour Midtown-on-Sea, he remembered the feeling of freedom that came from the swipe of cold air against exposed skin and the way their bodies moved together in a sinuous synchronicity.

He was weighing up whether to ask if she'd like to go for dinner one night after work, keeping a vague eye on the road, when he became aware that the bike had started to drift between lanes.

A wave of adrenalin pushed through him, focusing his

mind with a bright and painful clarity. With a thrum of urgency, he waited for Blue to correct the bike but it slid into the middle lane, narrowly missing a minibus. 'Blue.' He was sharp, insistent, his voice rising in panic, forgetting to use her real name. '*Blue.*'

But this young woman, who had not been afraid to speak up before, did not respond to Saul's entreaties. Instead her body – shockingly, unbearably heavy – tipped to the left and he was forced to pull her upright, his arm snaking around her stomach, holding her dead weight to him. A lone thought flashed through him, a neon flare of panic: if he didn't act quickly, they were going to crash.

His senses sharpened in the luminous afternoon air, the jaw of the bay just visible from the road. The sun – fierce but fading – was burning a hole in the sky. He caught the scent of petrol and the softer rush of Blue's deodorant. Cortisol freewheeled through him now, but it lent a simplicity to his thought process.

First priority was to regain control of the bike. With his free hand, he stretched forward as far as he could and reached for the handlebars, steering them towards the left. But with Blue's body in front of him, he was too unbalanced to drive with any sense of purpose and his hand jerked sideways in an uncontrolled motion. With a sickening lurch of awareness, he tightened his grip on Blue as the powerful machine skewed further off course and slid from between his legs, the narrow way between life and death stretched as thin as ribbon.

When Saul opened his eyes, the world was upside down. His leg hurt but it was a murmur of pain rather than a scream, and he could move it. He sat up. Removed his helmet. Cars were slowing but not stopping, the rubberneckers out in force. A schoolgirl in a scarf was peering at him, her brow furrowed in concern. She waved her mobile phone at him, her other hand propping up her bicycle.

'Shall I call for an ambulance?'

'Wait a minute.' He cast around for Blue. She was lying on her back, a couple of metres away from him. As he watched, her folded-up knees lengthened into a stretch and she pulled herself into a sitting position. That glimpse of cerulean as she removed her helmet. A rush of warmth ambushed him. In a minute, he would go to her. But first, using what little experience he had – those few weeks on Traffic – Saul assessed the situation.

The motorbike had careened through two lanes of traffic, clipped a dustbin on the edge of the grass verge and was on its side, wheels spinning. A couple of passers-by glanced at him but there was disinterest in their expressions. Saul blamed it on lack of blood and serious injury. Vultures were drawn by carrion. But no one had been hurt. He exhaled. Glanced up at the concerned schoolgirl. 'It's OK, I think. But thank you.'

The girl didn't need telling twice. She swung a leg over her saddle, adjusted her rucksack and was cycling into the descending dusk before he'd stood up.

He jogged over to Blue. Her helmet was on the pavement and she was sitting cross-legged, rubbing her eyes with the heel of her palm. 'Hey.' She didn't look up. 'Are you hurt?'

Still, she wouldn't meet his eyes.

He crouched by her, his voice gentle. 'It's not your fault.'

She mumbled something that sounded like, 'Yes, it is.'

Saul sat down on the pavement, ignoring the hardness,

the chill that crept into his thighs. The light was fading rapidly now. One by one, the lamp-posts flickered into life, watchful eyes in the gloaming. Cars droned past. He wanted to probe more deeply but he didn't know how to reach her.

Instead he scrambled back to his feet and retrieved her motorbike. If he couldn't tell her how much he liked her, he could show her.

The bike's tyres had stopped spinning. He noticed a dent in the bodywork and a violent flurry of scratches. He wheeled it over to where she was standing, fighting against a slight list from the handlebars. Blue's helmet was tucked under her arm and there was a rip in her tights, exposing the skin of her thigh. A cartwheeling sensation inside his stomach. He forced his gaze away and removed the key from the ignition, pressed it into her hand. She curled her fist, refusing to accept it.

'No,' she said, still unable to meet his gaze. But then she lifted her chin and stared at him, and he fell into the guilt and sorrow of her.

'What is it?'

She knuckled her eyes again, as if wiping away the last vestiges of sleep. Let loose a breath. Inhaled another, considered and slow, as if she was swallowing down a heavy weight, steeling herself to speak. 'I shouldn't have driven today. It was stupid and risky, and I'm sorry.'

Saul gave a dismissive shrug, his palms upwards and flattened. 'Don't apologize. Accidents happen. We're fine, aren't we?'

But Blue dug the fingers of her left hand into the front of her hair and screwed up her eyes. 'I shouldn't have driven.' He could hear the insistence in her voice.

He laughed, a nervous mistake – but a mistake, nonetheless. 'Why are you saying that?'

She turned on him, the cool fire of anger in her grey eyes turning them violet.

'Because I'm stupid.' The cry of a seagull tore open the silence. 'Because I've stopped taking my medication.'

'Are you ill?' The words were out before he could stop them, a concern that began as a ripple and eddied outwards, spreading through him.

'Define ill,' she said. And yawned.

A simple, everyday kind of gesture and he wasn't sure why it struck him, but he was reminded of finding her on Riva Holden's bedroom floor, and her late arrival at the briefing, cheeks flushed, and the way her body had slumped into him without warning while she was riding her motorbike. She took her hand away from her mouth, a wry expression on her face. He remembered an article he'd read in a weekend supplement a few weeks ago. THE GIRL WHO SLEPT. A preternatural knowledge settled on him.

'How long since you were diagnosed?' Questions ran through him like wind through grass. 'Does O'Neill know?'

Sarcasm edged her laughter. 'No fucking way.' It was the first time he'd heard her use a profanity. 'And there's no way I'm telling him.'

'But they'll understand.'

'Will they?'

'They'll make allowances—'

She exploded. 'I don't want allowances. Do you know how hard it was for me to qualify? I want this job.' She examined the hole in her tights. 'I need it.'

Saul didn't want to lecture her. He wanted to make sure she stayed safe. 'How many times a day?'

A quick rise and fall of her shoulders. 'Too many.' Those violet eyes met his and accepted the compassion in them. 'It's impossible to say. Narcolepsy isn't an exact science. A handful of times, or dozens.'

Saul watched darkness slip its net over the bay. He knew they should get moving to the Holden house, that O'Neill would be expecting to hear from them soon, but he wanted to know more.

'And you've stopped taking your medication? But doesn't that, you know, help control your symptoms?'

She took her crooked bike from him and started to push it up the road, limping slightly. 'We better get going. It'll take us a while to get there.'

They walked in silence for a bit. Through the town and edging into the kind of streets that were lined with money. Saul wanted to wheel Blue's bike for her, but he didn't think she was the type who would appreciate him taking it from her, so instead he said, 'I can do that if you're tired.' But she didn't reply.

He couldn't think what else to say and she was lost in her thoughts, somewhere far away. He wouldn't pry. He hated that himself, and her shuttered expression was one he knew well. On and on they walked. As they turned into the grid of smart streets that overlooked the bay, he said, 'Everyone thinks Gray Holden's killed his family but I'm not so sure.'

Blue shifted the weight of the bike to her other hand. 'He didn't write that message.'

'Who's your money on?'

She turned to him, narrowing her eyes, weighing up, he

suspected, whether she could trust him enough to share her early theories. 'I haven't mentioned this to O'Neill because I need to explore it further.'

He held his breath, not wanting to say something that might shut her down or cause her to run from him, but alight at her confidences, the faith it implied.

'The pressure was light, see, because the blood is thinned above the letter *S* and that tells me something. Grammarians will argue men prefer determinative words and women choose relationship words, and that's true, but sometimes it's more than that. When you study thousands and thousands of samples of handwriting, you develop an instinct, a recognition. My success rate is one hundred per cent.' Those eyes were fluid pools of colour. 'You know what I'm saying, don't you?'

She read the question mark in his expression and tutted, as if he should be as familiar as she was with linguistic nuance.

'It's female,' she said. 'No question about it. The message on Riva's mirror was written by a woman.'

23

A few hours before the Holdens disappeared

Julianne straightened the wedding photograph of her parents that sat on her dressing table. A black-and-white portrait, a perfect snapshot of the 1960s: her mother in a pelmet skirt and half-beehive, block-heeled Mary Janes and a posy of daisies; her father in a narrow black suit and white shirt, his hair curling around his ears. Pulsing and vibrant with their lives ahead of them. She touched the tip of her finger to the glass.

Quiller shouted something up the stairs. She was too far away to hear him. Why couldn't he come and find her instead of bellowing at her as if she was one of his employees? She pretended she hadn't heard him and sat on the edge of their bed, gazing at the picture of her mother and father. The smell of cooking – fried peppers and onions for the quesadillas – drifted upstairs. God, she missed them.

Julianne had been the first one to reach them, before the police and ambulances screamed into their cul-de-sac and a summer day's became a bloodbath.

Quiller shouted again, but his voice was opaque, like the square of obscure glass in her parents' front door. She contemplated getting up to see what he wanted, but found she couldn't be bothered. For once in their marriage, Quiller's needs would have to wait.

Her father had rung her, incoherent and moaning, as she was parking her car near their bungalow. Every now and then, she bought cakes, oozing with fresh cream and fruit, from the patisserie around the corner, and they ate them with gleaming miniature forks in the garden and coffee from the cafetière or a pot of tea.

'Your mother.' Two words. She could still remember the way they emerged from the primal grunt of his pain, twin injections of clarity. He stretched out the letters until they were elongated and cracked. And then his voice cut away, and she heard the thud of a mobile phone hitting the flagged stones that ran prettily up the garden, and the second, louder thud of her father hitting the ground.

The sound of thudding brought her back to the present. Someone was coming up the stairs and walking across the landing.

'There you are, sitting in the dark.' Piper was framed in the doorway of Julianne's bedroom. She switched on the light and thrust a gift-wrapped box at her friend. 'I know today is hard.'

She sat down on the bed. The springs gave way slightly, tipping Julianne towards Piper, who put an arm around her friend's shoulder and hugged her. 'How old would she have been?'

'Seventy-five.'

Julianne undid the box's ribbons. Inside was a silver

elephant figurine. Her mother had been a passionate wild-life advocate and collected them for years. The metalwork was cool to the touch. It was beautiful. She would put it on the shelf with the others. 'Thank you.'

Piper squeezed her hand and Julianne caught a trace of her perfume. She'd worn the same one for years. Sitting in her bedroom, her friend by her side, she was thrown back to the shadowy aftermath of her parents' death when Piper's strength had carried her during a time she'd been unable to carry herself.

Everyone – from the specially trained police officers to an endless parade of grief counsellors – had thought she was haunted by the blood, the stain of it blackening the grass, sticky in the heat, enfolding each blade in its viscous embrace. Even now, the smell of loose change or the butcher's shop in the high street, meat hanging dully from its hooks, dragged her into that moment when she unlocked the side gate and stepped into her parents' garden.

But it was the expression on her dead father's face that tormented her days and transformed her nights into dark valleys of insomnia and despair. A kind of rictus helpless-ness, a knowledge of what he had done stamped into his features like knife-scored wood.

Her father had hit the kill switch, the police later con-cluded. But his actions had come too late. The chainsaw, reeking of petrol fumes, had sliced against her mother's shoulder as it fell, partially severing her left arm, separating tendon and sinew from her body and resulting in major blood loss. But that wasn't the injury that ended her life. As it jack-knifed against her, the teeth of the blade became tan-gled in the lightweight scarf Julianne had bought her for

Mother's Day, pulling it taut. The chainsaw twisted and jerked across the lawn before her father reached it. By the time he had it under control, her mother's neck had snapped.

Her father – distraught, blaming himself for the freak accident – had managed to call both his daughter and the emergency services, but the traumatic events put pressure on his heart, and he suffered a catastrophic cardiac arrest. He, too, was dead by the time Julianne arrived.

When she'd walked into the garden, the family dog was licking her mother's blood and nosing the wound on her arm, his muzzle patchy and dark. She'd screamed at him and dragged him away, the thump of his tail against her bare leg, the rising heat of the afternoon and the earthy smell of death assaulting her senses.

With painstaking care, the specialist police officers involved in the case reconstructed the events of that day. They concluded that while the dog had been chasing his ball, he'd nudged against the stepladder her father was using to trim overhanging branches. That simple action knocked him off balance and he'd dropped the still-running chainsaw onto his wife, who was pruning rose bushes to his right and had no time to react.

The days that followed were lost to her memory. Julianne could not remember the specifics, only the fog of bleakness that enveloped her, occasionally punctuated by visits from the police, discussions with the undertaker, and a brief trip to court to hear the opening of the inquest into their deaths.

Selfish as it sounded, the fact she had two young children to care for had seemed unimportant. Quiller was working hard, trying to build up the business. 'I can't stay off work indefinitely,' he'd say. 'And it will be good for you to have a focus.' He believed the malaise afflicting her would clear when he wasn't around for her to rely on.

'Don't forget the children need breakfast,' he'd remind her every day on his way out. In some ways, she didn't blame him. The atmosphere at home was suffocating, her grief drawing all the oxygen from the room. He hadn't been close to her parents and she forgave his impulse to breathe in the clean air of absolution. If he couldn't *see* her distress, he was removed from the responsibility of it, temporarily, at least.

It was on a morning like that, a few days after her parents were buried together in the cemetery that overlooked Midtown's sweeping bay, that Piper Holden saved her again.

Her grief was a stone that morning, solid and weighty. It crushed her. When Quiller had left for work, he'd kissed her on her forehead, disappearing into the dawn, the high-pitched chatter of the birds a soundtrack to the rolling light that filtered through the curtains and hurt her eyes.

Even the sweet notes of Emelie babbling in her Moses basket couldn't penetrate the hopelessness that pinned her to the bed, muffling the world beyond. Her son had perfected the art of climbing over the bars of his cot and padded into her room. His toddler fingers groped at her hair, her closed eyes, trying to open them. 'Mama.' She ignored him.

Some time passed. She wasn't sure how much, only that the quality of light had changed and she was aware it was later. Emelie was crying, those rising wails that were impossible to ignore. She dragged herself from the bed and forced herself into her daughter's room. The baby was lying on her back, her cheeks flushed and shiny. A smell of ammonia, of sweaty, sharp distress. She pressed her into her shoulder, if only to silence the noise that filled every corner of her mind.

It wasn't until Emelie was gurgling on the changing mat, quiet dawdling through the house, that a thought streaked through her consciousness: *Henry.*

Her intake of breath made the baby look up from her teething ring. Without stopping to fasten the tabs on her nappy, Julianne heaved Emelie into her basket, flew from the room and down the stairs.

She shouted his name again and again.

In the kitchen, the back door was open. Henry was just tall enough to reach the handle. It should have been locked but Julianne had taken herself outside in the early hours when the mad grab of grief had kept her from sleeping, and she'd forgotten to bolt it on her way back to bed.

Her knees loosened, elastic. 'Henry!' Her cry filled their large garden that ran down to the sea and the cliffs that edged it. 'Henry.'

She ran to the swimming pool by the pergola, replaying the time she'd challenged Quiller about filling it in, and how he'd batted off her concerns, promising to install a fence and never quite getting round to it because the children were still too young to be left unsupervised in the garden, weren't they? Julianne scanned the water for a small body floating face down, convinced she would see him, sodden pyjamas, haloed by strands of his blond hair.

But the water was as still as the summer morning.

She stood for a moment, blinking, inserting herself into the mind of a two-year-old boy. She'd avoided going outside in the last few days, shying away from the bright, smiling disloyalty of the sunshine, preferring the shadows of home with its closed curtains. In a distant garden, a lawnmower droned and she caught the scent of the sweet peas and honeysuckle she'd planted in happier times.

Where would he go? Her head jerked upwards and she glanced towards the far end of the garden, its tangle of fruit trees and the silver strip of the bay beyond.

Quiller had fallen in love with this house because of its view of the sea. It overlooked steep cliffs that ran down to the bay and had a gate at the end of the garden that opened onto stone steps leading down to the water. Although the gate had a latch, the fence was broken in a couple of places. Henry's dummy lay amid the dead grass and fallen rose petals.

She ran.

The steps were badly maintained and she forced herself to slow down, stumbling on the cracked stones, almost losing her footing, scanning ahead of her all the time, scouring the water, the vast stretch of sand for her son.

A few dozen metres ahead she glimpsed a flash of colour and dismissed it, a buoy bobbing at the water's edge. But it was moving along the beach and she realized it was not a buoy at all, but the fire-engine red of his pyjamas.

She ran, her bare feet scraping against the shingle, the warmed-up smell of the sea: salt and seaweed and the fishermen's nets sprawled across the jetty.

'Henry!' She shouted his name over and over again, but her voice was lost to the ebb and flow of the waves, and the cry of the terns, and the ringing of the bells on the masts of the anchored fishing boats.

The beach was quiet for a summer's morning. It was market day in Midtown. The schools hadn't broken up yet and dog walkers were banned until end-of-season September.

The small figure bent down to collect a shell. At the same time, a woman came into distant view, jogging along the sand near the stretch of beach huts.

Julianne didn't stop running. But her breath was coming faster now, and she had a stitch in her side. It was a while since she'd done any exercise or eaten a proper meal, and her head swam with exertion. The tide was coming in, and although the day was calm, she knew enough about the sea to recognize only a fool would trust it.

He stooped to collect another shell and, without warning, a wave knocked him off his feet.

She screamed. Picked up the pace, running through the knife in her side. Her boy struggled to stand, his red pyjamas clinging to his body, dragging himself up from his hands and knees.

Although she couldn't hear him, she could see his face was crumpled with saltwater and tears. She shouted at him, urging him away from the water's edge, but he still couldn't hear her, the crash of the incoming tide drowning out her voice.

As he staggered to his feet, regaining his balance, he turned to her, a tremulous grin of triumph on his lips. 'No, no.' The moan slid from her even before it happened, although she had already guessed it would.

He didn't see the next wave coming because he was looking at her.

As it hit him from behind, he fell forwards, crying out as his face and palms scraped the shingle. This time, he wasn't able to stand before the tide came for him again, pulling him deeper into the water, the currents lethal on this stretch of the coast.

Within seconds, he was bobbing amongst the white-flecked waves, his head disappearing beneath the surface. If she'd been in the water with him, it would only have reached her thighs, but it was deep enough to submerge a small boy.

A cry of anguish slid from her. She was too far away to reach him. He would be dragged out to sea before she reached the shoreline.

Racked with indecision, she stilled, unable to decide which course of action to take next. If she swam out to him in her weakened state, she risked being dragged out herself. If she sought help, precious minutes – perhaps just enough time to save him – would be lost.

From the corner of her eye, she caught movement. Sprinting across the sand was the woman she'd noticed earlier. That woman was now wading into the water with strong, determined strides.

A release of breath. Her hand fluttered to her throat, scarcely able to believe it. She inhaled. Exhaled. Tried to calm herself, to control the panic that had been swelling inside her. The listing ship inside her stomach steadied. She'd recognize that face – that capable, *familiar* face – anywhere.

Piper.

By the time her friend had reached Julianne's son, the water was up to her chest. Piper grabbed him by the collar of his pyjamas, hauling him upwards, struggling to keep her balance as she held on to his limp body. Julianne could feel the frantic movement of her own heart as she willed them both to safety.

Piper pushed onwards, the waves knocking against her from behind, unrelenting as a playground bully. By sheer force of will, she managed to stay upright until she had staggered up the beach, away from the greedy reach of the water. Then she laid him down and collapsed onto her knees.

'Piper—'

It was the only sound Julianne could muster, but her gratitude, her impossible debt, was spelled out in those five letters.

She turned her attention to her son.

His eyes were shut, a ribbon of seaweed clinging to his cheek. Her beautiful boy, as pale and inert as the bleached pebbles she'd collected with her mother as a child. The sea had stolen his pyjama bottoms and his knees were scraped raw from the shingle. His lashes curled against his skin.

Dead.

That knowledge burned inside her gut and up her throat. She turned away from him and expelled the glass of two-day-old water she'd drunk from her nightstand before attending to Emelie.

It tasted of acid and bile.

'What are you doing?' Piper's voice was sharp, intrusive. Julianne didn't move. She stared at the horizon and thought about walking into the sea. Bare feet pressing into the clumped sand. The sting of a stone digging into her sole. An embrace that would draw her in until she could no longer breathe or feel. Her friend called her name again. 'For Christ's sake. Pull yourself together and give me a hand.'

Stung by Piper's cruelty, she swung around to face her, an instinct to scream rising inside her, a pressure that needed to be relieved. Her gratitude had evaporated. She wanted to fling herself at Piper and scratch out her eyes.

But what she saw instead was a miracle. Henry, lying on

his side, coughing, a trickle of seawater sliding from the corner of his mouth. Piper was crouched next to him, her hand rubbing his back.

'Good boy.' She stroked his hair. 'Good boy.'

'Mama.'

Julianne fell to her knees and gathered her son into her arms, trembling with relief.

They walked back up the stone stairs in silence. Julianne had tried to carry him but couldn't get further than a few steps so Piper, wet, covered in sand and with her own six-month twins at home, hefted the shivering child back to the house. He wrapped his legs around her waist and his arms around her neck. His cheek rested on her shoulder, but his eyes followed his mother everywhere.

Julianne wanted to thank her friend, but the words wouldn't come. She glanced sideways at Piper but she was concentrating on the steep climb back to the house, head down. As they passed through the gate and into the garden, a baby's screams filled the summer quiet through the open window. *Emelie.* She'd forgotten all about her. Piper looked up at her. Both women quickened their pace until they were inside the cool of the kitchen and the sounds of crying were amplified a thousand-fold.

Piper placed Henry on the table and ran him a beaker of water from the tap. One of Quiller's jackets was hanging on the back of the chair and she placed it around his shoulders.

'Go and see to the baby,' she said. But Julianne found her legs wouldn't move. A bolus of grief was expanding in her throat, making it difficult for her to breathe. She snatched at the air, a band squeezing her chest. Her limbs were rocks, freight she had no strength to carry. Piper came to her then, guided her into a chair, soothing her. 'It's going to be OK.' Julianne rested her arms and head on the table, and closed her eyes.

The next hour passed in a blur. She wanted to help but could not. She was aware of Piper boiling the kettle and placing hot, sweet tea in front of her. Her son came downstairs, smelling of freshly washed hair and wearing a clean T-shirt and shorts. The baby had been bathed and changed too.

Piper made up a bottle, and organized cereal and scrambled eggs and squares of toast. She played with both children and when Julianne was ready, she helped her upstairs and into the shower.

At one point, Julianne overheard her murmuring down the telephone, but she didn't catch the conversation and it didn't seem to matter.

Piper stayed all day. She played with the children, she tidied the sitting room and changed the beds, and when Quiller came home from work at the end of the day, the house was filled with the smell of roasting chicken and rosemary potatoes, a salad prepared on the side.

'Good girl,' he said to Julianne, who was sipping a modest glass of wine that Piper had poured. And to Piper, who was sitting at the table with her, pouring her own glass, 'Are you leading my wife astray?'

Julianne stared at the table, tracing the grain with her finger. She steeled herself, waiting for Piper to explain about the near-drowning, the hysterical baby, her own inability to do anything but sit still and allow her grief to swallow her.

But Piper said nothing except, 'She deserves a break, don't you think?' and Quiller had no answer to that.

Back in her bedroom, fast-forwarding from the past and into the present, Julianne placed the elephant figurine on the shelf and smiled back at Piper, who was still sitting on the bed. 'You're so thoughtful.'

In response, Piper touched her friend's arm. Her hand was warm. 'Are you still on for that drink tonight?'

The women smiled at each other, sharing a look of complicity. 'Of course.'

All these years later, they never spoke about that day when Henry had almost drowned. But Julianne would not forget what Piper had done for her until her dying breath. *Could* not. That knowledge was always between them. But it created an imbalance of power, like a shrub in a garden that seems harmless – beautiful, even – but takes over everything. Piper's grip on Julianne could not be loosened. The seed she had planted spread its roots, roping them together until their fates were entwined. Her act of mercy had cursed Julianne and reframed the dynamic of their friendship until it took on a different, more dangerous shape and they occupied new but opposing roles: those of ownership and obligation.

But Julianne did not see it that way. The truth was Piper had saved the life of her son. And with his life, Julianne's own. Nothing – not even murder – could ever be enough to repay that debt.

24

Monday evening

A few hours before the Holdens disappeared

Gray's father had been a crook. This knowledge had come upon him gradually as he was growing up, in the same way children realize Father Christmas is not real or their parents are not all-knowing gods, but humans with flaws and imperfections. Anthony Holden had many of these.

But he'd imparted one useful piece of information to his son. On those nights when the teenage version of Gray would come home late after his Saturday shift at the pub, or a gig with his friends, his father would still be up, counting cash into dirty piles.

In those strange, intimate moments, he'd rest his boots on the kitchen table, light a cigarette, inhale and blow out smoke through his nose, and talk about the cons he'd committed. Gray couldn't remember everything his father told him, but he remembered this: 'If you ever need to hide a dead body, son, you'd do worse than throw it off a cliff.'

That was how he found himself at the edge of Midtown

cliffs on a night when the clouds were running fast in the wind and the moon was obscured.

When it was late and full dark, he'd dragged the body from his office and into the car park at the back of the building, erasing the last twenty-four hours of footage from security cameras he'd installed after a break-in the previous year. Then he disabled them.

Her car was one of the two parked there. An idea came to him – something he'd seen on television – and when he'd retrieved her keys, he hefted her into the passenger side and fitted her seatbelt, the wound in his hand opening up and roaring in protest. Blood matted the side of her head and streaked the front of his shirt, his sleeve and forearm. When she was secured, he tossed in her handbag and slid himself into the driving seat, a hat jammed over his hair.

The drive took less than five minutes. He chose country roads, trying his best to avoid the built-up estates, the street lights and the risk of traffic cameras, keeping his head bent, his face hidden.

A wind was blowing off the sea when he parked up, nosing the cliff edge. The place was deserted, as he'd known it would be. A squall, full of rain, battered the windscreen. He sat for a minute, breathing darkness into his lungs, exhaling common sense.

There was no going back.

He opened the car door and stepped into the night. No artificial light here, just a muted glow from the moon that cowered behind the clouds. Rain touched his face. He didn't attempt to wipe it away but let it bathe him. For a second time, he scanned the cliffs. Not a soul. Except for the distant lights of Midtown.

He allowed his mind to empty, to disassociate himself from the task at hand. If he thought too much about what he was doing, he wouldn't be able to go through with it.

He leaned over and unbuckled her seatbelt. Her head rested against his chest and he fought against his instinct to swallow down lungfuls of air, to rail against the sky at this turn of events, upending their careful plans. An accident. That was all. He hadn't meant to kill her.

His heart felt squeezed. Suffocated. He snatched for a breath. And another. Was this a panic attack? Whatever it was, he couldn't afford to let it take over.

With immense effort, he slipped his hands beneath her armpits and pulled her from the car, revulsion rising in his gut. She was sticky with blood and much heavier than he expected, even though she was slight. In the still of the night, he could hear the wash of the waves below. High tide. A stroke of luck.

At first, he'd planned to throw her over the cliffs. Simple. Clean. Easy. But there was the small matter of her car, and the traces of DNA he'd left behind, and if he left it parked here, someone would call the police. His method would buy them a little extra time.

He half dragged, half shoved her into the driving seat. She lolled against him and he grimaced and pushed her upright. A twist of a smile as he clipped in her belt again. *Too late for safety measures now.*

He leaned across her and released the handbrake. Shut the driver's door. Took a step backwards and a long, deep breath.

Planting his hands on the rear bumper, he pushed with everything he had. The incline aided him. Without a sound, the car rolled forward. His shoes slipped against the wet grass and he fell to his knees, and then scrambled up again, gathering all his strength and fear and anger, and expelling it against the metalwork, freezing beneath his palms.

With a grumble of tyres against sandstone and chalk, the car tipped forwards, careering into the jutting face of the cliff about halfway down and rotating 180 degrees to smack into the water, landing on its roof.

He didn't know if the tide would take it, or whether it would float or become wedged into the rocks below, but he hoped the immersion in saltwater – for a few hours at least, *but please God, longer* – would erase any forensic trace of his presence.

Without looking back, Gray slipped away from the clifftop, threading his way across the sodden trap of the marshes towards town. With luck, he would see no one on his walk back, finish cleaning up his office, collect his car and be home before his sleeping wife even noticed he was late.

25

Wednesday afternoon

The day after the Holdens disappeared

In the embers of the winter afternoon, Seawings was a proud ship pushing through the gloom. Clover propped her dented motorbike against the wall and gazed upwards. The chandelier that dominated the grand hallway and staircase was illuminating the windows at the front of the house. She started, certain a fair-haired woman – Piper Holden? – was advancing from room to room, but it was only the light throwing out shadows that moved like ghosts.

Blue. He'd called her Blue. She liked that, tried it on for size again. *Blue.* It gave her a strange, exhilarated feeling to think he'd paid enough attention to take notes on her hair. And she'd respected the way he had handled her assault. Not pushy like some. Or overly solicitous. Kind and careful but with the heat of anger behind him.

His reaction to her narcolepsy had been revelatory too. When she was diagnosed six months ago, her mother had been full of hand-wringing doom, convinced it would cost her her hard-won career and relationships, but Saul had accepted the truth of it without asking too many questions. She liked people who didn't ask much of her. *Two* things she liked about him. That was progress. Most of the men she met didn't get beyond one.

'Shall we go inside?' Saul had dug his hands into his pockets but he was staring straight at her. She met his gaze. Something between them sparked and caught fire. Neither broke away until the police officer standing by the gates interrupted them.

'Are you two coming in or what?'

When she glanced at Saul again – a darting, sideways look – he was smiling at her. She fought against her instinct to turn from him and smiled back.

The hustle and bustle of the house had quietened. Most of the detailed forensics work had been done. Technically, due to an absence of bodies, it could still be described as a Missing Persons case but no one believed that anymore, especially since O'Neill had authorized the collection of evidence, and they all knew what that meant.

Riva's bedroom was a mess. Scenes of Crime was supposed to have tidied up, but clothes were strewn all over the bed and traces of fingerprint powder darkened the walls, the mantelpiece and her dressing table.

The blood was still on the mirror. Blue stood opposite it, head bowed like the devoted before an altar. Her eyes followed the loop and whorl of the letters, the pooling of the blood and the way the penmanship flicked and danced. She knew how difficult it was to write in blood because she'd tried it herself during her training. The police still had no idea who the blood belonged to but she was certain of one truth: the woman who wrote it must have had access to a plentiful supply.

That wasn't why she was here though.

A shadow moved in the brightly lit room. A masculine scent, a light sweat, the faint hint of deodorant. Saul was standing behind her. She was aware of him even though she couldn't see him.

'Have you found what you're looking for?'

She didn't answer him but moved closer to the writing, studying it. Something was firing in her brain, but it wouldn't catch. Riva's diary had been bagged and collated with the rest of the evidence, but she already knew the girl hadn't written this message.

Blue opened the drawers. They were full of cinema and theatre ticket stubs, and Polaroids of Riva laughing with her friends, and silver bangles and half-used lipsticks and hair elastics. She hadn't answered Saul because she didn't know what she was looking for until she saw it, and she rifled through the detritus of a teenager's life, waiting for the spark to become a flame.

After a couple of minutes, Saul joined in, opening cupboards and checking the pockets of Riva's coats and jeans. They worked in silence for a while, Blue feeling the tidal rise of frustration. But neither of them found anything of note.

'Let's go downstairs,' said Saul eventually. 'Take a break for a bit.' And she couldn't argue with that.

Seawings was keeping its secrets to itself. At least, that's what it felt like to Blue as she prowled its vast rooms, dissatisfied and out of sorts. She knew she was missing something, that it was all about looking in the right place instead of the wrong direction. Although she was clever, her inexperience was showing and she hated it. An instinct told her the answers were here if only she knew where to find them.

Riva's school bag was still in the kitchen, exactly where it had been left the previous day. Blue was surprised it hadn't been taken in evidence yet, but it wasn't possible to collect everything and the team would come back for it. Hesitating, not sure if she should touch it, she raised her eyebrows at Saul, who understood the question. 'I won't tell if you don't.'

Oversized, designer, it wasn't to her taste, but she could see how a teenage girl in an affluent community might attract friends with such expensive fripperies. She dug in her own rucksack for plastic gloves to reduce contamination. Folders, exercise books, a couple of textbooks and a pencil case. Some tampons. A hairbrush. Nothing out of the ordinary.

She sat back on her haunches, trying to remember what it was like to be fifteen and keep secrets. Where – if she'd had it – would Riva have hidden something important? She poked inside the bag again. At the back was a zipped pocket and inside her head, a bell clanged.

Heart drumming, she opened it. But it only contained a rusted safety pin and a sweet wrapper. Frustrated, she tore off the gloves and went looking for Saul.

She found him in the kitchen, replaying footage from the Holdens' security cameras that had been uploaded to his phone, a frown on his face.

'Look at this.' He played a snippet of the recording, Gray Holden arriving home gone midnight, his face a grey smudge. Then he rewound the tape until he found him leaving for work the same morning. 'What do you notice?'

'Um . . .'

'He's wearing different clothes when he gets home.'

'Perhaps he got changed at work and went out for the evening.'

'I don't think so. No one's come forward to confirm that.'

Saul played the recording again. 'This is weird too, right? O'Neill said the power cut happened at 3.49 a.m. But this camera stops recording at 2.47 a.m. Why? The cameras were still off when the police first got here. But that doesn't make sense. They should have come on again when the power did.'

Blue yawned. He gave a sudden laugh and shut his phone. 'Am I boring you?'

Side by side, they stood and gazed into the Holdens' impressive garden. Both young, inexperienced in their respective fields, uncertain what to do next. The light was almost gone, but Blue could see the pool house and a small wooden building to its left.

'I don't know what I'm supposed to be doing here,' Saul said suddenly. He was matter-of-fact but not embarrassed.

'Do you mean your higher purpose in life? Or on this particular case?'

'Both.'

'I hear you.' She pointed out of the window. 'What's that?'

'A shepherd's hut. You know, those expensive outside rooms for rich people who don't already have enough space. I think the Holdens bought it for the children and their friends. That's what one of the neighbours said.' Before he'd finished his sentence, she was disappearing through the back door.

Leaves silvered with rain littered the garden. Her boots sank into the grass with every step, moisture seeping in through a weakness in the leather. The garden, filled with the thin arms of deciduous trees, was several times the size of her flat. A suite of furniture stood next to a firepit and rose garden. *Money makes the world go round.* Or, in her case, grind to a sickening halt.

A key was protruding from the door of the hut, but when she tried the handle, it was unlocked. She stepped inside to a teenage paradise. A stereo system with top-of-the-range speakers, bean bags, a television and games console, a sofa bed and a small fridge were arranged in the well-designed space.

Saul whistled. 'Nice.'

Blue set to work, lifting up cushions and opening drawers, not certain what she was hoping to find, but driven by some instinct that convinced her the truth to the family's disappearance was hidden somewhere in the vicinity of the house.

The police officer was more methodical. While she was throwing cushions about, Saul focused his attention on one end of the hut and worked his way downwards. Patient. Logical. Ordered.

He lingered by the console, examining the stack of games. At one point, he shook the plastic casing of one of them, frowned and opened it up.

'Jesus Christ.'

Blue turned to him. 'What is it?' Wordlessly, he tilted the box towards her. Inside was not a metal disc, but a bundle of banknotes.

'How much do you reckon is there?'

'Got to be at least a thousand pounds.' He opened another cover to reveal a similar bundle of cash. 'Fuck,' he said. 'I need to put on some gloves.'

When he'd finished, five identical piles of money sat on the table. They both stared at them. 'This changes things,' said Blue.

Like the rent arrears she owed on her flat, the motorbike that now needed repairing and all the other things she could buy with that kind of money. She wondered if Saul felt the same pull of temptation. She wanted to ask him – she sensed there was a darkness in him – but she didn't want to offend him.

'Tempting, isn't it?'

She blushed, as if he'd caught her naked.

'Some people would give in to it, don't you think?' A flash of a grin before he picked up one of the piles and knocked it into shape, making sure all the notes were lined up with mathematical precision. 'I've got my own money, so—' He shrugged, leaving the rest unsaid. But it felt like he'd glimpsed into her mind and read what she'd been thinking. 'Lines are blurred sometimes,' he said. 'I'm hardly one to judge. But, in case you *were* tempted, they will find out it was you.'

'I wasn't,' she said, her denial too hot and fierce.

Blue turned away, cheeks flaming, annoyed with herself for allowing him to have this effect on her, even though her rational side understood he had no way of knowing what was in her head. She busied herself at the other end of the hut, picking up one of the glossy high fashion magazines she assumed belonged to Riva.

To cover her embarrassment, she flicked through the

pages, not noticing the models with their impossibly perfect bodies or the designer shoes, just needing something to do with her hands.

A small white card fluttered out and landed on the floor.

She bent down and picked it up. It was the type used by florists to tuck inside a bouquet, with a message handwritten on it. *Break a leg, darling. Love Mum, Dad and Artie x x x.* Heart running faster, she studied it, tracing the shape of the letters, the distinctive flick of the crossed *t*.

Saul was watching her. 'What is it?'

She held it out for him, forgetting he wouldn't see what she did, excitement rising through her like dozens of tiny air bubbles. 'I knew it.'

'Knew what?'

'That it was worth coming back to Seawings.'

He spread his hands. 'Help me out. All I can see is a card with a good luck message on it to Riva from her family.'

'That's right,' said Blue. She pointed to the handwriting, her face radiant with the joy of discovery. 'And the same woman who wrote this card left the message on her mirror.'

26

The day after the Holdens disappeared

Julianne dialled the number and let it ring four times before she hung up. She didn't leave a voicemail. She noted the time. Folded some pyjamas and put them away in her drawer. Dabbed some perfume on the insides of her wrists. Changed her earrings twice. It took him seven minutes and thirteen seconds to call back.

His voice was low. 'I missed your call.'

'Hello, David.' She made herself wait, a calculated pause, knowing the trick was not to appear too eager. 'I wanted to make sure you're OK. I hope I didn't impose earlier.'

'Not at all.' He hesitated. 'Actually, it was a relief to have someone else to talk to. Anoushka's family are doing the best they can, but they're suffocating me.'

Julianne smiled into the phone. A small and secret thing. 'Well, I'm always around if you ever need to chew things over with a neutral party.'

She screwed up her face, waiting to see if she'd misjudged it again. But as soon as he replied, she sensed her

183

tried-and-tested method was paying dividends, as it almost always did.

'Thank you.' His voice was soft. 'I mean it. I might just take you up on that.' A silence. She could hear music playing in the background and wondered where his children were. 'Did you—' Another pause. Experience had taught her it was wise to wait for these men to fill in the gaps, assume control of the conversation. 'Find out any more about that man?'

'I did.' She considered her words, weighing up whether this was the moment of revelation, or to wait, to string out the details for a little longer. The Holdens' disappearance had complicated matters. But the endgame was the same. If the news hadn't broken already, it would do soon. She made a decision. 'I can tell you exactly who he is, if you'd still like to know.'

'I looked him up. But I still have questions.' A sharp intake of breath. He was steeling himself, but she knew what he was going to say and admired his courage. 'I want to know everything.'

'Gray Holden runs an investment business in town. He's married with two teenage children. He lives in a property called Seawings in the bay area of Midtown.' She paused, knowing he would find this out with some superficial digging, so it was best to come clean now. 'I should have told you this earlier, but I didn't know how to. His wife is my best friend.'

'You *know* him?' She could hear the incredulity in his tone and regretted her earlier reticence. She *should* have told him. As a tactic to gain his trust. The next part of their exchange would be crucial.

'Was he having an affair with Anoushka?'

'I don't know. I haven't had a chance to talk to Piper about it.' Tears – spontaneous but genuine – clogged her throat. 'Piper – the whole family – has been missing since yesterday morning. I wanted to tell you, but you've got so much on your plate. I expect the news will break publicly soon, if it hasn't already.'

'Wow.' A beat to let it all sink in. 'Seriously?'

She imagined him running his hand through his hair, his face creased with confusion and worry, but she felt nothing for him, not even a twinge of shame. 'I'm sorry I can't tell you any more. I wish I could.'

'It's so out of character. She was always against this kind of thing, from a moralistic point of view.' He sounded crushed. 'I can't believe there was anything going on between them. I mean, how did she even know this guy?' His words were threaded with hurt. 'And I'll never be able to ask her.'

Julianne was quiet, letting the shock of it sink in. She glanced at her watch. Eight seconds, she decided. She watched the numbers tick by, resisting the urge to break the silence, and then, on cue, 'Oh no.'

'What is it?'

She mustered the perfect amount of concern and bewilderment. 'I don't know whether I should say—'

'Tell me. Please. I want you to.'

She watched herself in the bedroom mirror. Grey hair was beginning to push through at her roots. A trip to the hairdresser was required. And she definitely needed to redo her blusher. She refocused. 'It's just that something worrying has occurred to me.'

In the background, she heard one of his sons call to him, and sensed his distraction. He would hang up soon. But she knew his curiosity would keep him on the telephone for a few moments longer. 'What is it?'

'Look, I'm sorry for raising it, but if Anoushka was having an affair with Gray, it's a bit of a problem for you now, isn't it?'

He was sharp, defensive. 'I've got no idea what you mean. Why would it be a problem for me?'

Julianne held her tongue. Christ, she was good at this. She counted to five, to elongate the tension. 'Gray Holden, the man who was potentially having an illicit relationship with your wife, has vanished.' She let the weight of her words sink in.

'And?' said David. 'I'm still not sure what you're getting at.'

Julianne watched herself in the mirror as she dropped a bomb into the fragments of the widower's life. 'I'd say that makes you a suspect, wouldn't you?'

27

Tuesday, early hours

The day the Holdens disappeared

Seawings was in darkness when Gray parked his car on the driveway, the wind lifting his damp hair. He'd showered before he'd left the office, scrubbing every trace of her blood from his body, and then he'd disinfected the cubicle, pouring thick neat bleach down the drain.

Cleaning the office had been more time-consuming than he'd anticipated. He'd expended a great deal of effort on the floor and the door handles. Washing down. Vacuuming. Polishing. Then he'd double-checked he'd deleted the CCTV footage that showed her pulling into the car park at the back of the building, and of him leaving, dragging her body with him. He'd scoured the concrete outside with a wire brush in an attempt to obliterate those tiny forensic details, knowing that a strand of hair or a smattering of dead skin cells would be enough to place her at his office, but offering up a prayer of gratitude for the weather. The wind and rain would make life difficult if the worst happened and the police ended up at his door.

What the fuck was she doing in Midtown? It had been more than a year since he'd spoken to her, during that last meeting at a discreet hotel in Kent, and he'd never expected to see her again. She was bad news. Full of threats and histrionics. He'd given her money to go away, and she'd promised she would. Sworn it. It wasn't his fault she'd reneged on their agreement. Of course he'd reacted to that. She'd almost given him a heart attack. What else was he supposed to do? He knew what she was capable of. Anyone with a scrap of sense would have done the same.

But he hadn't meant to kill her.

A speck of blood was visible beneath his fingernail. He'd no idea how that had survived all the scrubbing and showering. It worried him. If he'd missed that, what else had he missed? He bit it off and swallowed it. Destroying the evidence in the only way possible.

As he walked up the path to Seawings, he tried to concentrate on the citrus scent of the evergreens that Piper had planted when they first moved in, but he was consumed by the memory of the smell of her blood, the feel of yielding softness beneath him. The horror of what he'd done slipped its noose around his neck. There was no going back now.

The house was full of shadows when he walked through the front door. Home. That smell of familiarity unique to those who lived there. Tears of self-pity pricked his eyes. People got away with murder all the time. Christ, there was even a cliché to that effect. If he didn't panic, if he could just hold it together, he'd be fine. He'd done everything he could. The police *would* come for him when they looked into her past. But it would take time. And that was in his favour. Now breathe.

He hung his coat on the hook and headed to the kitchen for a glass of water. He didn't see the shadow sitting at the table. When she spoke, he jumped and dropped his glass, scattering fragments everywhere. A sound of violence in the night.

'Where have you been?' Piper's tone was cool.

'At the office.'

'Until gone midnight?'

'I was finishing up some stuff.'

'What stuff?'

He waved an airy hand and then realized it was too dark for his wife to see. 'Work stuff. And all those loose ends, remember? We don't want Moore's goons coming back for his money.'

'You've been avoiding me.'

He switched on the light and began looking for the dustpan and brush. 'I thought that's what you wanted.' When she didn't reply, he crouched by her chair and grasped her cold hands. 'We agreed to make it look as if we'd had a falling-out. To muddy the waters, you said. Make our marriage appear weak. The art of misdirection now we've decided it's time to move on. Look, I'm happy to be the fall guy for this but don't make me out to be the villain here. We've both been playing our parts, haven't we?'

Piper gave him a steady look. 'Some better than others.'

'What's that supposed to mean?'

She shrugged, steel in her eyes. 'I'm not an idiot, Gray. Give me some credit.'

'I don't know what you're talking about.'

'Tell me what you were working on then.' She was ice. 'I'd like to know.'

His wife knew the mechanics of the business inside and out and wouldn't be fobbed off. He swept the glass from the tiles while he groped for a convincing lie to tell her, his cheeks aflame.

'Have you been seeing someone?'

'Of course not.' He sounded more defensive than he intended to. When he'd finished cleaning up, he put the dustpan on the counter. Piper was staring at him, her lips a thin line.

'If you've only been at work, where's your shirt?' The question hung between them, an airburst detonation.

Idiot. He should never have assumed she'd be in bed. Now he had all these questions to deal with. And how could he have forgotten he'd changed his clothes, stuffing his blood-stained work shirt into a plastic bag and swapping it for the spare running top he kept in his desk drawer? His mind emptied. He couldn't think of a single thing to say and he gawped at her, a vacant expression on his face.

'Who is she?' Piper laced her fingers together. No tears. No shouting. But that was his wife. Collected. Calm. 'I won't get upset, I promise. I just want the truth.'

His mind sought a response, frantic, panicked, but it wouldn't come. He collapsed into a chair at the table, conceding defeat. 'It's bad, but it's not what you think.'

Her face softened. The harsh light of the kitchen would have been unflattering to most women, but not Piper. She bewitched him still. 'There's solutions to everything, Gray.'

'Not this.'

She came around the table and sat on his lap, her arms sliding around his neck. 'Come on,' she said. 'Talk to me.' He shouldn't unburden himself. The only way to keep a secret was to tell no one. That's what they'd always said. But he trusted her with his life.

As if the wind had switched direction, her face changed. 'Is the money safe?'

'It's nothing to do with that.'

'What is it then?'

She was like a dog gnawing marrow from a bone. Relentless until she was in possession of every scrap of information, however small. But that was one of the reasons their marriage worked so well. She was a details woman, and by Christ, he needed one of those tonight. He made a decision, and with it came the instant hit of relief.

'There was an accident.' He was halting, eyes sliding sideways.

'What kind of accident? Where?'

He ran his hands through his hair, tugged at it. 'I didn't mean it. Honestly, Piper. It just' – he spread his hands in a gesture of hopelessness – 'happened.'

'Tell me everything.'

He stared at the woman he'd loved and trusted for sixteen years. Faint lines fanned out from her eyes. She scanned him with a shrewdness that he'd grown accustomed to over the years, but that still unnerved him with its intensity. 'Piper—' He didn't want to tell her because once he'd done so, he couldn't shove it back into the box. The lid would be open, exposing the filthy darkness within.

This wasn't a simple fraud. Stealing money from his clients was wrong. He accepted that, but he shouldered the risk because he and Piper had planned it that way. *Together.* In meticulous detail. The money they'd siphoned off was hidden in discreet offshore bank accounts they would access later. Easy to conceal. Just the right side of careful. Not enough to raise suspicion but just enough to fund their lavish lifestyle. He was so practised at it now, so used to dipping in and out of his clients' investment funds, that it had become second nature. In truth, he almost believed the money belonged to him. He'd worked hard for it, after all.

He and Piper were planning to leave Midtown with their children after a final fuck-it-all theft of Mr Moore's fortune. Gray had already begun the process of emptying the rest of their accounts. Except they'd got too greedy and Mr Moore was on to them.

But the act he'd committed tonight was much darker than theft. Most of his clients could absorb a loss. Every day, he gambled on the notion – the near-certainty – they wouldn't notice. But someone would notice a missing woman. And not just any woman. A woman with an irrefutable connection to him.

How much should he tell his wife? It wasn't his fault that women threw themselves at him. She'd been a mistake. One of his worst. She'd become obsessed with him. Delusional. He'd paid her a large sum of money to persuade her to stay away from him and she'd promised to abide by that agreement.

Until tonight when she'd turned up out of the blue.

Sixteen years of marriage was at stake. He loved his wife. But their relationship had grown stale, as these things often do. She was distracted by the children, by running a home, by the responsibility of the business, and she'd pushed him away when he pressed himself to her, and eventually – long after she'd stopped caring about that side of things – the penny had dropped for him, and he'd stopped trying.

Until that night in the hotel bar, he hadn't thought it mattered. Or that the distance between them was an inevitability of long-term relationships and must be endured. But the woman standing next to him was dark-eyed and new, and when she'd offered to buy him a drink, he'd surprised himself by accepting it.

A physical need, that was all it had been. A certain kind of relief that came from the mechanics of emptying himself into a woman's body. She could have been *any* woman. But she had been standing at *that* bar on *that* night, and he had been weak.

Her body had felt different from Piper's. Curvier. More welcoming. Her mouth had been warm with compliments, her hands massaging his body and his ego.

They hadn't exchanged numbers, but she had helped herself to one of the business cards he'd left on his hotel room desk in preparation for the next day's conference, and had messaged him a few days later. He should have ignored it, but he'd enjoyed the taste of forbidden fruit, was greedy for more of it. To gorge himself.

He'd had sex with her half a dozen times before guilt soured the sweetness.

'I'm sorry,' he'd said. 'It's not you, it's the situation. I can't do this to my wife.'

She had twirled the stem of her wine glass. 'I thought you were planning to leave her.'

He had thought of Seawings, of his children, his comfortable life, and released a bark of amusement. 'Of course not.'

It took him less than ten seconds to realize his mistake. The wine was warm and rich, and it dripped off his chin and down the front of his shirt, staining the fabric and the restaurant's white tablecloth.

'You can't do this to me.' Her mouth, which had kissed and sucked him a few hours earlier, was a tight line of disbelief. 'I'm in love with you.'

He scrambled to soften his words. 'You're beautiful,' he said. 'Incredible.' He reached for her hand. 'But I don't think I'm being fair to anyone.'

She had risen gracefully, her stare cool, her cheeks flushed. A couple of nearby diners were craning their necks, forks halfway to their mouths. 'So you used me?'

'No, I—' But he had no answer because that's exactly what he'd done. With no sense of shame at all.

She didn't wait for him to finish. She refilled her glass from the wine bottle on the table and drank it down in one violent motion. Then she walked away without looking back at him again.

The first photograph arrived that evening.

In it, Gray was asleep in a hotel bed, sheet tangled below his waist, exposing every part of him. Her face wasn't in the picture, but her manicured toes were. The intimacy between them was unmistakeable.

That was the beginning. Over the next few days, more compromising photographs arrived followed by a slew of screenshots of the sexually explicit messages he'd sent her, threatening to expose the truth to his wife.

Eventually, he'd agreed to meet her at that same hotel in Kent, and had written the first cheque to buy her silence.

A few weeks later she'd messaged again: I've been thinking. I'm worth a bit more than that. And so the cycle had begun. Months later, when he'd calculated how much he had given her and discovered it had reached almost £100,000, he was hit by the realization of what he was doing, the black hole of it. One day, he'd stopped, answering her threats with a blunt message. Tell my wife, then. And I'll tell the police you're blackmailing me. He'd expected her to put up more of a fight, but he hadn't heard from her for months now.

Until this afternoon when the chickens had come home to roost.

He raised his gaze to meet Piper's, but she had not buckled or turned from him. 'I'll help you,' she said, and he was so tired and frightened, and so used to leaning on his wife, who he'd always known was stronger than he was. He took a deep breath and told her everything.

When he'd finished talking, Piper placed the pot of tea she'd made on the table, her face a pale blur. 'She's definitely dead?'

Gray pictured the car pirouetting over the cliff edge. 'If she wasn't, she is now.'

His wife cocked her head. He wished he knew what was going on inside it. A part of him longed for her to scream at him, to rail against him for his poor judgement. He could understand that, would have welcomed it. But her cool-headed matter-of-factness was more difficult to gauge.

'We need to go. Tonight.'

Her words sounded unnaturally loud in the still of the sleeping house.

'We can't just disappear,' he said. 'What about the business?'

'You said yourself you've been tying up loose ends. What difference does it make if we go tonight or in two days? And what about Mr Moore? What if that man comes back? You might not be the only one he hurts next time.'

'We can't just disappear,' he said again.

'Fuck it, Gray, yes, we can.' She slammed her hand on the table to emphasize her words although her voice remained at the same steady octave. 'You cheated on me. On our children. You stole our money. You owe me, wouldn't you say?'

There it was then, the swell of her anger, the whiplash sting of it. He waited for a few seconds to see if she would change her mind, but Piper wasn't that sort of a woman. Once she'd settled on a course of action, she rarely wavered. If he was being truthful, he'd expected more of a reaction to his infidelity, but after sixteen years of marriage, he understood the way her mind worked. In the darkness of this moment – the shadow cast across the heart of their home by his revelations – the most pressing issue took precedence. In this case, the murder of his former lover.

'But where shall we go?' He was aware of how weak he sounded. But Piper was the organizer in the family, the dynamic force behind almost everything.

'Somewhere we can lie low for a while.' Her forehead furrowed, miniature cogs whirring behind her eyes. 'My mother's house.'

Marisa Sharp had died two years ago but she lived on in the farm that Piper had bought for her. Piper had not been able to bring herself to touch it, except for the animals, which she'd given away. She paid the utility bills and kept the telephone line running. The wardrobes were stuffed with Marisa's clothes and her car had remained in the garage next to the rusting ride-on lawnmower. Even her kitchen cupboards were stocked with tins, packets of pasta, and tubs of flour and custard powder. Two hours' drive from Midtown, it was an isolated haven, tucked away amidst fields and meadows grown unruly over time.

'I don't know . . .'

Piper planted both palms on the table and stood up, the fire in her eyes scalding him. 'What else do you suggest? Stay here until the police come calling for you?' Neither of them said it but the meaning was implicit. He might lie to himself but they both knew he would crumble under pressure within minutes.

He tried to come up with an alternative plan but his mind was as empty as a paper bag. He slumped into the chair opposite, defeated and exhausted, a grey ghost feeling his age.

Piper's face softened. 'Look, why don't you go now and I'll follow with the children. You know I'm good at sorting things out. I'll get your shirt from the office, OK? Don't worry, my love. Leave everything to me.'

He smiled at her, grateful. Relieved. 'Aren't you angry?' He was tentative, not sure whether he wanted to know the answer.

His wife pinched the bridge of her nose. 'I don't blame you for being unfaithful, put it that way. But that's a discussion for another time.' She sipped her tea. 'If your rash and stupid behaviour derails our future, though—'

She didn't need to finish. Piper had always been dismissive of fools, of impulsive and grandiose acts of sabotage.

'It won't. The money's safe, I promise.'

'In the same accounts we agreed?'

'The same accounts.'

She tossed a set of keys at him. 'Take Julianne's car.'

Gray hesitated. 'I can't just *take* it.'

'Yes, you can.' Piper's friend had left her car at Seawings that evening after a couple of glasses of wine, intending to collect it after they'd been for their run in the morning. She'd left her keys on the table, distracted by a call from Quiller, demanding to know when she'd be home. 'I'll square it with her.'

'But what about you and the children?'

'Don't worry about us. I'll take Mum's car.'

Ten minutes to throw some clothes into a bag and grab his toiletries. Piper said it was best to get on the road as soon as possible. As he prepared to leave, he hesitated by Riva's bedroom. These days, his daughter was often awake after he'd gone to bed, but it was late now and she was asleep, her door ajar. She'd forgotten to turn off her lamp and her face was bathed in a warm glow. It reminded him of all the times he'd read her fairy stories, his promises to protect her from the Big Bad Wolf. With a jolt, he realized that's what he'd become and he felt a sharp sensation inside his chest, a wire brush against his heart. But he trusted Piper. She would tell the children some made-up excuse and pick up the pieces at home.

In the dark of the night, he questioned how he could have been so stupid, risking everything for a cheap thrill, and now it was too late to go backwards, to undo that first drink, that first night with his lover.

He lingered, resisting an impulse to kiss his daughter goodbye, trying to shake loose that unsettling sense this might be the last time he'd see her. Artie's bedroom door was shut, as closed off to him as his son sometimes was.

'Goodnight, my darlings.' His whisper echoed across the landing.

Piper was waiting for him by the front door. An instinct to hold her claimed him but she shrugged him off. 'No, Gray.'

'I don't want to go without you.' There, he'd said it.

'What's the alternative?' A flicker of irritation crossed her face. He hated it when she looked at him like that, a piece of dirt on the sole of her expensive shoes. It made him feel small, less than. Contempt – the cold, sneering truth of it – pressed every button of his.

'I brazen it out.'

A bark of mirth, the joyless kind. 'Don't be ridiculous. The police will arrest you within hours, if Mr Moore's men don't get to you first. Admit it, Gray. You've fucked it up.'

He bristled at the cruelty of her words, the abrupt change in her now she'd had time to process the truth. 'That's not fair. I've worked my arse off for this family.' He waved an arm around. 'Without me, we wouldn't have any of this.'

'Without me, you'd still be working at the shitty company with no ambition. You never had the imagination, did you?'

She was taunting him now, with that sing-song tone he despised so much. A flare of anger became an inferno, the same roaring fire that had seen him shove that woman in his office. He stared at his wife – her expensive haircut and manicured nails and the diamond studs in her ears that he'd paid for – and he was overcome with an urge to place his fingers around her throat, to squeeze the life from her until she couldn't speak, couldn't breathe, couldn't make him feel any less of a man.

He took a step towards her and she backed away from

him. The power made him feel good. Better than good. Invincible. As a boy, he'd always been the last one picked for the football team, for the playground games of Bulldog, for the bike rides down the recreation ground. But he would be master in his own home.

He took another step towards her and she faltered, the words falling away. He could no longer hear what she was saying to him. Or perhaps he didn't care. He needed silence to think. To plan. She was pressed against the kitchen cabinets and he was struck by one of those stray thoughts, the kind he wasn't sure if other men had because no one talked about them: how much force would be required to rake his fingers through her hair, pulling until her scalp stretched, smashing her head into the glass over and over again?

Much later, when he'd arrived at Marisa Sharp's farm with blood all over his hands, he would insist to himself he couldn't remember what had happened next.

All he could recollect was the expression of fear in his wife's dark eyes.

28

The day after the Holdens disappeared

Saul considered steak but decided it was too expensive and chose fish instead. Blue was vegetarian.

The restaurant was tucked down an alleyway three minutes' walk from Blue's flat, where they'd just left her motorbike. He almost hadn't asked, but her stomach had rumbled and she'd laughed, and it had seemed the most natural thing in the world to invite her to dinner.

Candles flickered on a table covered in a red-and-white check cloth, but the place was saved from cliché by their waiter, who was the most strikingly attractive man either of them had ever seen.

Both of them watched him walk towards their table, carrying a tray of drinks. Blue leaned across to Saul. 'Do you think he's a model?' Blindsided by a white-heat prick of jealousy, he shrugged.

Blue waited for the young man to finish taking her food order. When he'd wandered off again, she rolled her eyes at Saul and picked up her shot of tequila. 'Not my type at all.'

The young detective felt the knot in his stomach loosen and raised his glass in answer before licking salt from his hand. Blue winced as she downed the spirit but Saul's face didn't change at all.

'When are you going to tell O'Neill?' Saul knew they would both be in the shit with the inspector for withholding information on a fast-moving investigation, but for one glorious evening he didn't care.

'About the assault or the narcolepsy?'

'The florist's card in the magazine.'

'When I've worked out what it means.' She tore open a bread roll, slathered it with butter and took an enthusiastic bite. 'I'm starving.'

The candlelight hollowed out the planes of her face. He wanted to stare at her, but he didn't want her to think he was being weird. Instead he contented himself with occasional glances when she wasn't looking.

She finished her roll and glanced at his. He offered it to her and she broke it in half. 'When are you going to tell him about the money?' Her mouth was full of his bread. 'And the CCTV?'

Saul shrugged. 'Tomorrow, I suppose. One night won't matter.'

For a few minutes, they talked about the Holden family and what might have happened to them, but their conversation drifted into more interesting waters, Saul blowing the sails in that direction. He didn't want to think about work. He wanted to know everything about the woman in front of him, and through the drip of conversation, he discovered she was newly diagnosed and resistant to that diagnosis.

'But you're taking care of yourself, right?'

Her face closed down. 'Shall we order more tequila?' She was already looking around for the waiter. Confused, he realized he'd strayed into dangerous territory but didn't understand why and was reluctant to probe further.

'Is that a good idea?' He hated that he sounded like her father. Fathers were a waste of space.

But in the handful of seconds it had taken for him to speak and for her to ignore him, she'd caught the waiter's eye and signalled for more drinks. And then he was carrying another tray over to them, two shots apiece.

'Chin-chin,' she said, holding up her two glasses, one in each hand, and indicating he do the same.

He shook his head. 'Not tonight.' He was gentle but he could tell she was, not offended as such, but piqued.

She half shrugged, mimicking his earlier nonchalance. 'I never drink alone. Somewhere, someone else is drinking too.' She downed them in quick succession. And when she'd finished hers, she reached across the table and drank his too.

His feelings disoriented him. He wanted her to stop, and to ask if she was OK, and to gather her up and kiss away the vulnerability he sensed, but he knew that was a line he hadn't been invited to cross. All he could do was to make sure she got back to her flat, safe and in one piece.

Their food arrived. Her eyes were glazed and unfocused, but she cut up her pizza and ate it in small, neat squares. His fish was overcooked but it tasted good because he was eating it with her.

Conversation between them slackened and stopped. Saul grabbed for words but he couldn't think of what to say to her. She ordered more drinks – wine, this time, and it stained her lips as she drank it down. He sipped his, not liking the woodsmoke taste of the rich red she'd selected for them both, but not wanting to say so, to appear gauche or unworldly.

He excused himself to go to the bathroom. His face looked thin in the mirror, older than his twenty-four years. He didn't want to fall in love. Especially not with her. He couldn't afford to. The choice was stark: drawing her down his dark path or keeping secrets from her.

When he returned, she was no longer sitting at the table. His stomach dropped away. After waiting several minutes it became clear she'd left him on his own. His cheeks flamed, not with embarrassment but with the shame of having been abandoned so publicly in the middle of – it wasn't a date, although it felt like one – dinner. His appetite died and he pushed away his meal, unfinished.

He beckoned to the waiter and asked for the bill.

'Going so soon? I thought you two were going to make a night of it.' A nod at the empty shot glasses. 'It's still early.'

Saul noted the young man's unblemished skin, the definition of his jaw, and decided he was not the type to be deserted by his date. An urge to sully this stranger's perfection, to run the edge of a blade against the jut of his cheekbone, reared up inside him, but he quelled it, accepting it was not the fault of the waiter but his own sense of inadequacy.

He didn't reply but left a generous tip to assuage his guilt.

As he rose to leave, the waiter hailed him. 'Don't forget that.' He was pointing to Blue's leather jacket, which had fallen on the floor next to her chair. Saul bent and picked it up, heard the clink of her flat keys.

'Shit.'

At the entrance to the women's toilets, he pushed against the door, hand on his warrant card. 'Police.' It was a friendly warning, not an official raid, but a young girl in jeans and trainers, washing her hands at the sink, yelped and bolted from the room.

She was in the third cubicle, her legs concertinaed between the tiles and the base of the toilet. The door was locked and so he kicked it once – rapid but hard – and prayed it wouldn't smack into her head.

Blue's body was slumped against the toilet bowl. A stray sheet of toilet paper had stuck to the bottom of her boot. He smelled piss and bleach and the sweetness of her perfume, and he was overwhelmed by an urge to protect her from the demons that chased her.

He wasn't sure if she was drunk or in the middle of another narcoleptic episode, but her eyes were closed, and so he slid his arms under her body and hauled her upwards, propping her into a standing position. When it became clear she was unable to walk, he hesitated, but only for a moment, and then hoisted her over his shoulder. He wondered if she always drank so much or whether it was to dull the edges of the assault. A fury at the officer who'd attacked her reared itself in him. But they didn't know who he was yet. When they found out – and they would find out – Saul would make him pay.

Night had fallen hard and cold when he got outside the restaurant. A blanket of stars lay across the sky and the moon was high and bright. His breath came in smoky gasps. The pavements were empty and he thought about the lonely Christmas that waited for him, and how it might feel to spend it with a woman like Blue.

Her flat was on the ground floor. He found the keys in her jacket pocket and carried her in. She stirred and moaned, and he waited for her to wake up, but whatever was keeping her under kept her there for a while longer, and she slipped into silence again.

Being inside her flat was like being wrapped up in the smell of her. He caught the scent of her perfume again, more strongly this time, and freshly washed clothes and oranges. It was sparsely decorated, a few pieces of furniture here and there, and hardly any clutter. He found the sitting room and didn't bother to switch on the light, laying her on the sofa.

The moon washed her face in its light. She moaned again and he slid a pillow under her head, and with tenderness, unlaced her boots and pulled them from her feet.

Such a long time since he'd met someone like her. Even longer since he'd burned for the touch of another's hand instead of the perfunctory familiarity of his own. He glanced around the flat for signs of a lover. When he used her bathroom, he noticed there was only one toothbrush in the glass and it lifted his heart.

A memory of Mr Silver ambushed him before he had a chance to close his mind to his old master's dark reach. A serial killer whose penchant for victims with medical oddities had seen him attempt to groom Saul as an heir – and almost succeed. Would Blue's narcolepsy have made her a contender for his collection, like Clara Foyle, the little girl he'd saved in return for the reward money? He pushed the thought away. He would have killed the evil bastard a dozen times over before he'd let that happen. A shiver, the fingers of fear playing their tune on his spine. He was gone now, long dead. Just the shadows of the past and nothing more.

Uncertain about what he should do next, Saul lingered, aware of what a vulnerable position he was in, but not wanting to leave her until he was sure she was going to wake up. He covered her with a throw and filled a mug with lemon squash, leaving it on the floor for her to find.

'Saul.'

Her voice – low, intimate in the darkness – touched something inside him, raising the hairs on his arm, the back of his neck. He crouched next to her. 'You're at home now. You're safe.'

'Thank you.' He caught the sour rush of alcohol, the pungent heat of garlic and tomatoes.

She struggled to sit up. 'What happened?'

'I found you in the toilets. Not sure if it was the tequila or the—'

'It wasn't the tequila.' Her eyes were dry but he heard the break in her voice. 'Fuck's sake.'

'Don't be upset. Or embarrassed. I don't care about it.' A smile, the curve of a scythe. 'We all have things about ourselves we're not proud of.' *Like killing men. And wanting to do it again and again.*

He held the mug of squash to her mouth and she let him. Their eyes met, that connection again, the cigarette-lighter spark of it, but this time he didn't look away and neither did she. The air between them thickened with want.

In bed that night, replaying it in his head, Saul wasn't

sure which of them broke first. If pressed, he'd have said it was Blue. But it could have been him. Or perhaps they had both moved towards each other at the same time. The moment had blurred and softened in his memory until he was overwhelmed by the sensation of her lips against his, the heat of her tongue in his mouth, the feel of her beneath him. He was lost in it, swept along by the fluid pull of desire, the loosening of the binds he had tied around himself after the traumatic experiences of his childhood. He couldn't explain why he felt so drawn to her, only that he recognized something in the dark behind her eyes, the magnetic attraction of it.

They kissed until the moon had risen and Saul was at the very edge of his control.

'I should go.'

She didn't try to stop him. Tiredness had settled on her, closing her eyes. He slid his arms beneath her and carried her to the only bedroom in her flat. Blue smiled up at him, sleepy, so intimate. And then she was gone again, pulled under into a world he would never visit, which dominated her without warning.

He'd looked it up – narcolepsy – during a rare quiet moment earlier that day. *A neurological disorder characterized by sudden attacks of sleep.* The French physician Jean-Baptiste-Édouard Gélineau had coined the term in the nineteenth century, taken from the Greek *narkē,* meaning numbness or stupor, and *lepsis,* attack or seizure. A rush of sympathy. He ached for her.

With an old-fashioned chasteness, he arranged the covers over her body. Her lips were swollen, the skin beneath reddened by the kisses they'd shared. His hands lingered at the hollow of her throat, and he closed his eyes, forced his breathing to slow. With restraint, he unclasped the choker she wore around her neck, resting the tip of his finger on the flutter of her pulse. He waited for a few minutes, savouring the feel of her life in his hands.

Wanting to make sure her jewellery was safe, he pulled open her bedside drawer, intending to put it away for her.

Every part of him stilled, except his breathing and his heart, which thundered in his chest, painful and insistent, powered by the rush of epinephrine.

A sheet of paper lined the drawer but his attention was not focused on that. He kneeled down, a soaring bird taking flight inside him. He didn't touch the items he'd discovered but his eyes were greedy for them. A fire-singed scrap of paper. A sealed plastic bag containing a lock of hair darkened with blood. Two or three fingernail fragments. Crime scene evidence.

All at once it became clear to him why he'd felt so drawn to her, that darkness he was sure he'd glimpsed, and then dismissed. Blue was a collector, just like him.

29

A few hours before the Holdens disappeared

Nightfall and the rain-dirty clouds rolled in, streaking the sky with their watercolour strokes. To Julianne, it felt like the atmosphere was freighted with pressure, bearing down on her until she found it hard to breathe. She'd planned to walk to Piper's but the downpour had started, falling in dense sheets that soaked everything within a couple of minutes.

A pair of golden orbs lit the gates as she drove into Seawings. In the intimacy of evening, the house looked beautiful and she squashed down a pang of envy. Piper always landed on her feet.

She parked her car on the drive and made a dash for the front door. Her friend opened it before she knocked, immaculate as usual. Quiller always insisted that looking good was easy if you had money and Piper gleamed with it.

The wine was poured. Her friend knew her tastes well. Still, it irked her every now and then. She might have preferred a gin and tonic or vodka with soda.

'Did you bring it?' Piper was tipping olives into a dish.

Julianne was struck by how poised her friend seemed, in spite of everything. But that was one of the reasons they fitted together so well. She calmed Julianne with her measured outlook, logic and strategic thinking, while Julianne encouraged Piper to take a lateral view.

Julianne pulled a week-old copy of *The Times* from her handbag. The rain had soaked into the edges, softening them, turning them to pulp. She spread the newspaper across the table and turned the pages, the newsprint smudging in places.

Piper leaned over it, scanning the Death Notices. 'Which one?'

Julianne picked up her wine glass and pointed to the announcement she'd ringed in red, third from the top.

ANOUSHKA LEE THORNTON, 42, MUCH-LOVED WIFE TO DAVID AND MOTHER TO SEBASTIAN AND THOMAS, SADLY PASSED AWAY ON 27 OCTOBER AFTER A SHORT ILLNESS. FUNERAL WILL BE HELD AT ST MARY'S CHURCH, MIDTOWN-ON-SEA ON 16 NOVEMBER. ALL WELCOME. FUNERAL FLOWERS OR DONATIONS TO SHINE CANCER SUPPORT.

'That's tomorrow,' said Piper. 'But is it too local?'

Julianne plucked an olive from the shining pile and popped it into her mouth. 'He's our best chance. No one else comes close.'

Piper returned to the table with a handful of cocktail sticks. Julianne ignored the passive-aggressive gesture and used her fingers to select another olive. Piper speared one with her wooden stick. 'You or me?'

'I'll go,' said Julianne. 'His wife had dark hair. I'm more his type, I think.'

'Is he worth it?'

Julianne pulled a folder from her handbag, withdrew a sheaf of printed papers and passed them to her friend. Piper flicked through them, chewing her bottom lip. When she was about halfway through, she stopped at a page, whistled and answered her own question. 'Oh, he's worth it.'

This irritated Julianne. Of course he was. Her meticulous research confirmed it. She and Piper had done this for years, scanning the newspapers for wealthy widowers who would be vulnerable to the targeted attentions of women. She was practised enough to know each mark needed to be worth a minimum amount of five million, and to cut their losses after a certain time-frame. Longer than six months and he wasn't going to break. If a man was going to succumb, it took about four months, sometimes much less if anonymous flowers were sent to his dead wife's funeral, implying a secret lover. Loneliness and physical need. A desire to remind themselves they were still alive. A listening ear from an attractive new friend who didn't push or demand things.

Julianne and Piper had been the recipients of large sums of cash, jewellery, cars, even property over the years. Because they were a partnership, they sold and pooled everything. The arrangement worked well.

Neither Quiller nor Gray had the faintest idea their wives ran secret bank accounts and secret lives.

Mostly, the women attended funerals during the day when their husbands were at work. If travel was involved, they explained they were going to a hotel for a couple of days away. In this way, they grew their secret escape funds.

Their motives were different but the result was the same. Encouraged by Piper, Julianne was trying to loosen the shackles of her abusive marriage, to muster enough financial independence to break free. Quiller was clever and sly, a devastating combination. He knew how to discredit her, to hide money and disguise their wealth. He would rather give his fortune away than share it with his wife in an amicable divorce. For the first time in her life, Julianne had control of her own money. Piper had shown her how.

Both women had agreed – in those painful early years of motherhood – these lives of suburban stultification were not for them. They loved their children, were indifferent to their husbands – at least, that's what they told each other – and dreamed of travel to Alaska, Svalbard, Thailand and the wide open roads of the American Midwest. As soon as the children were old enough to go to university, the women would flee. They would stay in touch with them, naturally. But theirs would be a life of no formal ties, moving from one place to the next.

They had taken shelter in their marriages, using these years of stasis to work towards their goal. The fates had smiled on them. Their lives had become entwined, their families growing together like the branches of two trees, but it was the women who were the roots of those trees, entangled in ways that bound them forever.

It wasn't about a sexual attraction to each other or denying themselves physical love, although they had kissed once after a vodka-soaked night in the early days of their friendship. Piper had laughed afterwards – 'that was unexpected' – and Julianne had blushed, but they had both misread the nature of their relationship with that misplaced kiss. What had drawn them to each other was not lust, but the recognition of a kindred spirit.

To the surprise and comfort of them both, this bond had not faltered. It had withstood the slings and arrows of marriage and parenthood, and deepened into an enduring platonic love. By some unspoken instinct, they both understood the misstep they had taken. If they hadn't been seduced by societal convention, they might have chosen to share a life together, in celebration of female friendship, the liberation of it.

Except, as the years had passed, the goalposts had moved. Julianne no longer wanted to leave her children and Piper – the least maternal of the pair – had become dangerously obsessed by money. Neither had been honest with the other about their change of heart.

And what Julianne had no way of knowing was that Piper – her best friend and loyal confidante – had promised exactly the same future to her husband Gray.

The front door slammed. Julianne gathered the papers into the folder and slid them into her bag as Riva appeared in the kitchen.

Her mother held out her arms. 'Have you eaten?' Riva ignored her and hefted her school bag off her shoulder. 'Hey, Julianne.'

'That looks heavy.' Julianne smiled at the teenager.

'Just some stuff left over from the show. I offered to bring it home because the school's hired out the theatre tonight. It's just make-up supplies and wigs.'

'Sounds interesting.'

Riva's face lit up. 'Did you know you can get stage effects for sweat and tears? And prosthetics that can change the shape of your nose or give you a wart.'

'Why don't you show us?' said Piper, trying to engage her daughter.

'I've got homework.' Her reply was curt. 'History. An essay on the British Empire.' She helped herself to an apple from the fruit bowl and disappeared upstairs.

Piper swallowed a mouthful of wine. 'So help me God.'

'She's just being a teenager.'

'Will you talk to her for me? Convince her I'm not the enemy.'

Julianne felt a twinge of sympathy. 'If you say so.' Relenting, she picked up a cocktail stick and speared her third olive. 'No Gray tonight?'

Piper's expression hardened. Something about her had become unreachable. Mask-like and impossible to read. A coldness spread over Julianne.

'What's happened?'

Piper wouldn't meet her eye. 'It doesn't matter.'

Julianne forced a smile and finished her wine. A long time ago, when Piper had starting seeing Gray as a lover instead of a friend, she'd wondered whether she would lose her to him. He was a charismatic man. They'd often disappeared together for weekends without telling Julianne, who'd been single at the time, and Piper's absence from their flat had stung. Even now, Piper and Gray shared many things that Julianne could not. Their marriage. Two children. The everyday intimacy that comes from sharing a home. She tried to ignore the prick of jealousy that sometimes overwhelmed her. But over the years, she'd come to understand that Piper had always put their friendship first. This knowledge reassured her now.

But she knew what an excellent actor Piper could be,

particularly skilled at masking her own pain or worry. She touched her friend's hand. Repeated the mantra that had steered their friendship. 'I'm here if you need me, OK?'

She couldn't know it yet but in six hours' time, Piper would call in the lifetime of debt her friend owed her and Julianne, reluctant but still weighted with gratitude, would find it impossible to resist.

30

Wednesday evening

The day after the Holdens disappeared

Saul shut the door to Blue's flat as quietly as he could manage and checked his watch. Still early, and he was at a loose end, all pent-up sexual energy and nowhere to put it. He wasn't ready to go home yet.

From his wallet, he withdrew a scrap of paper with that same scrawled address he'd carried around for a while now. If he closed his eyes, he could still hear that crying baby in her crib from all those months ago. He wanted to see it again for himself.

A boxy newbuild on the edge of town. Nothing remarkable. The windows were lit by the flicker of an oversized television. The front door was made from uPVC and the opaque glass glowed with light. Saul dug his hands in his pockets and watched as an older man emerged from the house. Under the street lamp, his face was notched with grief. 'I'll be home late.' Irritation hemmed his words.

The resemblance between them was striking.

As the grey-haired man walked past him, Saul shrank

into the upturned collar of his coat. The television flicker switched from the lurid green of a football pitch to the lurid colours of a game show. The man lit his cigarette and didn't trouble Saul with a second glance, even though Saul had visited his house the previous day in the course of his son's murder investigation.

He'd been there one week earlier too. Although no one at Essex Police had the slightest idea about that.

On that particular autumnal day, the type when leaves whirled and collected in corners, and the late-afternoon air smelled of bonfires and rain, Saul had watched a younger man wander down that same front path on his way to the pub.

Saul had followed him in his car and sat outside, watching customers come and go until dusk became evening, and the sky was black and soft with drizzle. It was eight months since that man had been arrested for beating a young woman half to death, three weeks since his conditional discharge, and 243 days since Saul had copied his address from a police file. When that man left the pub a few hours later, Saul had slipped from his car and tracked him along quiet, shiny roads. Several pints of lager had loosened the man up, rubbed off the edges of his awareness, and as they approached the entrance to a large public park, Saul had quickened his step and called out his name.

'Austin Kellaway.'

The man had turned, comically surprised, the alcohol in his veins making him sluggish and slow to react. He'd stared at Saul, almost invisible in the darkness, and recognition had flashed across his face.

'I know you,' he'd said, drunkenly stabbing his finger at the detective.

Saul had replied by moving behind the man, swift as the clouds scudding overhead, and looping a forearm around his neck. Using all of his strength, he'd manoeuvred the man through the park gates and into the undergrowth, shielded by trees and bushes. Saul was taller, but the man was bulkier and he'd fought back, all the savagery which pulsed beneath his surface roaring upwards in a wave of defiance. He was that easily identifiable sort of man, aggression leaping from him in arcs of static, always spoiling for trouble. But Saul was ready for him, and he'd allowed the man to pull at his forearm, allowed him to believe his actions were weakening Saul's grip. He wanted this man – no, he was much less than a man – to focus all his drunken energies on loosening the choke-hold because Saul was waiting for a moment so fleeting he would miss his chance if he wasn't alert.

In that breath of space between the man dislodging Saul's arm from his throat but before he'd had a chance to gather the fullness of his strength, Saul had acted. With a fluid, decisive motion, he'd kicked out the man's legs, forcing him to his knees. Using a restraint technique he'd learned in his training, Saul bent the man's arms behind his back until he'd cried out in pain, and cuffed him. With his other hand, he grabbed the spit hood he'd stuffed in his coat pocket and pulled it over the man's head.

The man had bucked like an animal fighting for its last breath. In some ways, he was. The spit hood – spit *guard*, the police called it, but Saul knew a euphemism when he heard one – covered the man's face like a carrier bag. While the fine mesh covering allowed air to circulate, the plastic shield across the nose and mouth, if positioned incorrectly, could – and had, in several cases – lead to suffocation.

Saul had paid careful attention to this detail.

His hair was damp with rain, the wind chilling his skin, but he'd welcomed the discomfort because the unkind weather had kept the park empty. Straddling the man, he'd turned his own face up to the sky and let the water cleanse him. The man had thrashed beneath the weight of Saul's body, trying to lift him off, but he was no match for the young police officer, who let out an exhilarated cry.

Saul had leaned forward, pressing the man's face deeper into the dirt, and counted to twenty. The plastic shield cut off his oxygen supply, and through mucus and muffled tears and an inflating sense of dread, the man whose picture would soon end up plastered across the Major Crime Unit's incident room fought with a ferocious hunger for his life.

As he'd felt the curve, the resistance, of the man's skull beneath his hands, Saul had faltered, the conscience that shadowed the Other Thoughts whispering to him, *warning* him. But then he'd remembered the butcher-shop smell of blood, and the shape of the baby against his shoulder, and the way the broken-up body of her mother had reflected in the dark spheres of her eyes, and a blankness came upon him.

He did not raise his hands from the man's head until he had stopped moving.

When it was over, he'd removed the spit hood and the handcuffs. An ornamental lake lay across a footpath and down a small gully, and he'd half kicked, half rolled the man's body until he was near enough to push it into the water.

Before he'd left the park, he'd changed his clothes, decanted his shoes, jeans, gloves and overalls into a carrier bag and dumped it in a recycling bin next to the supermarket on the high road.

The only thing he'd kept was the lock of hair he'd torn from the man's scalp during those last, violent moments before death had come for him.

When Saul had driven home to his old digs, still riding his high, he'd showered and changed before settling himself in front of his apothecary chest, where he'd reconstructed that crime scene from months earlier. Except this time, the pipe-cleaner woman towered over that worthless piece of scum and a pipe-cleaner baby – with a tiny tuft of hair – watched from a matchstick cot, clapping her pipe-cleaner hands.

31

The day the Holdens disappeared

Church Farm was at the end of a pot-holed track that teased obscenities from Gray with every jolt. Only when he'd pulled into the overgrown yard and killed the headlights of Julianne's car did he allow himself to relax. A security light announced his arrival although it didn't matter. The nearest property was two miles away.

Three or four tiles were missing from the eaves, the chimney stack was cracked, and a vivid sheen of mould clung to the brickwork. The metal of the cowshed roof had corroded and rusty tears rolled down the length of its white-washed walls.

Gray fumbled in his pocket for the key. The drive had taken longer than he'd expected as he hadn't dared to stray above the speed limit. His body was stiff from the journey and his hands were caked in dried blood.

His mind was racing. He wasn't sure if they'd made the right decision. But he was here now, so he'd better make the best of it. He thought about calling his wife but he'd turned

222

off his phone, remembering a documentary he'd watched once. *The police can tell where a suspect has been by triangulating the signal of the nearest masts.*

At least the power was on. The hallway was dusty with neglect, and smelled of damp and mice droppings, but there was light, and Piper had said the heating still worked. He found the boiler and switched it on. The pipes groaned but he heard the hot-water tank crank into action. At least he could wash the blood off his hands.

He didn't know what had happened at Seawings.

He loved his wife, of course he did, but she had a way of getting under his skin that triggered a rage inside him. She had always been smarter than he was, and it was true he found that difficult at times. He'd fucked up. Just when they were on the brink of their shiny new life. With Mr Moore's millions hidden away, he had more money than he'd ever dreamed off.

The kitchen was surprisingly clean. He'd expected a layer of dust or the smell of rotting food, but it was well kept. His stomach rumbled. It was so late, but he hadn't eaten since lunchtime and was too adrenalized to sleep.

After a bowl of tinned lentil soup – it looked old but tasted fine – and a glass of metallic water, Gray climbed the stairs, one creak at a time, to bed. He chose the smallest bedroom with a single bed – the idea of sleeping where his mother-in-law had died was unpalatable, and it was at the back of the house, protected from the blunt knife of the wind and rain. The sheets and pillowcases felt damp but not dirty. He lay on top of them, fully dressed, his coat pulled over him.

In the quiet of the night, a chill settled on him. He got

up again, searching for a blanket. On the landing was a linen cupboard. He remembered this from the last time they'd stayed here.

As he gathered up a pile of lambswool blankets, he stubbed his toe against something hard. He bent down to discover a Louis Vuitton suitcase, tucked behind the hot-water tank. Not Marisa Sharp's but his wife's, identifiable by its monogrammed initials. He frowned and then pulled it out, kneeled and clicked open the steel latches. Inside was a selection of clothing he'd never seen before and several rolls of banknotes, held together by elastic bands.

Piper Holden was not dead. She was angry. When Gray had advanced towards her with that expression of menace on his face, she had wanted him to think she was afraid because it tipped the balance back into her favour. She cowered. She flinched. Her very best acting. And then she threw a plate at him.

She hadn't intended to hurt him but to shock him, to force him into penitence and to consider the consequences of his actions, part threat, part festering distaste at his affair. But the plate, weakened through years of use, had broken down the middle when it struck his arm. Acting on instinct, he'd made a grab for it, to prevent the ceramic from shattering against the expensive floor tiles and cracking them. But the angle of the plate's sharp edges – and the force of it, propelled by her anger – had resulted in a freak accident which aggravated the existing wound on his hand. The bleeding was immediate and profuse.

'I'm sorry,' she said, wrapping a tea towel around his palm, pierced by guilt. But he didn't chastise her or even exclaim.

She wondered if his lack of reaction was in acknowledgement of his own poor behaviour. Bright blood soaking the cotton, head bent, he walked away from her.

She followed him out of the kitchen and into the shadowy cavern of their drawing room. 'I'm sorry.' And then again. 'I didn't mean to.' But he acted as if he hadn't heard her.

'Gray.' Sharper than she intended, but she hated to be ignored. When he didn't answer, she repeated his name again.

'What? *What?*' He swung around and threw the tea towel at her but misjudged his aim, and it caught one of the low-hanging icicle crystals on the chandelier, misting it with blood.

'I didn't mean to hurt you.' She reached for him. He tensed, still angry, but then her fingers curled themselves into the back of his hair, and he softened into her embrace. This was a familiar dance. They stood for a moment, two lovers caught in the shadows.

'It's going to be fine.' As she spoke, her mouth moved against his chest, feeling the warmth of him, his familiar shape. The security he'd always represented. She felt him relax into her. 'We'll work it out. We just have to hold our nerve.'

'We've got the money,' said Gray. 'We'll go to ground.' He smiled into her hair. 'Fresh start and everything.'

She let him talk, turning her head until her ear was pressed into him and she could pick out the steady march of his heartbeat.

'Let's do it.' His voice climbed in excitement. 'Wake the children up. We could go now. The life we promised ourselves. Travel. Excitement. Adventure.'

'What about Julianne?'

He laughed. 'What about her? She'll finally realize that your family comes first.' He chucked her under the chin, a gesture of tenderness. 'It's about time, don't you think?'

They stood a while longer until the bleeding had slowed. Piper found a bandage in the medicine cupboard and wrapped it around his wound.

'You should go,' she said. 'The longer you stay here the greater the chance of the children waking up. We don't want them caught up in all of this. I need to explain things to them first.'

'So you'll follow?' he said. 'With the children? And our passports?'

'I promise.'

'I love you.'

'I love *you*.'

When the lights of Julianne's car had disappeared from the driveway and Seawings fell into silence again, Piper picked up the bloodied tea towel and put it in the washing machine. She put the broken plate in the bin. For a long while, she sat in perfect stillness at the kitchen table. At 2.31 a.m., she dialled the number of her best friend from her mobile phone.

'I'm frightened, Julianne. Gray said he's going to kill me.'

32

Thursday morning

Two days after the Holdens disappeared

The nasal call of the kittiwakes woke him, those ghost-white birds that haunted the sea stacks rising from the sweep of water below the coastguard's lookout.

Saul stretched his body in the dawn dark of his bed, the feel of Blue's kisses still fresh on his lips. Would she want to spend an evening with him again? God, he hoped so, because he wanted that more than anything he could remember wanting in his life.

But that would have to wait. O'Neill had summoned them to an 8 a.m. briefing and he was going to be late if he allowed himself to linger over his memories of last night.

The wind slapped his face as he walked the coastal path, the seabirds cresting the thermals. He loved it here. The open skies and the taste of the early morning cockle haul and the salt spray drying on his skin. With Blue here too, he could imagine himself putting down roots and staying for a while, flying under the radar but paying off society's debts when the criminal justice system failed its victims.

Damp seeped into his shoes as he crossed the marshy flats. A lone cormorant flew overhead and he tracked its progress, transfixed by its throaty, rolling cry. He stood at the cliff's edge and followed it until it was lost to the seascape. A weak sun was pushing through the clouds, its diamond glints on the water. Something flashed in his eyeline and it made him stop, searching the waves for its source. Another flash as the sun broke through, not the glitter of reflective light but something much bigger, not belonging to water, unnatural and out of place, but the clouds filled up the sky again and it was gone.

The briefing was almost full when Saul arrived. He slid in the back, scanning the room for Blue. DI O'Neill was standing at the front, his trouser crease knife-sharp and an ironed shirt, but his face was crumpled from lack of sleep and progress. As he clapped his hands and the chatter ceased, Blue slipped through the door and stood next to him. Both looked forward, but her hand brushed his. A vibration of pleasure ran through him.

On the screen was an image of the bloodied writing on Riva Holden's bedroom wall.

'You told him?' Saul was surprised she'd checked in with her findings. Last night, they'd agreed to report their discoveries – the cash, the security footage of Gray in different clothes and the handwriting – together as soon as the briefing was over.

'Of course not.' She spoke out of the corner of her mouth. 'I don't know what this is about.'

'As you're all aware, the Holden family has been missing for two days. No one has heard from them. There have been no sightings. We have no sense of where they are, although we do' – he checked his watch – 'as of 7.21 a.m., have a warrant to search Holden Investments, which might shed some light on things.'

The briefing room was silent except for an officer who repeatedly clicked the mechanism on his ballpoint pen until he became aware of O'Neill's scowl.

'We've been working on the theory that the blood in Riva's bedroom belonged to a member of the family. Our aim has been to establish which family member.' His words rang out across the room, not a hint of tiredness, each syllable cutting through the expectant hush.

'The results of the blood samples have come back to us,' said O'Neill, his face unreadable. 'The blood on the mirror doesn't belong to Piper or Gray Holden.' A pause. 'Or either of their two children.'

A ripple of surprise made its way around the room. This was not what they had expected. A female officer at the front – Saul didn't know her name – asked the question that everyone was thinking. 'Do we know whose it is?'

'No,' said O'Neill, his tone brusque. 'Do you know why?' He stared around the room at his team. Not one of them answered. They didn't dare when he was in this kind of mood.

'Because it's not real blood.' Saul felt a swoop of exhilaration in his stomach. His instincts had been true. 'It's fake.' O'Neill was pacing now. 'Hydrolyzed corn starch. Propylene glycol. Methylparaben. Potassium sorbate. Do I need to go on?'

He looked from one officer to the next until the air rang with silence.

'Which begs the question: what else about this set-up is staged?'

For the last day or so, the police officer Blue and Saul had been surreptitiously searching for had eluded them. Saul had managed to ascertain he was a detective constable working on the case of the mother killed by her husband with a propane cylinder, but because they were involved in separate investigations, their paths had not crossed. So far.

This morning, however, a stroke of good fortune meant their team was filing out of the briefing room at the exact moment this particular police officer was waiting to go in.

The young detective, who'd just finished sharing the evidence they'd uncovered the previous night with O'Neill, felt a pinch to his hand. And a whisper. 'That's him.'

An officer with a shaved head was smirking at Blue in such a way that Saul was left in no doubt who it was. Every fibre in his body urged him to confront him and he was forced to exercise extreme self-restraint.

The man winked at Blue, who looked away. A senior officer strode up, calling out to him. 'Lynch.' His voice was sharp, insistent. 'Doug.' The officer in question turned around. 'Can I have a word?'

So now, at last, they had a name.

33

Tuesday, early hours

The day the Holdens disappeared

Moonrise. The light flooded through the window and pooled on their bed. Quiller liked to sleep with the curtains open, but Julianne preferred the secrecy of darkness. She listened to the clamour of the wind, banging its drum on the roof. The rise and fall of his snores. Sometimes they woke her up, but not tonight. Tonight, she was awake and waiting.

When her mobile phone rang at 2.31 a.m., that shrill call to action, she jumped, even though she'd been expecting it. She didn't answer it immediately, but let it ring several times until she felt Quiller stir into wakefulness, and then she reached for it, feigning sleepiness. 'Piper? What's going on?'

Quiller switched on his bedside lamp. She felt his eyes on her, but she didn't look at him. She frowned, pushed herself up and back against her pillows, and cocked her head.

'Slow down, I can't understand what you're saying.'

A pause. 'Are you safe?' Another beat of silence. It was a dance. A rhythm. And she was practised at its steps. 'Piper?' And repeat. 'Piper?'

Eleven seconds later, she lowered the phone, concern indenting her forehead. Rain sprayed against the windows like gunfire. The moon was dulled by a cavalcade of clouds, racing across the sky, faster than her heartbeat. The wind – a riled, aggressive creature – clattered the tiles on the roof.

'What's going on?' Quiller was rubbing his eyes, his hair sticking up in tufts. 'Is Piper OK?'

Julianne considered her next words with care, weighing them out. 'It sounds like Gray has lost it.'

Quiller's interest waned. He yawned, low-key and sleepy, and settled back into the bed. 'A fucking domestic. Nice of Piper to drag us into it. I've got an important meeting first thing.'

'Do you think I should go down there and make sure everything is OK?'

'I think you should keep your nose out and go back to sleep. They're probably drunk or something.'

Quiller switched off the lamp and rolled away from his wife. A few minutes later, his breathing was steady and even. Julianne silenced her phone, set her alarm for 4.30 a.m. and smiled into the darkness.

The wind drowned out everything, but she turned off her alarm before it sounded. She'd barely slept, the taste of stale wine in her mouth. A light doze, drifting in and out for an hour or so, but mostly she had lain still until the appointed time.

Her clothes were in the spare room where she'd left them before going to bed. She checked her phone, listening to a voicemail left by Piper at 3.37 a.m., and dressed as quickly and quietly as she could.

The streets were an empty canvas, painted with rain. She ran until she reached Seawings and did not see another soul. The grabbing fingers of the wind pulled her hair from its ponytail, the brined air soaking her face. Her mind pulsed with all that she had to do.

The house was as Piper had promised it would be. In darkness. No tell-tale electronic beep of the alarm. The red recording light of the CCTV cameras extinguished. She listened – for Piper and Riva and Artie – but there was silence.

Working methodically, using the torch she'd brought with her, she laid out bowls and spoons on the kitchen table. Piper's oversized Tupperware containers of cereal and a pot of jam. She reached up to the cupboards for china coffee mugs and checked their mobiles were plugged into their sockets and put Piper's car keys on the counter.

She checked her phone for Piper's list.

Answer first call in earshot of Quiller (witness)
Silence phone to allow me to leave voicemail (evidence!)
Put school bags by front door/kitchen
Lay out breakfast things
Untidy our beds
Turn on the radio
Collect cash from the hut
Delete this message

She ran upstairs. It felt strange to be alone in Seawings during the hollow hours of the night. The house still held the scent of them. Riva's bedroom was a mess of teenage chaos. Nothing untoward. She spotted the overflowing bag of stage make-up the girl had shown her earlier, half unzipped and spilling across the floor, and her pyjama bottoms inside out on the bed, as if she'd removed them in a hurry. Along the corridor, Artie's bedroom was surprisingly ordered for a teenage boy. Nothing more than a couple of dirty mugs and a mud-streaked rugby kit shoved in the corner.

Piper and Gray's bedroom was in darkness. Julianne wasn't sure whether to risk switching on the light because it would place a time on movement inside if it was seen by a passer-by or neighbour, but then she decided it didn't matter. She could hear Piper's voice in her mind.

'Authenticity, that's what we're aiming for. The police have to believe we left – or were taken – in a rush. So what if there's activity inside the house in the early hours? Do what you need to.'

The bed was neat. It was clear neither Gray nor Piper had slept in it, so she pulled back the covers and mussed up the sheets, indenting each pillow with her fist. Gray's cologne was on the dresser and she lifted it to her nose, inhaled the scent of him. Piper always landed on her feet: the better house, the better husband.

But that was the past. This was for their future. Although a treacherous voice acknowledged this was now Piper's dream and not hers.

The first birds were singing by the time she'd ticked off nearly everything on the list. She made coffee in the stovetop pot and poured it out, wondering if the mugs would hold their heat until the Holdens' vanishing act had been discovered in – her eyes flicked to the kitchen clock – a couple of hours or so.

She put slices of bread in the toaster and deliberately burned them, so the kitchen would smell of toast.

As she placed the coffee pot back on the hob, a scraping noise caught her attention. Julianne froze, the horror of the unexpected drumming through her veins. She stilled, every sinew of her body straining to listen. She had almost finished, but being caught now would be catastrophic for them all. There it was again, a scratching metallic sound. Fear walked its way up her spine. She held herself as still as she could manage, buttoning down her breath. But the security cameras were switched off, the interior screens blank, and she had no way of checking who or what it was.

A split second to make a decision.

She bolted for the front door, not daring to linger, knowing the key to success was a convincing set-up. She had the presence of mind not to slam it, but to close it with care, the wood barely whispering in the frame, the lock mechanism engaging with a click, and then she was sprinting up the road, faster than she'd run before.

Back home, all was silent and as she'd left it, Quiller snoring softly, the children's bedroom doors still shut. She slid beneath the covers, a light sheen of sweat coating her body, and despite the cocktail of adrenalin and panic, she surprised herself by falling into a deep sleep almost as soon as her head touched the pillow.

Daylight was flooding the bedroom when she woke later to a cold bed. Quiller had left a while ago – his 'important meeting' – and when she went downstairs, she called to her children.

Henry appeared, a slice of toast in one hand, his bag in the other. 'I'm off to school now, Mum. I've got music practice tonight. And I might stay at Jake's.'

'Where's Emelie?'

'Dunno. I think she's left already. I haven't seen her this morning.'

Julianne tried to ignore the needle prick of hurt that neither daughter nor husband had bothered to say goodbye. She watched her son, a lovable puppy of a boy, walk down the path. If she had known what the next few days would hold, she might have run after him and held him in her arms until the threat had passed, as she'd done when he was a baby almost lost to the sea.

But she didn't. Instead, she raised a hand in farewell and didn't even wait for him to reach the end of the path. All she could think about was covering for Piper, the key in the lock and the setting of their trap.

She changed into her running clothes, her friend's voice a commentary in her head. 'You need to keep to your schedule. Head to my house as if we're going on our usual run, *come what may.*'

It was only when she was jogging down Seaview Avenue and into Marine Parade, as she did every Tuesday morning, that she remembered. In her hurry to take flight from Seawings, she'd forgotten to retrieve the hidden bundles of cash.

34

Tuesday, early hours

The day the Holdens disappeared

The children were confused at being dragged from their sleep. Piper had considered leaving them behind, but the family's 'disappearance' would not be so dramatic then. And what if Mr Moore's men showed up? It didn't matter what Riva and Artie said to the police later – it would be over then – but it needed to seem as if they'd been abducted by Gray for the next stage of her plan to work.

'Come on,' she said, coaxing them from the 3 a.m. warmth of their beds with thick jumpers, the lure of hot chocolate, and lies. 'It's a surprise. Dad's organized it.'

'I've got a maths test tomorrow. And my history homework is due in.' Riva was rubbing at her eyes, pulling off her pyjama bottoms. 'Why do we have to go in the middle of the night?'

'It's a long journey. We need to set off now to get there in time.'

She left Riva dressing herself and woke up Artie. He was less resistant than his sister, but bemused. 'Where's Dad?' A yawn. 'Where are we going?'

Piper soothed him with the promise of a day off school. 'It'll be fun.' His protest was weak but heartfelt. 'I'm supposed to be going to Joe's for band practice tonight.'

'You'll have to miss it, I'm afraid. This can't be rescheduled.'

She'd always been good at juggling things. After she'd hustled the twins from their beds, she checked again that the security cameras had been disabled and made sure the kitchen was tidy and clean.

While they were upstairs getting ready, she shut herself in Gray's study and searched her mobile for the audio file she'd recorded earlier that day. Finger poised on the play button, and this time using the landline, she dialled Julianne's number. At 3.37 a.m., she left a voicemail.

When the children had zipped up their jackets and were waiting in the hallway, she held out her hand. 'Give me your phones.'

'What?' Riva was outraged. 'Why?'

'Because we've decided it's about time this family spent some time together instead of staring at screens.' Riva rolled her eyes, but Piper wasn't having that. 'And because I told you to.' She could project steely fury better than either of them. Not for the first time, she thought how much freer her life would have been without children. 'Give.'

Piper left them charging on the kitchen counter. 'They'll still be here when you get back.' She held up her own to show them. 'See, I'm doing the same.'

The street was cold and dark when Piper led them out of the front gate. A sharp wind lifted the leaves.

'Where are we going?' Riva was surly. 'Why aren't we taking your car?'

'All part of the surprise,' she said. Her daughter wasn't ready for the truth.

A battered Land Rover – Piper had driven her mother's old car from the farm a few weeks ago and hidden it in a lock-up she'd rented in town in preparation for a night like this – was parked outside the entrance to Seawings. The door was unlocked. Piper felt in the glovebox for the key and started the engine, suppressing a smile. Julianne was so reliable and had done as she'd promised. Even the tank was filled with petrol.

She drove away from Seawings, her home for the last decade, without a backwards glance.

The children were asleep within minutes. With no phones, the lateness of the hour and the rocking motion of her mother's car, it was an inevitability.

In her head, she ticked off her mental checklist. Everything had gone smoothly. Even if the police decided to search her mobile phone, they would find no incriminating messages. And it would take them days to recover the ones she'd deleted. It had all fallen into place. But that didn't surprise her. Being organized brought its own rewards.

Except she couldn't relax, worry gnawing at her. She struggled when it came to being dependent on others. Would Julianne have the composure to hold everything together? Their plan – crafted with such meticulous care – depended on it.

Within half an hour, they'd hit the motorway, the miles to Midtown stretching behind them like contrails of cloud, thin and insubstantial, fading into the night. If she had her way, she would never go back.

She'd promised Gray she would stop at his office before driving out to the farm. *Don't worry, my love. Leave everything to me.* In spite of all that he'd done, he'd believed her. Probably because she'd never broken a promise to him before. But there was no chance of her retrieving that bloodied shirt from his desk. None at all. It could not have worked out more perfectly if she'd planned it.

Her mind drifted back to the events of that afternoon, her husband so stupidly trusting, so pitted with guilt and remorse that his logic was clouded.

Piper had watched Gray exit the front door of his office and walk down the high street. She had checked the time. By her reckoning, if he went to buy lunch at his usual sandwich shop, she'd have around twenty minutes. Half an hour, if she was lucky. She would have to be focused and efficient. No distractions.

Charlotte was sitting at her desk when she walked in. 'Hello, Mrs Holden.' Her smile was bright and practised. 'Mr Holden's gone for lunch, I'm afraid.'

She'd feigned disappointment. 'What a shame.'

'I'm sure you could catch up with him. He's only just left.'

She had waved a hand, loosened her scarf. 'It's fine. I'll wait for him in his office.'

A flicker of uncertainty had crossed his PA's face. 'I've got a doctor's appointment in a bit.' Gray had made his views very clear, it would seem. *Nobody is allowed in my office without me. No exceptions.* She could almost hear him say it. That's what he impressed upon each new personal assistant when they started working for him.

'I know Mr Holden doesn't like anyone poking around in his office.' A warm smile, inviting trust. 'But he won't mind if it's me.' *Smile again to emphasize the point.* 'You go to your appointment. Take the afternoon off. I'll square it with Gray.'

Charlotte had blushed, as if Piper had somehow read her mind. She'd hesitated. Then a tentative smile in return. 'Thank you – go right in.'

Gray had many failings, but he was a scrupulous keeper of records. He had his own coded system, but Piper was as familiar with the business as he was. She was the one who'd encouraged him down the path of investing clients' money – and defrauding them. She knew about every client, every deal and every transaction, however minor. Insisted upon it. Which was why she was here now. Something didn't add up.

But it suited her that Gray was the face of the company. Behind the scenes was more her *scene*. The business was in Gray's name too. He'd offered to make her a director for tax purposes, but she'd declined, even though it went against her best interests. When the shit hit the fan, she didn't want to be caught with her fingers in the till.

She had closed the door behind her and sat in his chair. Through the window, she could hear voices in the street, the hum of passing traffic. She'd stayed longer in Midtown-on-Sea than anywhere in her life. She hadn't expected that. But Gray had somehow persuaded her to stick around.

Children had never been on her radar. She could still remember that wintry Saturday evening when they'd swapped Maldivian sunsets for the January pall of Heathrow airport. After a missed period, she'd bought a test as soon as they'd passed through customs, and had sat with her knickers around her ankles in the cold public toilet, picking at the peeling skin on her tanned thigh, stippled by goose flesh.

Three minutes was all it took to alter the course of her fate.

Her first reaction had been denial, the emergence of that faint line a hallucination brought on by a twelve-hour flight and tired eyes. By five minutes, that hallucination had become a certainty.

When she had emerged into the arrivals hall, Gray, then her boyfriend, had been leaning against the wall, reading the newspaper. His eyebrows had disappeared into his hairline when he'd seen the expression on her face.

'It's positive?'

'Yes.'

'Oh fuck.'

She didn't know what she had expected, but there was no moment of joy, no flinging their arms around each other, no wrapping up the package and labelling it 'To Daddy'. Instead, all she had felt was the sharp click of handcuffs closing around her wrist, chaining her to domestic life.

There had been no question she would go ahead with her pregnancy. Even though she did not judge others, her devout Catholic upbringing meant it was not a possibility she was able to entertain. And so he had proposed and they'd married as quickly as time would allow, before her bump had begun to show.

She loved them. In her way. But having children had forced her into putting down roots when, in the past, she had always cut herself loose.

The statements were locked in a metal cabinet in the corner of the office. With efficient fingers, Piper flicked through several pages, clocking dates and names and sums of money. She recognized them all, but none stood out or caught her eye. If her instincts were correct, she would have to go back further.

May. April. March. February. January. Still nothing. Her eyes flicked to the clock. Five minutes, at most. Or less, if she was unlucky.

She was about to give up her search when she noticed the tell-tale white triangle of a corner of A4 paper, slipped between two dividers and tucked at the back of the cabinet. Piper pulled it free.

Typed in neat rows on a single sheet was a list of transactions she'd never seen before collected under the heading 'AUTUMN'.

Her mouth dried. These were not regular payments but chunks of cash here and there: £9,000 in September, £7,500 in October, £6,500 in November. Mentally, she totted up the amount of money. It came to almost one hundred thousand pounds. She looked for winter, for the rest of the seasons, but there was nothing. Of course there wasn't.

With trembling fingers, she noted down the account number and dates. The payments had all been made to the same bank account but there was no name. It was not enough. Not yet. But it confirmed her suspicions and now she had a place to start.

The electronic beep of a mobile phone. But it wasn't hers. She opened his desk drawer and there it was. Gray's phone. He was rarely without it and this was a gift. She tapped in his passcode – they'd always been open that way – and searched for a name: Autumn.

Messages. So many messages.

Cool as always, she scanned them. Blackmail was such an ugly word. It disgusted her more than the sex. Thinking on her feet, she fired off a message from Gray's phone, inviting Autumn Ellis to come to the office that afternoon for *further discussions to their mutual benefit regarding the financial situation*. She then pocketed it, planning to return it later.

Voices sounded in the hallway. *Gray*. Her heart thumped, a painful sensation. She closed the drawer with a controlled movement, wincing even then at the sound it made, and turned the key in the lock.

By the time her husband entered his office a few seconds later, she was twirling around in his chair, grinning at him as if she didn't have a care in the world.

Once she had said goodbye to her husband, Piper spent the afternoon watching the entrance of his office from the coffee shop opposite and had seen Autumn Ellis arrive on time – but not leave.

When Gray had hurried out a few minutes later – alone, his face pale with shock – she'd left some pound coins on the table and slipped across the road for the second time that day. Charlotte was at the doctor's, as she'd known she would be. Piper was the one who'd persuaded Gray to let her take the afternoon off.

The woman was lying on the office floor, hair matted with blood, a bruise blooming at her temple like the lilac roses Gray used to bring home every week.

She had crouched over her, careful not to touch. Autumn's eyelids had flickered and opened. Her eyes were so pretty, flashes of hazel and amber. Piper could see the appeal, a bland kind of beauty that didn't age well. She had smiled down at her. 'Did you enjoy fucking and blackmailing my husband?'

Autumn had struggled to sit up, a darkening around her pupils, a shrinking of her spirit. She opened her mouth but it was clear she was struggling to form the words, still reeling from the blow to her head.

'Where's Gray gone? To fetch help?'

With effort, the younger woman shook her head. Her voice was raspy, as if it was pulled from somewhere deep within her. 'Ice.'

Piper observed her with dispassion. The elegant neck, the stylish clothes. It might have been her, twenty years ago. 'Tell me, did you receive a message from my husband inviting you here?'

The woman – still a girl, really – hesitated, confusion playing across her features, but under Piper's gaze, she conceded the truth. 'Yes.'

'And you *wanted* to see him?'

'Promised I'd come if he asked me to.'

Piper kneeled over her husband's lover, brushing a strand of hair from her forehead. Her voice was low, conversational. 'I bet he was surprised to see you.' Autumn's eyes gave her away, that subtle flick to the left, a subconscious acknowledgement.

Piper's face was almost touching hers. 'Do you know why?'

She blew sharply at Autumn, startling her and making her blink. 'It's because he didn't send you that message.' The room was silent except for the injured woman's rapid breaths and the hum of the traffic outside. 'I did.'

Piper removed her phone from her handbag and placed it on the floor.

'Look at me.' Her voice was scalpel sharp. Autumn did as she commanded but fear radiated from her.

The women locked eyes. Again, Piper was drawn into the well of her stare. Had Gray gazed into those pools of floating amber as he'd fucked her? That thought hardened her heart and her resolve.

She removed the woollen scarf from around her neck. Activated the audio recording app on the handset. Autumn Ellis watched her, a wariness in her expression, a primal instinct for what was to come next.

With the righteous strength of the wronged, Piper pressed her scarf against the young woman's mouth and nose, the full tilt of her body behind it, grunting with the effort of it.

The blood on the floor thinned and spread.

Autumn bucked a couple of times, kicking out. She tried to say something, her voice rising in protest, but it was just a series of unidentifiable sounds, muffled against the scarf. One foot caught the leg of a chair, tipping it over with a blunted thud.

Still fighting, Autumn rolled herself towards the phone but Piper stopped her, pressing down harder. Slim fingers clawed at the scarf but weakened almost as soon as they'd touched the fabric. Piper kneeled on Autumn's arms and sat across her chest, grabbing her hair and hitting her head repeatedly against the floor. She let out a scream at the thrill of it, the adrenalin kick.

Dazed from the repeated blows to her head and the lack of oxygen to her brain, Autumn's strength faded like the dying sun. Within a few seconds, she'd stopped moving and instead looked into Piper's eyes with the limp resistance of the damned.

As intimate as sex, perhaps more so, Piper held her gaze and watched that light dim, their eyes locked in mutual understanding, not a climax of sexual gratification, but the last sunset.

When it was over, Piper lifted the scarf from the woman's face and wound it back around her own neck. It smelled of Autumn's scent. 'God help us all,' she said and turned off the recording.

With her trademark cool-headedness, Piper noted a couple of things. The woman was in the same position as she'd been when Piper had arrived. Good. Gray had to believe she'd died by his own hand.

The second was her own surprise. She'd forgotten how much she enjoyed the power of turning off someone else's light.

35

Thursday morning

Two days after the Holdens disappeared

Saul was sent back to the Hilliers' house instead of DC Williams. He was joined by O'Neill. The subtext was that this job was too important for a new recruit to handle alone – but he was showing promise. Blue had returned to Seawings.

The sky was the flat grey of a winter morning, empty of colour, but the air was rich with the brine of the sea and the pungency of estuary mud. Saul could smell it as they walked up the garden path, even though he couldn't see it.

Mrs Hillier was startled to see the men but invited them in. It was the second time Saul had been here, but she seemed jumpy and distracted this morning. Her friend's disappearance was taking its emotional toll. Or perhaps she sensed the snake-like striking instinct of O'Neill, an ambush waiting to happen.

The detective inspector indicated she sit down.

'Mrs Hillier.' Gone was his sympathetic tone. 'We've identified the source of the blood at the Holden house.'

Julianne paled. 'Oh God. Whose is it?'

O'Neill didn't beat around the bush. 'No one's. It's fake.'

She frowned, then understanding dawned. 'That's a good sign, isn't it?' No one answered. She looked between the men. 'Riva's stage make-up. So Riva did it then?'

Without warning, Saul withdrew a set of keys from his pocket and tossed them in her direction. 'Do these belong to you?' Instinctively, Mrs Hillier reached out to catch them. With her dominant hand. O'Neill nodded at him, grudging thanks for his flash of insight.

'You're left-handed,' said Saul.

'Yes.' She sounded bewildered.

O'Neill face's was blank, but Saul caught the glint of respect in his eyes. The older man was sharp and picked up the baton the younger detective had handed him.

'No, it wasn't Riva,' he said. 'Because Riva's right-handed, and the "blood" on the mirror was written by someone who's left-handed.'

'It wasn't me.' Her protest was hot and immediate.

'Nobody suggested it was,' said O'Neill, a deceptive mild-ness to his tone. 'Except you.'

The implication of his words hung in the air. Mrs Hillier shook her head, pushed back her chair and thrust the keys at Saul, who gave her a level gaze.

'You and the cleaner let yourself in to Seawings, is that right?' O'Neill folded his arms, but Saul sensed permission to continue from his superior, not censure.

'I've already told you this.'

'What time was that?'

'About 7.45 a.m. The time we usually go for our run.

Emelie's teacher, Adam Moran, can confirm that, if you need him to. He saw us.'

'So you weren't at the house any earlier in the day?'

She stilled, held eye contact. 'I was there the night before, having a drink with Piper.'

'What time did you leave?'

'I've told you this,' she said again. 'Ten, something like that.'

'And that was the last time you were in the house? Until the morning, when you raised the alarm?'

'Yes.'

But she looked down at her lap when she answered. Saul didn't believe her and he suspected O'Neill didn't either. His boss lifted his hand to pause Saul's line of questioning and stepped forward, a carefully choreographed dance.

'Can we listen to the voicemail again? The one Piper left on your phone? We have a recording of it back in the incident room, but I'd like to hear it now. Full volume, please.'

'Of course.' Mrs Hillier reached for her mobile and played the message. Saul watched her. Her hands were trembling.

'What time did you get this?'

She didn't answer but replayed it, the electronic voice filling the quiet of the kitchen. '*One old message. Received 3.37 a.m. on Tuesday 16th November.*'

'I thought so,' said O'Neill.

Saul waited for the detective inspector to strike. He still didn't like the man – his arrogance and dismissiveness were traits he could never admire – but he'd warmed to him, impressed by his acumen. He knew where the senior officer was going with this and held his breath, waiting to see how Mrs Hillier would react.

'If Piper Holden left that message so late at night, why is there daytime traffic noise in the background?'

Julianne Hillier did not move. She did not blink or fidget or react. She was a statue. 'I don't know.'

It wasn't immediately obvious. Not on first play. But now that O'Neill had drawn his attention to it, and with the volume at maximum, the hum of background traffic was unmistakeable. There was no way that recording – the thumps of moving furniture and the cry for help – was made in the small hours of the night.

'What's going on, Mrs Hillier?'

But she was resolute. 'I honestly don't know what you're talking about. You know what time I received the voicemail. You've heard it yourselves.'

'Is your daughter here?' Saul watched her carefully.

Julianne Hillier busied herself with brushing non-existent crumbs from the table. 'She's at school. You've already spoken to her and she doesn't know anything.'

'But she'd fallen out with Riva before she disappeared, is that right? One of her classmates mentioned that in an interview yesterday.'

'Do you have daughters, DC Anguish? Girls have arguments all the time.'

O'Neill gave her a searching look. 'If you remember anything you think you'd like to share with us, I suggest you get in touch. Failure to do so now might harm you later.'

But Mrs Hillier flattened her lips and when they left a few minutes later, she didn't say goodbye.

* * *

O'Neill was striding towards the car. 'Something's going on, but I'm damned if I know what it is.' Saul was inclined to agree. The pieces of the puzzle were scattered everywhere. They just needed to find them and fit them together.

'Right, sunshine. Now's your chance to impress me. Tell me what we know. And what you think.'

Saul considered his words with care. Despite his antagonism towards O'Neill, he *wanted* to impress him. He knew how important it was to keeping his coveted position in the murder squad. Counting them off on his fingers, he said, 'Fake blood, background noise on the voicemail, the stacks of cash, burglar alarm and cameras switched off: it all sounds a bit contrived.'

O'Neill banged the base of his palm against the steering wheel. 'Exactly.' He turned left at the roundabout. 'Do you buy it? The disappearance, I mean?'

'I'm not sure,' said Saul. 'Was Gray violent to Piper? Possibly. And why was he wearing different clothes in the security footage? That's got to be a red flag. But I don't have any theories as to what's happened instead.' The lie thickened in his mouth. He had an excellent idea but he wanted to test it first.

Still, he needed to prove to O'Neill he was on the ball, and so he threw out a bone. 'Although I wonder if we should have another chat with Emelie Hillier.'

'What makes you say that?'

He told the inspector that one of Riva's classmates had mentioned some ruined flowers on the night of her show. 'She might have an idea if Riva had any enemies. And remember what Dr March said. The card with Riva's bouquet and the message on the mirror were written by the same woman. But it wasn't Piper Holden.'

O'Neill agreed. 'We'll head back to the Hilliers' later. I'm not finished with Julianne.'

Saul tucked away his smile of satisfaction. During his brief interaction with Emelie, he couldn't help noticing she gave off that air of closeted secrecy he recognized from his own childhood. It was more than teenage truculence. He sensed an uneasiness about her, a jagged edge.

O'Neill was on the telephone, barking orders through the Bluetooth as he drove towards the offices of Holden Investments. 'I want a full background check on Piper Holden, anything you can dig up and as far back as you can go. And the same for Julianne Hillier while you're at it.'

Saul watched the houses blur and fade as they drove further into town. In the distance, the tide was out and he could see the mudflats pockmarked with geese.

For a few minutes, they drove in silence. Until O'Neill's phone rang again and a police operator patched through an urgent call for him.

'Hi,' said a hesitant male voice. 'My name is David Thornton and I think I might have some information for you in connection with Gray Holden.'

36

Tuesday, early hours

The day the Holdens disappeared

The moon on the wet surface of the night-time roads made it seem as if Piper was driving on water, but the wind and rain kept the traffic at bay.

Despite the lateness of the hour, she was not tired but hyper-alert, running through the plan over and over again in her head. Gray would be waiting for her. Ready for him and the children to begin a new life, and put the past behind them. Away from Mr Moore's need for revenge and the murder of Autumn Ellis. She hoped Julianne would understand why she'd run when she had. Her hand had been forced.

It was gone 5.30 a.m. when she pulled into the yard of her mother's farm. When Marisa Sharp had moved here from the poky flat of Piper's childhood, it had felt like a personal victory. Her money might not have been able to save Clodagh but it had paid for her mother's retirement. She might not have been an actor but she'd put those considerable talents to work in other ways instead. Some might have called her a con-woman but she preferred to see herself as an artist, playing a role with her particular set of skills.

Her sister's death had left its scars, paper-thin knife wounds upon her heart. The pain of losing Clodagh had rendered her incapable of feeling that intensity of love again. But she would not change that now, even if she could. Those scars were a part of her. They had thickened and twisted inside her until the damaged tissue had become impossible to separate from the healthy. The tragedy of losing her sibling had altered – *hardened* – her in ways that no one had foreseen. Not just in the weeks and months that followed but for the rest of her life.

The farm animals had all gone. In the folds of her memory, she heard a distant whinnying. She'd wanted to keep the horses – had practically begged – but Gray had put his foot down. The cows, pigs and chickens had been given away too. One day soon she would have what she wanted. And no one would be able to stop her.

In the windswept rural pre-dawn, she stood alone under the clouded skies. Both children were lost to sleep, tucked under their coats, soft and even breaths. A flash of tenderness. It was not their fault. She felt love for them. Of a kind. But she was not a natural mother, not a natural caregiver. She was an actor. She had wandered into this life, played her part, and now it was time to move on.

The farmhouse was dark. The wind rattled the thin trees and they bowed to her, a welcome. She left the car parked under the barn, next to Julianne's. At least he had made it here. He had done something right.

Houses held the souls of their occupants in the walls. At least, that's what her mother had always told her. Marisa had died alone here after a bite from her cat had turned septic, and Piper could feel her presence inside the farm. In the old kitchen, a pan was drying on the draining board and Gray's shoes were paired by the door.

Piper, in her coat and thick scarf, climbed the stairs to the bedrooms. She found him in the spare room, his arm flung over the side of the bed, a shadow of stubble on his chin. His wedding ring gleamed as the moon lit the window and was gone again, carried off by the wind into darkness.

She sat on the edge of the bed, staring at the face she knew so well. She didn't love him. She didn't want a future with him. She didn't want *anything* with him. He just didn't know it yet.

He stirred, opened his eyes. 'Piper.' Her name was laced with the slow sweetness that comes from being only half awake.

'Go back to sleep,' she said, soft in the night. 'We're here now.'

With efficient hands, she made up the twin beds in the attic bedroom, covering the damp mattresses with linen she found in the closet. It was a strange room, high in the eaves, the birds scratching their claws on the roof, with a small, square-latticed window that wouldn't open but gazed onto the rolling curve of the hills. Its wooden door with a fat, rusted key that had squatted in the lock for as long as Piper could remember made it seem like a hideaway from a fairy tale.

The children had slept up here when they were small, but there was no trace of their past adventures now, their story-books with torn and scribbled pages, and the soft yellow stack of nursery blankets thrown out long ago. All that remained was a chest of drawers crowned with a vase of dusty silk flowers.

When she had finished preparing the beds, Piper filled a large jug with water and carried it with two glasses up the stairs. Then she returned to the yard at the front of the farm-house and stood in the first blush of dawn, the air cold against her skin. *Hold your nerve, Piper.*

She woke her children and helped them, stumbling with tiredness and stiff from the journey, up the stairs, thrown back to a memory of when they were little and she'd carried them to bed, two monkeys that had clung to her, all arms and legs.

Even now, they were still young enough to want to settle themselves into the comfort of their pillows. She pulled their duvets over them, shut the curtains and kissed them both, her heart weighted with guilt but not grief.

Then she closed the door behind her and locked it.

A pink winter sunrise was painting the walls when she returned to Gray. He'd changed position and was lying on his side, his lips apart, blowing out air in soft, rhythmic bursts. She watched him sleep and listened to the first bright song of the robin.

Despite the early rays of sun, a chill hung over the room, but she removed the coat she was still wearing and draped it across the back of the chair. Next, she unwound her scarf and held it loosely in her hands.

Gray had been such a catch. Handsome. Ambitious. Just the right side of malleable. But a little too fond of other women. Even her friends. Autumn Ellis wasn't the first. She could have lived with his infidelity. Turned a blind eye. But she'd always been motivated by money – and it was that theft of their money that had tipped her into darkness. Anything she might have felt for him because of the years they'd spent together had vanished when she'd discovered the truth about that.

When she looked back at him, his eyes were open, shining in the darkness. 'Aren't you coming to bed?'

She shook her head, just once. 'Not now. I'll never sleep. Too wired from the drive.'

He pulled back the covers, inviting her in. 'Come on. Just for a few minutes.'

Piper hesitated and then slipped into bed beside him, her face pressed against his back, wrapping her arms around his waist. She felt him relax against her. 'This is nice.' He was murmuring, sinking back towards sleep. It would be harder now. She thought about waiting until he'd drifted off again but she couldn't be certain he would. He'd always been an early bird, rising with the lark. If he got out of bed now, her chance would be lost.

She loosened her arms, feeling around for the scarf she'd left on the bed. Her fingers closed around it. So soft. Cashmere. She remembered buying it last winter with Julianne. A Christmas shopping trip to London. Cocktails at Claridge's. The young choristers in their pleated ruffs and robes. Afternoon tea, glazed confections as pretty as jewels.

And Julianne prattling on and on about Gray.

'What do you think he'll buy you for Christmas? Do you mind that his PA's so young? He doesn't deserve you, you know. You could do much better than him.'

Piper pulled the scarf upwards until it was bunched in her hands. Holding each end, she looped it over Gray's head until the fabric pooled at his throat. He murmured again. 'That feels nice.'

She stroked a wayward tuft of hair at the back of his head. 'Go back to sleep, it's still early.'

Eyes closed, he smiled into the shy flush of dawn. 'Love you, Piper.'

'I love you too.' The lie tasted sweet, not bitter at all. She tightened her grip on the scarf and with no fanfare, no sense of drama, she drew it towards her until it became a garrotte around his neck.

At first, he did not react. But as she summoned every sinew of her strength into constricting his airway and the blood-flow to his brain, his body stiffened and his hands rose by instinct to the makeshift noose, trying to free himself from its hold.

Piper did not flinch, did not turn from the task at hand. She executed her duty with the same callousness, the same air of moral depravity as those monsters who haunted the newspaper headlines before they were banished to the dark hiding places of their prison cells. She concentrated on the purity of that moment with a single-minded determination to achieve her purpose: the death of her husband.

A grunt. Gray struggled to raise himself and sit up, but the awkwardness of his position made it impossible for him to move. She felt his panic in the wild flutter of his pulse as she pushed his head forward, one hand pressed against the heat of him, the other pulling the ligature tighter and tighter still, her feet braced in the small of his back.

An indistinct word: two syllables, rise and fall. Her name. 'I'm here.' Another grunt. Anger. Frustration. Fear. She wasn't sure which one. Perhaps all of them. He bucked once. But he couldn't find the strength to resist as his wife of sixteen years squeezed the last vestiges of life from him.

It didn't take long for Gray to stop moving. Even an unfair fight has its victor and its victim. His left leg convulsed, a farewell dance out of time with the music. His fingers closed around the bedsheets, gathering them close as a kind of comfort in his final moments. His wedding ring glinted again, this time in the morning light. He wouldn't see another moonrise. And not once did she slacken her hold on the scarf or soften the tensed muscles of legs made strong from running. 'Let go,' she said. 'It's time to let go now.'

The bedroom was on fire with sunrise. After it was done, she watched the rays spread across his face, rinsing him of the paleness of death. His eyes were open. She stared into them, not compelled to close them, as some might, but to probe them for the secrets of the afterlife. He did not yield them.

She rolled up his body in her mother's rosebud-patterned sheet, knotted each end and dragged it to the edge of the bed. The noise of her busy feet against the floorboards echoed throughout the house. He was a slight man, but death had made him too heavy.

With all that she had, she pushed the bed on its wheels until it was under the pair of leadlight windows that looked out onto the front of the farmhouse. The yard below was streaked with shadows and colour. Not long until the full force of daylight arrived.

She unlatched the metal catches and pushed open the windows, as wide as they would go, the sting of cold air against her skin.

Reaching for one knotted end, she climbed onto the bed and hefted the still-warm corpse of her husband towards the open window. The weight of him almost defeated her. She could not move him, could not ease the bulk of him upwards, as she'd intended. She lost hold of him and his body tumbled backwards and knocked into her, his hand flopping out of the sheet.

Steeling herself, she dug for the reserves she called upon when running those last miles and the bite of the lactic acid was almost enough to make her stop. Almost but not quite. She tried again, pushing and heaving and dragging. She did not stop until she'd hauled his body onto the lip of the windowsill.

The farmhouse – remote and silent – was typical of its kind. Honey-coloured walls and a slate roof. A clear drop from first floor to yard below.

With a burst of strength, she shoved her dead husband through the unlatched window. He hit the ground like a sack of grain, his body lolling from its makeshift shroud, the sheet unable to contain him. The sight of his hand – the hairs on his knuckles and neat half-moons of his nails – was a powerful reminder of what she had done, but it did not faze her. She retrieved his phone from the bedside table, ran downstairs and folded him back inside the sheet, not looking at his face at all.

The rest was easier than she'd expected. She drove Julianne's car over to the battered remnants of her husband, as close as she could park it. She unlocked the back door, crawled into the seat and reached down for the sheet, stained with dust and leaking blood, and dragged him inside.

And then she drove across the overgrown fields of her mother's farm to the fishing lake in the middle of the property, released the handbrake, and watched the car roll down the slope, into the water and disappear.

37

Thursday lunchtime

Two days after the Holdens disappeared

Swearing under his breath about the delay to the investigation but not able to ignore the possibility of a significant lead, O'Neill took a detour from Holden Investments to the address David Thornton had given them over the telephone.

He was waiting for them on the doorstep when they arrived. Saul's first impression: handsome, wealthy, and awkward with whatever truth he was about to impart.

O'Neill indicated to Saul to take the lead, which surprised him, and he flushed with pleasure. He would need to watch that. In the past, he'd never cared about seeking approval from an authority figure, but he *wanted* O'Neill to rate him. The feeling unnerved him. 'I gather you have some information you'd like to share.'

David Thornton's dark eyes clouded. 'To be honest, it's uncomfortable but I think it might be something you need to hear.'

When he opened up to them about becoming a widower, about how it had felt to lose half of himself, O'Neill's face creased in empathy. 'I know what that's like.' And Saul realized how little he'd known about the older detective until now.

'That's what makes this even more difficult,' said Thornton. He pushed a pile of laundry from the sofa and sat down, gesturing to the police officers to do the same. 'It seems my wife may have been having an affair with Gray Holden, the missing man.'

Saul flicked a glance at O'Neill. He managed to keep his expression neutral but the young officer knew his mind would be in overdrive. He continued his line of questioning.

'Are you sure?'

Thornton's eyes filled with tears. 'No. I can't bring myself to believe she would do that to me. It's blindsided me, to be honest. I didn't think she was the cheating kind. But it looks like it's a possibility. And now she's dead and I have so many questions but I can't ask her any of them.'

'When did you find out about this?'

'On the day of my wife's funeral.'

O'Neill removed a piece of Lego from beneath his thigh. 'I'm sorry. That's a kicker.'

The sounds of children laughing floated down from upstairs. Footsteps thudded across the landing followed by a shriek of joy and a thump. Saul guessed the brothers were jumping off a bed.

'They don't know anything, obviously,' said Thornton. 'I'm glad they're laughing. It's been a while.'

'So how did you find out?'

'He sent a floral arrangement to the church. I found the card and Julianne told me.'

'Julianne Hillier?' The edge to O'Neill's voice was sharp as broken glass.

'That's right. Didn't she tell you? She's close friends with his wife.'

'No, she didn't.' O'Neill had taken over now. 'And was there anything else to make you think they'd been having a relationship?'

Thornton rubbed his finger in a circular motion on his temple, as if he had a headache. 'That's the weird thing. There weren't *any* signs. I checked her mobile and computer afterwards but there were no messages or emails. Nothing at all. She didn't even have his number stored. I suppose she must have had a second phone or something. And she was with me most of the time, so I've got no idea when it happened.'

An idea struck Saul. He waited for the grieving man to finish and then asked, 'Do you still have the card?'

Thornton rose from the sofa and rummaged in a bureau in the corner of the room. On the front of his trousers was a stain. Toothpaste or washing powder that hadn't been properly rinsed away. A wave of compassion surprised the young detective.

'Wait, I've just remembered. I gave it to Julianne.' Thornton fished in his pocket. 'But I do have a photograph of it.'

The officer examined the screen of Thornton's phone, heart thumping. 'Do you mind sending it to me?'

As soon as it arrived, Saul forwarded it to Blue, asking for an urgent reply. He wavered over whether to write a more intimate message, uncertain of etiquette, both professional and personal, but something compelled him to let her know she'd filled all the space in his head since last night. I'm looking forward to seeing you again.

David Thornton made coffee while they waited, but O'Neill's left leg was jerking in tiny rhythmic beats and Saul could tell he wanted to leave. He drank his coffee in three quick mouthfuls and it scalded his throat. His mug was almost empty when his phone buzzed in reply.

I'm looking forward to seeing you again too. What about tonight?

His stomach performed a lazy flip at the prospect of what might happen between them in a few short hours. He read the rest of it, the thrill of anticipation humming through his veins.

Judging by the syntax, the vocabulary choices and the flicks, I'd say it was written by a woman. But I don't think it's the same person who wrote the other card or left the blood on the mirror. And whoever wrote that message, it wasn't Gray Holden.

38

Tuesday morning

The day the Holdens disappeared

Night was a memory now, but even as a milky sun was curdling the winter fields, its secrets lingered. A lark spiralled skywards, seeking seeds and insects in the fallow earth of neighbouring farms.

The lake was a living thing, its surface broken by the wind's undulations, but the car and Gray Holden had vanished, lost to its silted bed.

Piper dawdled through long grasses that bent and swayed. No one had cut them for months. The last time she was here, she'd considered hiring some extra help, but now she was glad she hadn't bothered. When their disappearance became public in a few hours' time, no one would know where the Holden family was, not even Julianne. She gambled on the fact that the police wouldn't think to look here. As far as her old friend was concerned, Piper had sold her mother's farm two years ago.

Julianne would be expecting to hear from her – they'd agreed to see how it played out and had planned a call today

– but her friend would have to wait. In any case, Piper had left her phone at Seawings and Julianne would know that. She couldn't risk contact between them now.

Two days to convince the authorities of the authenticity of their disappearance. That was all. Piper could hold her nerve until then. She'd been doing it for years.

Artie was shouting for her. She could hear him from outside the farmhouse, the low rumble of his fear. But she felt nothing, no flicker of maternal concern and no compulsion to react. They had water. And each other. They would survive.

The noise was louder inside. Her son was banging against the solid wood of the bedroom door and even from the attic, the sound reverberated throughout the empty spaces. She shut the kitchen door and boiled the kettle. Made herself some toast with bread from the freezer which she ate with Marisa's plum jam in precise bites. The noise did not concern her. They were too far from anyone or anything to be overheard. A cry, high-pitched but distant. Now it was Riva's turn, screaming for her mother and father.

She turned on the radio.

Later, when the children had quieted and the afternoon sky was bruised with the threat of rain, Piper rummaged in her mother's boot room until she found a walking stick. She breathed in, composing herself, and stepped into the hallway.

The beams creaked and shifted. If Piper was a fanciful woman, she might have said the house was her audience, waiting for the performance to begin. She might not have been on television or at the National Theatre or the Almeida, but that didn't mean she couldn't give it her all.

She screamed, the sound slicing through the air, carving it up into pockets of fear. Then she ran up the stairs, dragging the walking stick behind her, its rubber ferrule thumping against the parquet.

'*Mum.*' Shouted by one of the children. Riva. And then again, with urgency and streaked with fear. '*Mum.*' Piper called out her children's names, an answering cry. A muffled reply: Artie, this time. 'Upstairs. In the attic.'

Her mother had collected the kind of populist art beloved of the masses. Claude Monet. Pink and purple irises. She lifted a picture off the wall, threw it on the floor and cried out again.

'Stop it, Gray.'

Then she hit the tip of the walking stick against the glass, the walls amplifying the excited shatter of it. Then silence.

Perhaps it was cruel of her. But she had to convince them too.

Winter dusk had edged into the house, painting some rooms with a luminous golden light, filling others with shadows. She crept down the stairs and into the dark spaces of her mother's library, pulling an old favourite that was losing its pages from the shelves and ignoring the cries for help of her children.

39

Two days after the Holdens disappeared

As soon as the police officers had left, Julianne began to shake. She leaned against the countertop, head bowed, drawing in one breath after another, but it was several minutes before she regained control of her body.

She hadn't considered the significance of the traffic noise in the background. In fact, she had barely noticed it, so consumed with all that her friend had asked of her. In a rare misstep, Piper had overlooked it too. Julianne had no idea what Piper had been up to in the recording and she wasn't sure she wanted to know. Except this time her friend wasn't here to hold her hand or come up with a plausible explanation. If Julianne wasn't careful, their plan would unravel with one tug on the thread. She wouldn't mind so much if she wasn't implicated in their disappearance. But she'd begun to feel that while she was ready to leave Quiller, she did not want to leave her children. And she was concerned about Piper's reaction. They had been planning their escape for years. But it was only when Piper announced that night that she was bringing the plan forward that Julianne recognized her own feelings had changed.

And what about the writing on Riva's bedroom mirror? Julianne knew she hadn't done it. She'd felt sick since the police had told her about it. When she'd gone upstairs on that night to check the bedrooms, it hadn't been there. So who was responsible? More importantly, had they seen her?

A cocktail of frustration and panic bubbled inside her. If she knew where Piper was, she would go to her now and ask her what to do. The promised phone call hadn't material-ized, perhaps because Piper couldn't speak freely with her husband around. But she couldn't understand why her friend was so intent on delaying. Everything was in place for Gray to take the fall.

'What's going on, Mum?' Emelie appeared in the kit-chen, dark patches beneath her eyes. Sometimes, on the spur of the moment, she came home from school for lunch. Julianne was struck by how much she had grown in the last few weeks, body curving, face narrowing. She looked so tired though. 'Why do the police keep coming here?'

'Don't worry, sweetheart,' she said. 'It's just routine.'

She began to prepare lunch, chopping vegetables and buttering bread. Emelie lingered in that awkward way of teenagers who want to talk but don't know how to open up.

'Do you think the Holdens have been murdered?' She blurted out the question, not meeting her mother's eye.

'Oh, sweetheart.' She tried to fold Emelie into an embrace, but she was stiff and unyielding. 'You poor thing. This must be awful for you.' She stroked her daughter's hair. 'No, I don't think that at all. The police will find them.'

'But how do you know?' Julianne sensed a challenge in the

girl's voice. Emelie was staring at her, bold and questioning. She looked away, discomforted by what she saw in her expression.

'Because that's what the police do.'

'No, I'm serious, Mum. How do you know?' Her demeanour was odd, unstable, full of spiky aggression, that hallmark of teenage bravado. But she was on the verge of tears too, and that made her vulnerable.

Julianne concentrated on slicing mushrooms. Her knife slid through their springy flesh, an earthy smell of sweet decay rising up to her. 'I don't know,' she said. 'None of us do. But we have to hope, sweetheart, because sometimes that's all we have.'

'Except you *do* know, don't you?'

Julianne froze, the paring blade hovering above the chopping board, its neat pile of pale caps and the exposed underside of brown gills.

'I'm so sorry, Emelie. Clearly, this is all getting on top of you and I've been too wrapped up in myself to notice. You must be so worried about your friend. Do you want to talk about it?'

'I've told you. She's not my friend.'

'Well, I miss Piper like hell and you must—'

'You were at the house. On the night they disappeared.' It wasn't a question. Julianne's instinct was to deny every accusation, but it was clear her daughter knew much more than she'd realized. 'Have you told the police that, Mum?'

'I had a couple of glasses of wine with Piper, that's all.'

'At 4.45 a.m.?'

Julianne's heart gave a painful thump. 'Why on earth would you say that?'

Emelie began to cry, a hot river of tears that would not stop. 'Because I was there too.'

40

Monday afternoon

The day before the Holdens disappeared

Riva had always marvelled at the speed her school emptied when the final bell rang. One minute, the corridors were filled with the shouted noise of hundreds of teenagers, giddy with freedom; the next, the parquet floors and clanging lockers fell silent, as if they'd always been that way.

As joint president of the Drama Society, she'd promised to take some of the make-up and props home because the school's theatre was being hired out. Ordinarily, they might have left them in the dressing rooms, but there had been that spiteful attack on her flowers, and it wasn't worth the risk. Some of the make-up and prosthetics had been imported from America and had taken weeks to arrive at great expense.

Would Emelie be waiting to walk home with her tonight?

Her oldest and best friend – the one who had seen her through everything from being dumped by her first boy-friend to the paper-cut sting of playground slights – had been so distant lately. She'd wanted to ask her what was

272

wrong, but even that seemed too difficult to broach. Perhaps she was jealous of Riva's starring role. But she wouldn't have been any good at that part. *Cabaret* needed decent singers and dancers, and Emelie was neither. She'd done her a favour talking to Mr Moran. But then, a flicker of guilt. Perhaps she *had* spoken out of turn and should have checked with her first. She dismissed the thought, not able to acknowledge, even to herself, that she'd overheard Emelie singing to herself a couple of weeks earlier and feared the competition. Riva collected as much of the make-up as she could carry and headed towards the gates.

As she walked through the leafy school grounds to the exit, she could see her friend's familiar shape in the distance. Her heart gave a joyous knock. But then Scarlett Colman appeared. She watched the girls embrace and set off down the road without a backward glance.

Her mother would have warned her to leave it alone. But Riva had a fiery temper – she'd belonged to the school's Volcano club when she was younger, to help control her outbursts – and she couldn't resist running to catch them up.

'Thanks for waiting,' she said, her sarcasm as biting as the wind.

Scarlett started to apologize but Emelie responded with a cold look. 'We've both got a lot of homework, so we're in a bit of a hurry.'

'Since when have you bothered about homework?'

'We can't all be naturally bright, Riva. Or good at acting. Or beautiful.' Emelie dropped compliments as if they were insults. 'We've got exams coming up, remember?'

'How can I forget? But you don't need to be so nasty. It's not my fault Mr Moran chose me for the show.'

Emelie gave a sarcastic laugh and shook her head in disbelief. 'Really? I don't know how you can stand there and say that with a straight face.'

'I'd better go,' said Scarlett, shifting awkwardly. 'My mum wants me to go to my grandma's tonight, so I'll see you both tomorrow.' She hoisted her bag over her shoulder and made her escape.

'Thanks a lot,' said Emelie. 'You've just scared off my friend.'

'You don't even like Scarlett.'

Emelie didn't answer.

'Have I upset you in some way?' Riva tried to hide her confusion, but she couldn't disguise her hurt. 'What have I done?'

'Two words. Mr Moran.'

'I didn't—'

'He told me, Riva.'

Riva went cold. *Shit.* She would have to ride it out by pretending it didn't happen. 'Whatever he told you wasn't true. Anything else?'

Emelie rolled her eyes. 'It's just hard living up to the amazing Riva Holden with her amazing talents and amazing house and amazing mother. I need a break from it sometimes.'

'Wow.' Silence stretched between them. 'I had no idea you felt that way. But there's no need to bring my mum into this.'

'Why not? She's either at our house all the time or dragging my mum to yours.' She muttered something under her breath that Riva didn't catch.

'At least have the guts to say it out loud.'

'I said, "*At least* my mother likes me, though."'

'What the fuck's that supposed to mean?'

The two girls squared up to each other. Riva could feel a fire rising inside her. She fought to lock it down but Emelie wouldn't stop talking.

'Your mum's always so busy, isn't she? Getting everyone else to do her dirty work. She couldn't even be bothered to pick up your flowers.'

'What are you talking about?'

'That bouquet of white roses everyone was losing their shit over. *My* mum picked it up from the florist and dropped it off at school. And I wrote your card in the car while we were driving here.' There was a taunting quality to her tone that was too much for Riva.

'Your mother's a lying bitch, but I don't go on about it. Ask her about the funerals. They think I don't know, but if my mother's bad, yours is worse.'

Emelie's eyes flashed, triumphant. 'Don't you dare attack my mother when yours is so messed up she cut up your roses with some nail scissors.'

'You're lying.' Riva's face was pale with shock.

'I saw her. When I went back to the dressing room to get my drink.'

'She would never do that.'

Emelie raised her eyebrows. 'Believe what you want but it's true.'

Riva pushed down on her pain, wanting to hurt her friend in the way she'd just been wounded. She arranged her face into a smirk. 'You're going to get a nasty shock when you find out the truth about your mum. She's a thief, Emelie. Stealing money from men whose wives have died. That's pretty low.'

It was a relief to finally say the words out loud to some-one, even if it was Emelie.

The other girl stared at her. 'I don't believe you.'

'I don't care if you believe me or not.'

'How do you know?'

'Heard them talking about it on the phone.'

Riva's anger vanished as quickly as it had arrived. A long-ing for the peace of her bedroom filled her up. Weary of their argument, she turned around and walked away, leaving Emelie open-mouthed on the pavement.

For hours that night, Emelie stewed over the words of her oldest friend. She didn't want to confront her mother but she couldn't stop thinking about what Riva had said.

When Julianne arrived home from Piper's at ten thirty, expansive from too much wine and too little to eat, Emelie waited for her to take herself off to the sitting room. As soon as she heard her parents talking over the rising notes of the record player, she ran into the kitchen, looking for her mother's hand-bag. She rummaged in it, seeking out some kind of evidence – she didn't know what – but there was nothing except a folded newspaper which she tossed on the table.

It was only when she heard her father's voice – heading towards the kitchen, asking Julianne if she wanted another glass of wine – that she slipped the newspaper back into her mother's bag and spotted a funeral notice ringed in red pen.

She couldn't bring herself to kiss her mother goodnight and went to bed early with a stomach ache that didn't exist. Riva was refusing to answer her phone. 'Please call me back.' When she tried again a little while later, her number had been blocked. Emelie didn't blame her. If she was Riva, she wouldn't talk to a bitch like her either.

The night marched on, the wind stamping its feet on the roof of the house. Emelie heard her parents come to bed and the scraping of loosening roof tiles. She must have dozed off because when she woke up later, the curtain of the night had closed around her. Still no messages from Riva. The phone's clock told her it was 4.33 a.m.

She could not sleep, lying in the noisy darkness. A compulsion to question her friend, away from the dramas of the school playground and the pressures of their families, seized her. If Riva wouldn't speak to her, she would go to her instead. It wouldn't be the first time they'd visited each other during the night without their parents' knowledge.

The front door was off the latch which was unusual as her mother was meticulous about locking up after a spate of burglaries in their affluent enclave, but Emelie checked her key was in her jeans pocket and didn't think about it again.

Over the years, she and Riva had flitted between their two homes all hours of the day and night, as if they belonged to both, but, like her mother, she'd always preferred the grandeur of Seawings.

The streets were quiet, but the route felt less familiar in the dark. The sound of the wind and the rush of the waves competed for supremacy. When she rounded the corner, the house was in darkness, and she almost changed her mind and turned back. But as she glanced upwards, a light came on in the bedroom window and a woman with distinctive hair and a slight frame was silhouetted against the glass. Her mother.

Questions – one after the other – jostled for her attention.

What was her mother doing there at this time of night? And why? Did her father have any idea where his wife was?

The light was on for less than thirty seconds before it blinked out. If Emelie hadn't been there at that precise moment, she would never have seen it.

The gardens at Seawings were dripping with rain. Emelie found the key in its usual place and let herself in.

Self-preservation silenced her instinct to call out. Finding out why her mother was there was important, but so was talking to Riva. Was this part of what her friend had warned her about? She burned to know more. But when she reached Riva's bedroom, it was empty. The bed had been slept in but her friend was not there.

And no sign of her mother at all.

Was there some secret she was being kept in the dark about? Frustration and hurt bubbled up inside her. Once they'd told each other everything. But Riva, her oldest friend and confidante, the school's most glittering success story, had not confided in *her*.

On the floor by Riva's unmade bed was the holdall of stage make-up she'd brought home that afternoon. A bottle of fake blood nestled at the top, near the open zipper. In a maelstrom of emotion, she picked it up, intending to 'accidentally' spill it over Riva's sheets and carpet, to teach her a lesson not to exclude her, but when she shook it up, the cap, which hadn't been properly closed by the last person who'd used it, flipped open and sprayed the mirror instead.

Vivid splashes of rust coated the glass.

In shock, she balked at what she'd done. She would need to wash her hands in the bathroom. To clean up the mess of it all. She replayed those words in her head. *The mess of it all.*

Could it be true? Were her mother and Piper doing what Riva had insinuated they were? No. It was wrong. Criminal. They were their mothers. They loved them. Didn't they?

But Riva wasn't in her bed. She'd blocked Emelie's phone. Almost certainly, she'd ignore her at school tomorrow.

On impulse, she picked up the bottle and using its pointed tip, she scratched out a message to her friend: *Make Them Stop.*

41

Two days after the Holdens disappeared

Gray Holden had been dead for fifty-three hours when things started to unravel. Piper was making herself a winter salad with the lamb's lettuce she'd found growing in a sheltered spot in the garden, and so she didn't see the man approaching the farmhouse until it was too late.

He knocked, a brisk but loud rap against the wood. Piper dropped the knife she was holding. She listened for the children, praying they wouldn't react. They'd been silent for hours, most likely asleep, but this would disturb them.

She considered not answering it, but he knocked again, more aggressively this time, and in the distance she heard Artie shouting, and so she stepped onto the front step, pulling the door to behind her. Fair hair. Young. About twenty-five.

Don't over-react. Be pleasant. Forgettable.

'You're a bit off the beaten track. What can I do for you?'

He was wearing a uniform and carrying a package, and at first, he didn't look up, staring down at the electronic pad in his hand. 'Is this Lower Manor Farm?'

'No,' she said.

'Do you know where it is?'

'No idea, I'm afraid.'

He sighed, as if it was her fault. 'Why are these places always so difficult to find?' She didn't answer, and was about to turn away and go back inside when he looked up. A spark arced between them, not of physical attraction, but recognition. He eyed her with a curious expression. 'Do I know you?'

He *did* know her. He'd been working at the butcher's in the village the last time she'd stayed here overnight. Her mother had introduced them. But would he remember her?

He scratched his head. And then: 'There was a woman on the news this morning who looks like you.'

'Poor love.' She ran her fingers through her unwashed strands. 'I hope she has cleaner hair than me.'

He laughed with her, not sure what he was laughing at, but following her cue. 'Well, I suppose I'd better be off now. Try and find that farm.'

'There's a place two miles down the road. They might know it.'

She watched him saunter back to his van and climb inside. An excellent performance from her. Not a flicker of unease, nothing to arouse suspicion. Light and friendly. But would it be enough? With luck, he'd be drinking pints with his friends in the pub by tonight and have forgotten all about her.

But as he started the engine, the attic window exploded in a shower of glass. The jug she had left upstairs with Artie and Riva shattered as it hit the concrete, the noise explosive in the still of the afternoon. And then Artie began to shout, his voice far away but clear.

At the entrance of the farm, the young man got out of his van, indicator still flashing.

What a fucking disaster.

'Are you all right?'

She tried to think, clear-headed, smart. If she hurt him, attempted to *kill* him, he might fight back. She wasn't prepared, no weapon to hand except surprise, and if she failed, he would be a dangerous witness. To him, she was not a woman in distress, held captive against her will, but a smiling if harassed mother. And so her best option would be distraction, to send him on his way and hope he didn't give them a second thought.

'Don't worry.' She jogged over to the van, determined to keep him as far away from the house as possible. She injected a note of disapproval. 'Let me apologize for my children. They were playing a game that's got out of hand. I'll go up in a minute and tell them off.'

A voice tossed forwards and backwards by the wind, too distant to be distinct now. But she knew it well and could pick out the rigid consonants, the looping vowels of his cries. *Help us.*

The faint lines of his forehead deepened into uncertainty. 'If you say so.'

A quicksilver smile. 'I'm sorry if it startled you. Must have been a shock. Don't give it another thought.' Another smile for good measure, to convince and reassure.

Two minutes later, he'd returned to his van and was gone, disappearing down the narrow tree-lined lane, not knowing he'd brushed up against death in female form, and how she'd almost closed her fingers around his heart.

* * *

Piper had run out of time. Even she could see that. But the children had gifted her an opportunity. She ripped at her tights until the nylon was torn, and tugged buttons from her blouse. Scooping up dirt from the yard, she rubbed it into her face, the dry skin of her knees, the bleached fabric of her skirt, and finally, into the parting of hair she'd deliberately left unwashed.

She retrieved the suitcase she'd hidden in the linen cupboard during her last visit and removed the women's clothes, folding them carefully into her mother's drawers. Unless she came back for it, she would have to write off the money for now. But it couldn't be helped. When the police arrived at the farm, they would find it, but they'd assume – and she would tell them – that the rolls of banknotes had been packed by Gray, and take it away as evidence.

Piper had always planned to frame Gray for her murder and assumed the children would escape – or be discovered. But the delivery man had put paid to that. It was too much of a risk. He had witnessed her alive, smiling. What if he went to the police and told them what he'd seen? Yes, in theory her murder could have happened after he'd visited Church Farm, but it would raise questions. Too many of them – and ones she didn't want to answer.

And then there was Julianne and the rest of the money. She would have to go back.

Using a short length of rope she'd found in the barn, she bound her wrists with it, using her teeth to tighten the knots, the fibres getting trapped between the gaps and cutting into her gums. In the furthest corner of the barn, she'd left a threadbare horse blanket and the bucket she'd been pissing in since arriving at Church Farm.

And then, steeling herself for the performance of a lifetime, she stumbled up the stairs to the attic, screaming the names of her children.

The key was in the lock, exactly as she'd left it. Limping into the bedroom, tears tracking through the dirt on her face, she fell onto her knees, bound hands in front of her.

Riva was lying on one of the twin beds, matted hair and listless. Artie was by the broken window, still shouting, but to no avail.

The room smelled of human waste and sweat and despair.

'Oh, fuck, Mum. What has he done to you?' Artie was at her side, holding her elbow and guiding her to the opposite bed. As his fingers worked to loosen the rope's knots, his face darkened. 'Where is he now?'

'He's gone.' Her voice was a whisper. 'When you broke the window, he took the car and drove off. I don't know where.'

'Fucking coward.' More than two days in captivity, the skin had stretched across his cheekbones. Effects of dehydration. 'Who was at the door?'

She tried to think, seeking a plausible answer, a convincing lie. 'I don't know,' she said. 'But whoever it was, I think they scared off your father.'

Artie said something she didn't catch. Her son seemed older, more authoritative, despite his ordeal. Her daughter was a different story. She had not changed position or uttered a word.

Artie unwound the rope with tender hands. She winced, as if stiff from hours of holding her wrists in the same position. 'Where was he keeping you?'

'In the barn. Outside.'

Artie swore again and put his arm around her 'You're safe now, but we need to get some help.'

Piper thought about the phone she had retrieved from the bedside table after she'd strangled Gray and deposited on the kitchen table. 'He's left his mobile downstairs.'

With tentative steps, she crossed the room and sat on the bed next to her daughter. 'How long has she been like this?'

Artie's lips were cracked and dry, a fresh drop of blood forming as he spoke. 'A while. She just sort of shut down a few hours ago.'

Her daughter's forehead was burning. She laid her cool hand across it. 'She needs something to drink. Help me get her downstairs.'

Between them, they persuaded Riva to her feet and manoeuvred her down two flights of stairs. She didn't resist but there was an absence to her that Piper found disconcerting.

Her son poured glasses of water for the three of them. 'Don't gulp it. Small sips.' He switched on his father's mobile phone. Piper wondered if the police were tracking his signal and if it would triangulate between masts and give away their location.

Artie handed her the phone. 'You do it.'

She nodded, accepting the responsibility as hers. She searched on the internet for the incident room number. It didn't take long. Their disappearance was news. Dozens and dozens of stories about them, their faces staring out from a family photograph Julianne had taken at the beach last summer, all smiles and freckles and ice-cream cones: MISSING, FEARED DEAD.

A bored-sounding female voice answered the telephone. 'How can I help you?'

She drew in a deep breath and started to cry. For once, the tears were real, except they were not from trauma or pain or hurt, but relief that her meticulously detailed plan was holding together.

'My name is Piper Holden. My husband has been holding me and our two children at a farm against our will for two days. He's disappeared for now, but we don't know when he'll be back. We're terrified of him. Please send someone to collect us. Tell whoever is running the investigation we've come back from the dead.'

42

Thursday afternoon

Two days after the Holdens disappeared

News of the Lazarus-style resurrection of three out of the four members of the Holden family spread rapidly amongst the jubilant Midtown murder squad.

Before O'Neill had time to delegate tasks and organize a briefing, he'd spoken to Mrs Holden over the telephone from the car park of Holden Investments.

'We're on our way to pick you up and take a statement,' he said. 'Don't move. The local police will be with you in five minutes or so. You're safe now, OK?'

'My husband—' Her voice – already distorted through the speakerphone – cracked in the pin-drop silence of the car. 'He killed a woman.'

Saul, who'd been instructed to take notes, almost dropped his pen, but recovered his composure to record and time-stamp the allegation.

O'Neill was sombre. 'That's a very serious accusation, Mrs Holden. Are you able to provide any proof of this?'

'Yes,' she said. 'I am.'

*   *   *

The shirt was in the drawer at Holden Investments, exactly as Piper Holden had said it would be. They found a record of the financial transactions in the filing cabinet and three empty bleach bottles in the bin. CCTV footage of Gray Holden buying bleach in a supermarket had also surfaced as a result of publicity. Within forty-five minutes, a specialist search and recovery team had been dispatched to the area of the cliffs where Gray Holden had confessed to disposing of Autumn Ellis's body and car to his wife.

Two hours later, O'Neill and Saul were pulling into the yard at the front of Church Farm. Two patrol cars were parked by the barn, their livery bright against the overcast day.

Piper Holden had a blanket wrapped around her shoulders. Dark circles shadowed her eyes. Her son Artie was sitting close to her. Riva Holden sat with her eyes shut, her head resting on her brother's shoulder.

Saul observed it all.

The Scenes of Crime team photographed the attic bedroom, the barn and the unmade bed where Gray Holden had been sleeping for the past three nights. They photographed the broken glass from the Claude Monet picture and the shards from the jug on the yard floor. The washed plate on the draining board and the wilting lamb's lettuce and the tyre tracks of the vehicle in the dust.

They photographed and documented everything, and O'Neill and a couple of specialist officers walked the family through the events of the past two days, making notes and asking questions. When the family had returned to Seawings, been examined by a medical professional, eaten and slept, they would interview them again.

Piper Holden was composed when relating her husband's abuse. She had a memory for forensic detail. He'd kept her bound and gagged in the barn for two days. Yes, he'd been violent to her before, although never in front of the children. Artie Holden bridled when asked about his father, expressing that angry energy of a teenage boy with nowhere to put it. Furious at being held against his will. Humiliated at having to shit in the corner of a room he was sharing with his sister. Hurt at his mistreatment at the hands of someone who was supposed to love him. Riva Holden said nothing.

Through extensive questioning and several telephone calls, the picture they built up was this: Gray Holden was a killer. He had been living a secret life in which he embezzled money from his clients, had extra-marital affairs, was physically violent to his wife – Julianne Hillier's statement corroborated this – and had emptied their joint bank accounts so he could escape to a new life. If he hadn't been interrupted by the delivery driver at Church Farm, it's likely he would have killed his family too. The evidence checked out and it was damning.

And yet an instinct twitched in Saul when he thought about Mrs Hillier and the voicemail recording and the writing on the mirror at Seawings.

O'Neill and Saul drove the Holdens back to their home in Midtown-on-Sea. Essex Police's offer of a family liaison officer to stay overnight with them was declined. Piper had made a statement but they would interview her again in the morning. Their priority now was to find and arrest Gray Holden.

'It's going to be a late one,' said O'Neill, stopping at a

Turkish takeaway for grilled lamb kebabs and hot sauce. 'Eat something now.'

Saul messaged Blue while O'Neill was in the toilet. Tomorrow instead? Her reply took twenty minutes. Already looking forward to it, DC Anguish. A warmth he wasn't used to spread through him. So am I, Dr March.

The briefing room was full of the buzz that swelled and spread throughout the station when an investigation took flight. Saul relished it, especially because it diverted attention from Austin Kellaway's murder.

O'Neill called for quiet and ran through the tickets that were active in locating the suspect. ANPR on Julianne Hillier's stolen car. Fresh checks on Gray Holden's bank cards and accounts. Investigations into the frequently contacted numbers on his mobile phone call log to flush out potential lovers. An INTERPOL Red Notice in case he tried to evade justice and leave the country. Forensics teams were at Holden Investments and Church Farm.

'And – as of two minutes ago – search and rescue divers have found a car registered to Autumn Ellis.' O'Neill was fired up, talking rapidly. The excitement rolled off him in waves. 'Let's find the bastard.'

When the briefing was over, Saul checked his voicemail. He listened to it, intent and alert, and then he walked up to the inspector and quietly made his point. 'Some things don't add up, sir.'

O'Neill chewed on his thumbnail. 'Go on.'

'Dr March says the messages on the cards and the mirror were written by two different women.'

The senior officer shrugged. 'Did you check with the florist?'

'Yes. She gave *both* cards to Julianne Hillier apparently.' A thought slid into his brain and clunked, like those penny-push machines at the arcade. He tried out his theory. 'So it's possible she wrote the anonymous card sent to Anoushka Thornton's funeral.'

'Why would Mrs Hillier do that?'

'Revenge on behalf of her best friend? To make it seem like Gray Holden was having an affair when he wasn't? In the same way that voicemail wasn't actually recorded at 3.37 a.m., and the security cameras at Seawings were switched off.' He waited a beat. 'And what about Mrs Holden? How did she manage to free herself if her husband was keeping her captive?'

'What are you saying?' O'Neill narrowed his eyes.

Saul tried to shape it into words. 'It's very neat and tidy, isn't it?' He paused. 'There's something else you need to know.' He explained the message he'd just received.

To his credit, O'Neill didn't flinch but pursed his lips. For a minute, he considered what Saul had said. 'What do you want?'

'Permission to speak to Julianne Hillier one more time.'

'It's yours. But only if I come too.'

Night had settled over Midtown. The wind and rain had stopped and a filigree web of stars lay across the clear, cold sky. Quiller opened the front door.

'Is your wife in?'

'This is beginning to feel like harassment. What do you want?'

'We can either do it here, or make it more formal and take it down the station,' said O'Neill. Quiller huffed but stood back to let them in.

'Found my wife's car yet?'

Saul felt the pulse of his anger as he walked past him.

Julianne was washed out. The Mallen streak in her hair had widened, ageing her by ten years. She was wearing her coat, as if she was about to go out.

'Off somewhere nice?' asked O'Neill. She didn't answer but sat across from him at the kitchen table for the third time. Her manicured nails were chipped and her make-up was patchy, darkening the creases by her eyes and the folds in her neck. 'You found them,' she said. 'It's wonderful.'

'It is,' said O'Neill, 'but we've got a couple more questions we'd like to ask you, if we may.' He lifted an eyebrow in Saul's direction.

'Is it correct to say that you sometimes organize flowers for Piper Holden?'

She eyed the young detective with a wary expression. 'Yes. She has so many commitments she occasionally asks me to sort them out for her.' Defensive. 'I'm happy to help her if she's pushed for time.'

'Did you arrange the flowers and card for Riva?'

A complex wave of emotions crossed her face. Saul had already checked with the florist. Mrs Hillier was smart enough to know that. 'Yes.'

'And the teardrop arrangement for Anoushka Thornton's funeral?'

The effect was immediate. She paled, eyes flicking between the two detectives like a frightened rabbit.

'A forensic linguist has confirmed the style of language and handwriting on the card sent anonymously to Mrs Thornton's funeral matches yours.' Saul watched her. 'Did you tell David Thornton that Gray Holden was having an affair with his wife?'

To her credit, she didn't hesitate. 'Yes.'

'How did you know that?'

'Piper told me.'

'So you took it upon yourself to send flowers to her funeral, designed to stir up trouble. Why did you do that?'

She was silent, but her fingers were plucking a loose thread on the cuff of her jacket in compulsive jerks. Saul leaned forward, a neutral expression on his face.

'You've already told us you had a couple of glasses of wine with Piper on the night the Holdens disappeared.'

Mrs Hillier folded her hands in her lap, glad to be on firmer ground. 'Yes, that's right. I stayed for a couple of hours.'

'Can you remember what time you left?'

'About ten, something like that.'

O'Neill steepled his fingers. Saul shifted in his chair. The air in the kitchen thickened in anticipation of a storm. 'Can you explain why data from your mobile phone company places you in or around Seawings between 4.40 and 5.30 a.m.?' Both men watched her.

Mrs Hillier sat very still. 'I must have left it there earlier in the evening.'

'But you received a call from Piper in the early hours while you were in bed. Your husband has confirmed that.'

Fixing on a spot above Saul's shoulder, Mrs Hillier made a performance of frowning, then chewed the inside of her cheek. 'I must be getting confused. Perhaps I'm thinking of the night before.'

Neither man challenged her, but all three of them knew the facts did not lie.

O'Neill stood up. 'You've been very helpful, Mrs Hillier. I'd like you to come to the station to be formally interviewed under caution tomorrow at 10.30 a.m. You're entitled to legal representation. In fact, I'd recommend it. We can arrange a duty solicitor if you'd like.' He softened. 'Don't look so worried. We'll untangle it all.'

The two police officers were walking down the garden path when Julianne Hillier's teenage daughter appeared at the gate. O'Neill smiled at her. 'Good news about Riva Holden, isn't it?'

Emelie shot an anxious glance at the house and then at the ground. 'Yeah.' Saul, more attuned to the behaviour of teenagers than O'Neill, stopped. 'Are you OK?'

The girl shrugged, still staring at the ground. 'I don't know.'

His instincts ringing, Saul tried to catch her eye, but she wouldn't bite. He pulled out a card from his pocket. 'Listen, if you need to talk to us or you feel concerned about something, you can reach me on this number. Nothing formal. Just a chat.'

Emelie Holden thanked him and took the card. She disappeared into the house without looking at them once.

43

Thursday evening

Two days after the Holdens disappeared

Julianne heard her daughter come in through the front door, but decided against confronting her. They'd barely spoken since Emelie had confessed to seeing her at Seawings. The teenager had refused to reveal why she'd been out of bed so late but Julianne didn't want to get into another argument. Piper's carefully laid plans were unravelling. Talking it through with her friend was her priority now.

Since the police had informed her of the Holden family's miraculous return, she'd called her friend several times until, finally, Piper had answered.

'What's happening?' Julianne took her phone into the bedroom and tried to conceal her panic. 'You were supposed to get in touch. I haven't heard from you in days. The police are getting suspicious.'

'Leave it to me.' Piper had been her usual cool self. 'All you need to do is stick to the story. Give it a day or two, and then we'll meet up, OK?' She laughed, a soft sound. 'You worry too much. Everything's under control.'

Except it wasn't. Not at all. And now the police had come calling again and she was being formally interviewed tomorrow, and the situation was escalating in a way that neither of them had anticipated. She couldn't think straight. She messaged Piper. The police are on to us. We have to go tonight. And Piper had replied: Yes.

But a tiny treacherous part of her had realized that, while they'd agreed to frame Gray for Piper's murder, they hadn't thought about how to explain Julianne's disappearance in anything more than the vaguest of terms. This realization stung, but it was too late now.

The four of them ate supper together. A lasagne that had been in the oven for so long the pasta had burned and curled at the edges. Julianne tried to eat, but it stuck in her throat, and she couldn't swallow it. Emelie did not speak but picked at a green salad.

'What the hell's wrong with everyone tonight?' Quiller poured himself a glass of water. 'You all look so bloody miserable.'

Julianne couldn't bring herself to tell him about the police interview planned for the morning. Emelie refused to meet her eye. Her son Henry was oblivious, shovelling down second helpings and asking for dessert.

She spat her undigested food into a napkin, cleared the plates and got on with the washing-up. No one offered to help.

Much later, when the children had gone up to bed, their doors shut, hiding bedroom secrets, and Quiller was snoring, unaware of his wife's turmoil, she went downstairs and put on her coat. She didn't kiss any of them goodbye. She chose one small photograph of her children, and collected her passport from the safe, and her purse. She did not take her house keys and removed her wedding ring. She walked out of the door with only the clothes she was wearing and a suitcase containing almost £90,000 in cash which she'd withdrawn from their joint account that afternoon at Piper's request.

The waves were crashing against the cliffs as she walked the familiar route to Seawings. How many times had she made this journey over the years? The streets were quiet, glittering with frost, and she could hear the echo of her footsteps. She slid the back off her mobile phone and stamped on both parts until they were cracked and broken before placing them in a dog bin. She stopped by the postbox and slid in a letter.

It was happening too soon. She didn't want to leave. But staying was no longer a possibility. In framing Gray, they'd sacrificed the luxury of choice. She wondered where he was. Hiding, probably, like a rat in a trap. He was a killer now. For real. Not just in their imagination. Piper had told her what he'd done to that young woman. A sigh slipped from her. Julianne would miss Midtown-on-Sea and the life she had built here, but mostly she would miss her beloved children. But she was too frightened to leave her fate to chance.

Piper was waiting for her in exactly the place she'd promised, her car parked near the shelter by the beach, scarf wrapped around her neck, winter coat buttoned all the way to the top. The windows of the car had steamed up.

'Have you got the money?'

Julianne slung her suitcase onto the back seat. 'It's all there.' She gave her friend a sideways look, testing her. 'How do you think Gray will feel when he finds out what you've done? Do you think he'll dare to come home?'

Piper laughed. 'I don't think there's much chance of that.'

They didn't talk much. They didn't need to. In the end, Julianne decided not to tell Piper about Emelie's night-time visit to Seawings, a protective instinct towards her daughter stirring in her. What purpose would it serve now, anyway? Through the internet, they'd booked a last-minute Channel Tunnel crossing to France. By the time the police realized what had happened, they'd be long gone.

When they arrived in Calais, they stopped for tiny cardboard cups of coffee. Julianne offered to drive for a while, but Piper batted off her concerns. 'We should try and get some sleep at the next rest stop.'

The *aire de repos* was basic and almost deserted, a patch of woodland with a block of toilets that stank of urine. Piper parked her car close to a bank of trees and away from the lights. One or two long-distance lorries were parked up, their curtains closed. Julianne had dozed off, breathing through her nose.

Piper watched her sleep for a few minutes. Then she slipped off her coat and unwound her scarf, not quite ready for sleep herself.

One hundred and twenty miles away, Saul Anguish was letting himself into the coastguard's lookout. It was 2 a.m. and there was still no sign of Gray Holden. O'Neill was losing his shit.

He would suggest in the morning they refocus their attentions on Church Farm. He didn't believe Julianne Hillier's story but he couldn't unpick the truth. He remembered again that he'd planned to press her on the whereabouts of her car and why it had taken her so long to tell them it had been stolen from Seawings. He suspected – hoped – she would crumble at being interviewed under caution. He recognized a weakness around her mouth. She was easily led and easily broken. Failing that, he'd suggest a tap on Piper and Julianne's phones. Or covert surveillance of the Holden house.

It was late but he wasn't tired, his brain wired from a long day at work. He couldn't settle. He prowled the rooms, not yet ready for sleep.

He lit the woodburner in the sitting room, stoking the flames. He made himself a sandwich and ate it, watching the glow of its fiery heart. The rest of the house was freezing, and so he brought his pillows and blankets downstairs, intending to sleep there. In less than five hours, he would need to be back at work.

He hoped he would get to see Blue.

Their paths hadn't crossed at all today and he'd missed her, more than he'd expected to. His mobile phone was on the arm of the sofa and he noticed the blinking light of two new messages. One was an email from Jasmine Faraday, a clerk at the General Register Office, subject line URGENT, which he ignored, and the second was from Dr Clover March.

His heart thumped harder and faster.

Blue. It's tomorrow now. Are you free?

44

Tuesday morning

A week before the Holdens disappeared

Piper removed the dough from the proving drawer she'd persuaded Gray to install when they'd upgraded their kitchen and placed it onto the floury surface, pressing her knuckles into the yielding mixture.

She pounded all her emotion into that dough, rolling and shaping it with her fingers, the fragrance of custard rising from the pan on the stove in a cloud of memory. When she'd moulded and filled a dozen neat buns, she put them in the bamboo steamer, a private ritual for one.

Seawings was looking its best, gleaming and freshly tidied. From the window, she watched the geese take flight, their black wings carving up the flat, wide sky. They flew every winter to the Essex coast from Siberia, making the journey across the miles, migrating in family groups, loosely formed pockets of darkness. She admired their loyalty, their commitment to unity.

Mila had lit the fire in the snug at the back, overlooking

the garden. For all the house's grandeur, Piper was happiest here, sprawled on the sofa that Gray thought too scruffy for the rest of the house. It reminded her of her childhood home, the mismatched furniture donated by friends and the leather armchair that had belonged to her late grandmother, worn thin and cracked from use.

Piper had been finishing her homework when the news came through. All these years later and she still remembered every detail. It was a project on Kew Gardens for Geography, sketching the lilies in the Waterlily House, colouring their petals with purple and yellow pencils made soft through over-use. They had spent the day there, wandering through the vast grounds, eating their lunch by the Palm House and buying ice creams from the shop. She had come home and told her sister all about it.

And now they were in the midst of a June heatwave. The afternoon was swollen, heavy with it. Clodagh wasn't in hospital, not then. But she was pinched and weak, lying on the sofa watching an Australian soap opera. Her sister hadn't been to school for weeks. Her grandmother had died nine days earlier. A stroke, most likely brought on by extremely high blood pressure caused by stress, the doctor had said. Piper, drowsy in the soaring temperatures, rested her head on arms sticky with heat and closed her eyes.

She awoke to the sound of shouting. Her mother. Then a deeper male voice. Her uncle Jack.

'Calm down, Marisa. There's nothing we can do about it now. I've talked to the police and the bank. She gave it away willingly.'

Piper sat upright, listening with interest. When she had jerked awake, she must have jogged her pencil and it had left an unsightly mark across the paper. She would have to start again.

Her grandmother was the wealthiest person Piper knew. She lived in a grand house with a huge garden in a place that took hours to drive to and was cold in the winter. She did not share her money, believing her children should earn their own living instead of relying on handouts. Even when Marisa had begged for help when Clodagh fell ill, she was unmoved, unable to understand why her granddaughter didn't just eat her dinner and be grateful. But it had always been understood the money would pass to the family when she died.

'Clodagh needs to see a specialist.' Her mother's voice was a hiss but Piper could hear it from the kitchen. She glanced at her sister to see if she had noticed but she was engrossed in the television. 'I was going to use that money to pay for it.' Her voice cracked. 'I was relying on it.'

'There's nothing left. It's all gone.'

'All of it?' Her mother was disbelieving.

'Every penny. She gave it all to that fucking charlatan.'

Looking back, Piper could see that was where the dark blot in her family's history had begun. Because her mother drove herself half mad trying to raise money to pay for her sister's treatment while her father watched from his armchair, benignly inert. Clodagh died a few weeks later, her parents' marriage never recovered, and that blot spread until it stained everything.

Piper brushed the memories of her childhood away, like fallen crumbs from her lap. She picked up the box on the table, another part of her past. No one would think twice if they saw it. Perhaps they might consider it a place to store keepsakes. Even now, all these years later, an electric thrill pulsed through her.

Memory box. Steamed custard buns. A tray of pretty tea things.

She watched the spitting tongues of fire, remembering that day exactly two decades ago. Piper poured out the fragrant tea and ate one of the smooth white confections.

Then she leaned forward and opened the box.

Even after all these years, still that curious scent of salt and stagnation. With careful fingers, she pulled out the faded copy of the passenger manifest the Thai authorities had given to her after the accident. A leather wallet stiffened with seawater. A pair of men's Gucci sunglasses with a lens missing. A rusted Rolex watch. Two wedding rings sealed inside a transparent plastic bag.

Piper opened the bag, removed one of the platinum rings and slid it onto her middle finger. It was too big. She flicked it and it spun like a penny on a hard surface.

His name was rubbed soft, blunted by time. *Patrick Clarke.*

Piper watched the flames bow and rise in a complex dance. Twenty years on and she'd never once missed this ritual. Her house was much grander now but she was still the same woman who'd eaten sweet custard buns for breakfast at the hotel and ordered pitchers of rust-coloured iced tea, a newly-wed widowed by nightfall.

Piper never talked about that humid afternoon in November: the sort of day where a thin cotton dress might stick to the river of sweat between the shoulder blades, and the soft hair at the nape of the neck is damp. Her second husband – Gray – knew nothing of it. And never would.

They'd hired a boat for a couple of nights. The idea had been to enjoy dinner under the swollen gaze of the full moon and to explore some of the islands.

Patrick had called to Piper, waving his beer bottle, leaning against the side of the catamaran, his teeth white against his tanned skin, his expensive linen shirt unbuttoned to expose the dark line of hair on his stomach. His voice was excited, urgent almost, but slurred.

'Come and see. It's a leopard shark, I think. Or is it a tiger shark?'

He turned back to the clear waters, following the flick of its tail as it darted beneath the left hull, its striking black saddle-bag markings vanishing from sight. 'Quick, Piper. You're missing it.'

As he'd called out, he leaned over the side of the boat, straining for a better glimpse. Piper, cool in a yellow sundress, appeared from below deck, Martini glass in hand. It wasn't clear what happened next. One minute, he was smiling and pointing in the afternoon heat, the next, he'd tipped overboard, arms flailing, the ocean pockmarked by a series of panicked splashes until he disappeared from sight.

Piper screamed. Patrick, a strong swimmer under normal circumstances, was drunk. His reactions were slowed, his limbs weighted with beer and rum, his heart like brushed wire in his chest. By the time the crew had thrown the life ring and raised the alarm, he'd been missing for several minutes.

It took three days to recover his bloated remains, made buoyant by the gases that had built up inside the cavities of his decomposing body. The skin on his forehead and nose, his elbows and the tops of his feet had been abraded by coral and the sharp edges of stones as they were dragged along the ocean floor and then upwards, to the surface.

Despite evidence of anthropophagy – the fingertips, lips and eyelids were marked with the tell-tale jagged wounding consistent with fish feeding – investigators were confident about the cause of death. They determined that Patrick Clarke had drowned while intoxicated after suffering a fatal heart attack.

Piper, married for less than three weeks, inherited his apartment in New York and his lucrative business shipping expensive wines across the globe, a business, he'd told her, that had been funded from a large sum of money he'd 'persuaded' an elderly woman to invest. He'd laughed when he'd told her, amused. He didn't know that elderly woman had been her grandmother.

It had taken her a year to find him. She had discovered his name and address amongst the letters in her grandmother's possessions and, when she had tracked him down, she inveigled her way into his life.

She made herself everything he wanted in a woman. She dyed her hair three shades lighter. She wore the clothes he picked out. She learned that her acting skills were Oscar-worthy and more than enough to convince him of her love. Not once had the mask slipped until she pushed him overboard. For her sister Clodagh. And her grandmother. His life for theirs.

The £15,000 Rolex watch he'd received for his twenty-first birthday was never recovered. At least, not by the police. In the days that followed, the two-man crew of the catamaran – brothers who had grown up in poverty on one of the islands and painstakingly built their tourism business from a run-down shack – were both arrested for theft, but after detailed questioning and the quiet exchange of bribes from extended family, they were never charged.

Piper had always maintained to the Thai authorities she had not seen what had happened when her husband had fallen overboard.

That wasn't true.

Piper had seen *everything*. She'd witnessed his face transform into that now-familiar expression of ugliness at odds with the landscape, arguing with her in a quiet but vehement voice about the low-cut dress she was wearing, the way she'd looked at the captain at lunch, the amount of alcohol she'd consumed, the flowers in her hair. He'd shoved her so hard that she had stumbled, spilling her drink, and Piper – already regretting her marriage – pushed him back with a ferocity that knocked him off balance. 'This is for my sister, you thief.'

And she'd registered the surprised cry of a falling man breaking the surface of the ocean.

When she inherited the money that was rightfully hers all along, she used some of it to buy her mother the farm. The rest she'd put into a bank account. But once she'd tasted wealth, she wanted more. She was intoxicated by it. The freedoms it promised. And so she set about looking for a man with the same ambivalence towards morality as her. Although he wasn't rich – not then, at least – she recognized it in her old university boyfriend Gray. When they'd reconnected and she'd accidentally fallen pregnant with twins, it had felt like a sign from Clodagh and her grandmother. And so she had stayed, watching their fortune grow. But she'd wanted it all for herself.

The first forty years of her life had been for her family. The next forty would be for her.

A bird's call – solitary and harsh – broke the spell of silence. A crow with a hooked beak that disembowels the soft underside of lambs and drags at their tongues and eyes, seeking out weakness. Just like her.

Piper shifted on the sofa and raised her cup of fragrant tea. '*Chon gâew.*' She recognized the truth of this moment: that through the corridor of time, her past, present and future selves collided, and by marking this day every year, she celebrated exactly how far she'd come.

45

Three days after the Holdens disappeared

When Saul awoke, a winter sun was streaming into the lookout, transforming Blue's hair into a riot of colour. He eased an arm from under her, the numbness replaced by a sensation of loose sand, and checked the time on his phone.

Six missed calls from O'Neill. *Fuck.*

He was late. And this was not just any day. This was his chance to shine. He should have been at the station by now, prepping for his interview with Mrs Hillier. As he cleaned his teeth, he read the email from the clerk at the General Register Office and swore again. He showered, dressed, brewed coffee for Blue, and then took a deep breath and rang O'Neill back.

'I'm sorry,' he said. 'Late night, I overslept.'

'Never mind that.' O'Neill was irritable. 'But get down here as soon as you can. It looks like Piper Holden and Julianne Hillier have done a moonlight flit.'

Saul crouched by the sofa. Blue was waking up and her

308

morning face – crumpled, soft around the eyes – was the most beautiful sight he'd ever seen.

'Hey, sleepyhead. I've got to go in a minute.'

She coiled her arms around his neck and drew him to her. A kiss, long and deep. He didn't want to leave her. 'Stay as long as you like. Make yourself at home.'

Blue yawned and offered up a lazy grin, eyes still closed. 'Do you want to do something tonight?'

He'd been on his own for so long that her interest felt alien to him, but the light she radiated warmed him in ways that no one else had been able to before. 'Yes.' He couldn't think of anywhere he'd rather be.

At the station, there was uproar. O'Neill was a bear with a sore head. The humiliation of having three suspects on the run when he should have brought two of them in was driving his fury.

He fired orders at the team like machine gun rounds. If they were slow to react, the fallout was bloody.

A traffic camera had picked up Piper Holden's car near Folkestone and O'Neill had scrambled resources in that direction. But the women had a head start on the police and the fact they were on French soil complicated everything. 'I don't want fucking excuses,' he said to one officer who'd dared to raise the possibility that accessing cameras on the Continent might mean time delays and red tape. 'We're up against the clock.'

Their first break came mid-morning. The desk sergeant patched through a call from a delivery driver who was convinced he'd seen Piper Holden the previous day at a farmhouse in the Hertfordshire countryside.

'She didn't seem in distress. She was chatting away, a bit embarrassed by her children, I think. No, her clothes weren't dirty, and of course she wasn't restrained. Do you think I would have left her there if she was?'

The results of a background check came in soon afterwards. As Jasmine Faraday from the GRO had confirmed in that email to Saul the night before, Piper Holden had been married before and her first husband – a wealthy young man – had died in a boating accident.

By mid-afternoon, the forensics team at Church Farm had discovered tyre tracks by a lake in the middle of the property. By late afternoon, a diver had found Julianne's car. His flashlight had cut through the murk inside and picked out what looked like the shape of a body.

Saul was willing to bet a year's salary it was Gray Holden.

By the end of the day, floodlights were trained on the lake and a recovery operation was underway. Saul, who'd been sent back to the farm by O'Neill – 'keep an eye on things, see what you can pick up' – remembered how it felt to abandon a body to water. The disinterested coldness of it.

As night spread its dark curtain, they brought Gray Holden out. When Saul saw what was left of him, he felt nothing but a creeping revulsion at the sight of his skin, bloated and incomplete. He wondered if the man had deserved it. When he bent down to see if anything of the father and husband in the photographs at Seawings remained, he clipped a tiny section of his hair and slipped it into his pocket.

He'd tried to reach Blue a couple of times during the day but she hadn't replied. Both of them had been busy with work and so he didn't think too much of it. As he drove back along the main roads to the coastguard's lookout, the street lamps, a necklace of distant orange suns, marked his way. He had stopped at a house on the way home, paying the breeder with a thick chunk of cash, and he wanted to show Blue what he'd collected.

A smile played across his lips when he remembered the feel of her bones under her skin, and her intimate softness beneath him. He burned to see her again.

When he'd parked outside, he stood for a minute, watching the moon turn the water to mercury. He checked his phone for what felt like the hundredth time. Still nothing. He was reluctant to message again. She would reply when she was ready. He carried in the food he'd bought for them – a late-night supper of fresh bread and cheeses, wine, olives, a rich chocolate cake.

The sitting room was cold, the unemptied ashes a reminder of the fire between them last night. The cushions of the sofa had been plumped up, their mugs left upside down on the draining board. Seeing those domestic touches gave him a warm feeling.

He walked up the stairs to change his clothes, humming under his breath. Despite the darkness of the day's discoveries, an unfamiliar lightness filled him.

In his bedroom, the duvet and pillows were folded neatly on his bed. He imagined laying Blue across those sheets, his mouth and hands moving over her body.

From the jacket he'd hung on the back of the door, Saul fished out an evidence bag and wandered into the box room. Gray Holden's hair, fragile and smelling of stagnant water, would be an excellent addition to his collection.

Or what was left of it.

His heart beat out a wild tattoo.

He'd forgotten to lock the apothecary chest and its drawers were pulled open, their contents spilling out. Each of the tiny crime scenes he'd painstakingly recreated had been broken up or obliterated.

His fingers traced the scattered remnants of the baby's hair.

But he had no compulsion to check on his insects. He knew enough about human nature to recognize Blue wasn't one of those kinds of girls who enjoyed cruelty for cruelty's sake.

A weakness in his legs surprised him. He stumbled over to the bed, steadying himself, drawing deep breaths into his lungs. His collection could be rebuilt – it was a tragedy of the human experience that there would be other crime scenes and other murders – but was it possible that his relationship with Blue, a fragile, precious thing, could not?

How could he have misjudged it so badly? No wonder she'd been quiet today. She was not the same kind of collector that he was. The idea of her revulsion undid him.

Saul was not the type of man to cry, but his eyes stung and hurt burned a hole in his chest.

When he'd recovered himself, he began to tidy up the detritus, salvaging what he could, scraps of hair and cloth here and there. It was only when he'd finished that he realized all traces – all *evidence* – of Austin Kellaway's murder had been removed.

Which left him in a very dangerous position indeed.

The cool fingers of night stroked his cheek, comforting him. He packed up his apothecary chest, put on his jacket and climbed back into his car, driving the coast road towards town, a pain sharpening inside him.

Blue's flat was in darkness, but it was on the ground floor and its weaknesses were simple to identify – an unsecured window at the front, a vulnerable back door. And she was much smaller than him, easy to overpower. A hand round her throat. A knife in her side. She wouldn't stand a chance unless he chose to give it to her.

As a teenager, he would have walked that path of violence without a second thought. Removed the problem before it became one. But he was a man now, albeit a conflicted one. Across the bay, he could see the distant square of light he'd left on in the coastguard's lookout. How he had loved it here. Meeting Blue. The grudging respect in O'Neill's eyes. For the first time in his life, it had felt like home.

With a pang of regret, Saul Anguish, avenger of brutal men, a contradiction who trod the blurred lines between light and darkness, imagined himself disappearing into the night as quietly as he'd arrived, alone, as he always was.

Was it time to run again?

A light came on in the window. A shadow moved against it. He pressed his fingers around the cold metal handle of his car door and waited, ready to flee at a minute's notice. It was Blue, searching in the darkness for something. Or someone.

He didn't move, couldn't. She stilled, catching sight of him in the spotlight of the moon. She was wearing a nightshirt, unbuttoned at the front, hanging off one shoulder. He could see the outline of her clavicle, the hollow between her breasts. He waited for her to turn away from him – from the darkness inside him – but she did not. She beckoned to him, calling him forward, and then she disappeared from the window and the door to her flat opened.

He walked towards her like a thirsty man in the desert.

Her mouth was against his before he could speak or offer up explanations for his secrecy, the twisted truth behind his collection, her cool hands resting against the heat of his cheeks. The kiss lasted until he was dizzy with it but he would not pull away until she did.

When she had finished, she glanced up at him and he glimpsed something in her expression: compassion, interest, and that flash of light-resistant opacity that matched his own.

'My stuff . . .'

He didn't want to hear the answer but he had to know. He wasn't sure if that kiss was hello – or goodbye.

She looked down, but a smile twitched her lips. In the midnight shadows, her eyes were black and her pastel hair looked grey. A monochrome beauty.

'It's a good job you've got me watching your back. You shouldn't leave those kinds of things lying around. Especially evidence relating to an ongoing murder investigation, even if he was a piece of shit.' A beat. 'It could get you into a lot of trouble.'

In that moment, he felt a surge of relief. No, it was more than that. A sense of coming home.

'That's another thing you should probably know,' said Blue – and this time her eyes met his, those deep pools he could lose himself in. 'I live for making trouble.'

* * *

INTO THE DARK

Detective Constable Doug Lynch's house was in darkness when Saul and Blue arrived outside. Once they'd had a name for the man who had sexually assaulted her, it was easy enough to find an address. Police officers loved to gossip, even when they should know better.

Forty-five minutes from Midtown-on-Sea but that suited them both. Their combined knowledge meant they knew how to evade cameras and avoid a paper trail. They had come in Saul's car for two reasons: because he'd wanted to protect her and because there wasn't space on her motorbike for what he had planned.

They hadn't discussed what was going to happen next. But Saul knew they couldn't kill him. At least, not yet. A murder of one of their own did something to the police, galvanized them until no stone was left unturned in their hunt for a perpetrator. They couldn't risk it. And it wasn't a conversation he could have with Blue. It was too soon. He didn't want to scare her away. But that didn't mean they couldn't seek their own kind of vengeance.

A more subtle campaign than violence or arson. But a targeted one. Enough to strike terror into the heart of a man who deserved nothing less. Saul's old mentor had taught him a trick or two.

He had come well prepared. He'd been waiting for this moment since Blue had told him what had happened. For all his own misdemeanours, his knowledge of the darkness that haunted the world, Saul remained outraged that a man could touch a woman without her consent. Sexual assault. A physical attack from the weakest sort of individual. For safety's sake, they both wore balaclavas and black clothing, but he could still see her eyes and he could tell she was smiling.

His house was in a rural setting. Detached. Nearest neighbours half a mile away. After a brief recce, they deduced there were no security cameras trained on the front door, just a burglar alarm. Lynch was divorced after having multiple affairs and lived alone. His three children preferred to reside with their mother.

He also suffered from ornithophobia.

There were six cages in the boot and back seat of Saul's car, each containing five birds, incessantly chirping, driving him to the brink of distraction. Budgerigars, lovebirds, canaries, zebra finches and conures. Small enough to fit into the palm of a hand. Or through a letter box.

With quick and gentle fingers, Saul and Blue pushed each of the tiny birds through the slot in Doug Lynch's front door. When he woke up in the morning, thirty of them would be flying around inside his house.

And that was just the beginning.

46

Three days after the Holdens disappeared

The woman staring at herself in the mirror had newly darkened hair and an upturned nose. She cleaned her cheeks
with alcohol, applied the adhesive and waited until it was
touch-dry before she pressed on the silicone prosthetic,
working outwards and smoothing away the air bubbles. By
the time she'd opened the bottle of acetone, dabbing on a
tiny amount to blend out the edges, her nose was elegant
and thin.

Even in the harsh light of the service station's family
toilet cubicle, Piper looked like a stranger. Julianne's Mallen
streak would be harder to disguise.

Piper packed away the stage make-up she'd taken from
her daughter's bedroom and combed her wet hair. Not long
until the hotel in Bruges would open for check-in. She
would need to abandon the car, but her new life was so close
now, within touching distance, and she was confident the
Belgian police would be slow to find it in the cramped car
park of the upscale Hotel Navarra.

Snow, shimmering and barely there, was falling as she navigated the stone bridges and canals that criss-crossed the medieval city.

The police would be hunting for them. Piper had switched off her mobile and disposed of it in a service station bin near Folkestone and was travelling with cash, not cards. At some point, she would acquire a fake passport. Julianne had thrown her phone away, but had set up access to her secret account on a second pay-as-you-go burner. She'd told Piper about it last week, using the same codes she'd used since the days they'd lived together, sharing everything.

Even so, it would not take the authorities long to find them. Staying ahead would require deftness and smart thinking, but money smoothed the way and there was plenty of that.

What a clever illusion she'd constructed to fool the police into believing her version of the truth.

That first phone call to the bank when she'd already instructed Gray to empty their joint accounts, knowing it would be recorded and logged.

The flowers she'd crushed at the school theatre to cast suspicion on her daughter's friends after their disappearance. A risk of discovery, perhaps. But one worth taking to distract the police.

Luring Autumn Ellis to her husband's office as evidence of his infidelity. She could not have predicted the accident but she'd turned the unexpected events in her favour, manipulating Gray into believing he was responsible for her murder.

Implicating him in an affair with Anoushka Thornton to allow Julianne to target her wealthy widower. Repeated suggestions Gray had been physically violent to muddy the waters – and the set-up of their captivity at Church Farm.

Convincing both Gray and Julianne she was planning a new life with each of them when the opposite was true.

The gleaming white majesty of the hotel was a welcome sight. A historic listed monument, they'd always promised themselves they would stay here on their first night. Sauna and swim. Cocktails and piano music. Neither too stuffy nor too elite but the perfect place to hide themselves in plain sight.

Piper pulled into the car park and rested her head against the wheel. A twenty-year journey to reach this point. Framing her husband for murder. Rinsing him of everything. Getting caught had been Julianne's fault. She'd made repeated mistakes, unable to think as deftly as she might, to divert the police with plausible explanations. Decades of friendship had not been enough to save them this time. Gray and Julianne. Weak and dull-witted.

Piper had not been able to conceal her anger in the dark of the car at the *aire de repos* last night. 'Why did you take your phone to my house? So stupid of you.'

'I know that now,' said Julianne. 'But I wanted to have it in case you needed to reach me.'

'But it undermines everything. That simple, foolish act. Because it implies it wasn't a kidnap but a set-up.'

'I'm sorry. But we'll be OK, won't we? We just need to lie low for a while. Disguise ourselves. Let the dust settle.' Julianne had sounded almost pitiful. Pleading.

'You're right.' She'd relented, bored of her friend's distress. 'I'm just tired. We've covered our tracks as best we can. We just need to keep being careful.'

Piper opened the car door and stepped into the afternoon gloom of the hotel car park. The snow was falling more thickly now and she held out her tongue to catch the flakes.

Glancing around to make sure no one was watching, she unlocked the boot to retrieve her suitcase and the one containing Julianne's money.

The bloated face of her dead friend stared back, her body curled like a comma in the cramped space.

Piper had believed in their shared dream. But as with everything she'd learned over the years, the only person she could depend on was herself.

Neutral observers might ask themselves why Piper had stuck with Julianne and Gray for all these years when it was apparent they were both a liability, a millstone around her neck. Or how a woman could lock up and abandon her children. But to ask that question was to exhibit a profound lack of understanding about Piper's motives. It was never about friendship or love, although she had felt both of those things in her way. It was about other base desires: money, bitterness, revenge, obsession.

She closed the boot and locked the car. In a few days, she would get rid of it, the last link to the truth, but for now, she wanted to celebrate.

In the letter she'd left on the table at Seawings, addressed to Detective Inspector Angus O'Neill, she'd explained how Julianne had always coveted her life, and had targeted lonely widowers for money, and how she'd suspected Gray and Julianne were more than just friends, and were planning to kill her and be together.

That if she were to disappear again, Julianne Hillier

should be considered his number one suspect. Not a word of it was true. But Piper Holden had thought of everything.

If they believed she was dead, no one would come looking for her.

The receptionist was warm and welcoming. The bedroom was exactly as advertised. Silk sheets and fat pillows, and a bucket of champagne on ice. She would stay here a week or so. Perhaps longer. They would have no idea where she was. No idea at all.

Using Julianne's phone, she checked her bank account. With the stolen millions from Holden Investments and her friend's suitcase full of money, Piper was now an extremely wealthy woman.

Her conscience did not prick her. She felt no remorse, except, perhaps, a flicker of guilt for her children. In the end, it had come down to her or Julianne.

And one simple truth.

The only way to keep a secret is to make sure there's no one alive to tell it.

EPILOGUE

Monday morning

Six days after the Holdens disappeared

The letters arrived on the same morning, four days after Piper and Julianne had absconded.

The first was addressed to Riva and Artie Holden, Sea-wings, Marine Parade, Midtown-on-Sea. It was thick and rectangular, and it plopped through the mailbox at the edge of the property on the morning of the twins' sixteenth birth-day, when they were officially old enough to live unsupervised.

There was no accompanying note but there were details of a solicitor in London and a copy of the Deed of Trust.

Artie rang the number at the top of the letter.

'Ah, yes,' said the man, clearing his throat. 'A minor cannot legally hold property in their own name but it's pos-sible for a property to be held in trust for you.'

'Sorry, what does that mean?'

'It means the mortgage has been paid off and as soon as you're both eighteen, ownership of Seawings will formally pass to you.' He cleared his throat. 'Please accept my condol-ences. I was sorry to read about your parents. It seems your mother had the extraordinary gift of foresight in arranging this before her untimely . . .' He tailed off, unable to articulate exactly what had happened to Piper Holden, who had since been declared a Person of Interest by the police.

But the twins, who had been left in a state of bewilderment and shock at the drowning of their father and the second unexplained disappearance of their mother, were at least provided for in a financial sense, if not an emotional one.

A second letter – written in a different hand – landed twenty minutes later on the mat of the Hillier household, addressed to Emelie.

By chance, she'd been at the bottom of the stairs when the postman delivered it. She recognized the writing immediately and snatched it up before her father, who'd spent the last couple of days white-lipped with anger, could read it.

It was from her mother.

Dearest Emelie,

If you've got as far as opening this, please don't tear it into pieces before you read it. There's a couple of things I'd like to explain. Firstly, I'm so sorry I didn't say goodbye. When you're older, I hope you'll understand, but I had to leave before the police arrested me for things I shouldn't have done. We all make mistakes, sometimes terrible ones, but having you and your brother was never one of those, and I'd hate you to think I'm abandoning you. I'm leaving because I have no choices left to me now. I love you both so much.

I will stay in touch when I can, even though Piper would kill me if she knew. But I know you're good at keeping secrets, my beautiful girl. You've kept mine and I've kept yours. So here's another one: a new number so you can contact me if you'd like to. I know I've upset you and I will never stop regretting that, but I hope one day you'll forgive me for everything that's gone wrong.

Piper is different now. She's not the woman I used to know. I'm not sure I trust her anymore. She frightens me, but I don't know what else to do or where to go. Sometimes I catch her looking at me with an expression of anger or regret, I'm not sure which. Piper says we shouldn't tell anyone where we're going. That we'll stay at our destination for a week or so before moving on to another city. We'll keep moving, I suppose, until we're caught or we die, whichever comes first.

If you decide to reply (I hope you do – please do) but don't hear back from me within a day or two, alert the authorities and don't share this information with anyone except the police.

We'll be staying at this hotel, my love: Hotel Navarra, Sint-Jakobsstraat 41, 8000 Bruges, Belgium

ACKNOWLEDGEMENTS

This is a novel written in lockdown. Yes, during *that* pandemic, in which we were confined to our homes and there were food shortages and far too many deaths, but also during a personal lockdown in which the shadow of a virus we didn't understand, fear for loved ones and strangers, a near-constant anxiety, insomnia and the complexities of home-schooling drained me of creative focus.

But as I write this, death rates are dropping, millions have been vaccinated and spring promises, at least, a ray of hope. To misquote Charles Dickens, the last year has been like one of those April days when the sun shines hot and the wind blows cold: when it's summer in the light, and winter in the shade.

During the last months, I've finally been able to write again.

Thanks to my agent Sophie Lambert and my editor Trisha Jackson for gentle encouragement but absence of pressure: I could not have asked for a more considerate pairing and these wonder women make publishing a warmer place. Gratitude, as always, to the Pan Macmillan team of Rosie Wilson, Elle Gibbons, Stuart Dwyer, Lucy Hale, Jayne

Osborne, Claire Gatzen, Samantha Fletcher, Neil Lang and Rebecca Lloyd for their continued hard work and faith, and to my literary agency C&W, especially the foreign rights team.

Thanks also to Fiona Sharp, Waterstones bookseller extraordinaire and champion of authors, who planted the seed of 'Detective' Saul Anguish. The character Marisa Sharp is for her.

A shout-out too, to my friend Emma Chong, who bought me *Wordcrime* by John Olsson, which inspired forensic linguist Dr Clover March, aka Blue; to Stuart Gibbon for all his help with police procedure and new recruits; and to Elizabeth Dodd for allowing me to borrow Miss Meow and the urinating-in-the-toaster story.

And thanks to all booksellers, librarians, reviewers, bloggers and readers. We couldn't do it without you.

This book is dedicated to my brother Steven, a port in any storm; my sister-in-law Ceinwen, a warrior in the true sense; and my favourite niece Meredith. Shine Cancer Support, the charity mentioned at Anoushka Thornton's funeral, was co-founded by Ceinwen after she was diagnosed with stage IV Non-Hodgkin's lymphoma eleven years ago.

During the toughest of times this year, my family – especially my children – have provided unstinting love and support: they've given me plenty of time and space to write while knowing the door to the Writing Shed – built by my husband Jason so I had a room of one's own when everyone was home – is always open.

This time, though, it's my fellow authors who've pulled me through the writing of this book, word by reluctant word. I couldn't have done it without my friends in the crime community, who make me laugh every day and are always on hand to lift me up, offer words of encouragement, a shoulder to cry on and advice on how best to dispose of a body. You know who you are.

And lastly, a reminder at the end as well as the beginning, especially to my daughter Alice and my niece Meri, that women – all of them – are equal to everything.

April 2021